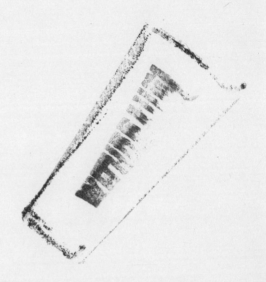

# Hiding
## Mr. McMulty

BERNIECE RABE

# Hiding

# Mr. McMulty

**BROWNDEER PRESS**

**HARCOURT BRACE & COMPANY**

*san diego    new york    london*

*Browndeer Press* is a registered trademark of Harcourt Brace & Company.

Library of Congress Cataloging-in-Publication Data
Rabe, Berniece.
Hiding Mr. McMulty/by Berniece Rabe.
p. cm.
"Browndeer Press."
Summary: In 1937 in southeastern Missouri, eleven-year-old Rass, son of a proud
sharecropper, proves his worth when a flood destroys his family's home and forces
his best friend, an elderly black man, into hiding from the Ku Klux Klan.
ISBN 0-15-201330-X
[1. Family life—Missouri—Fiction.   2. Farm life—Missouri—
Fiction.   3. Race relations—Fiction.   4. Floods—Fiction.
5. Missouri—Fiction.]   I. Title.
PZ7.R105Hi   1997
[Fic]—dc21     96-49144

Text set in Electra
Designed by Camilla Filancia
First edition     A B C D E F
Printed in the United States of America

## ACKNOWLEDGMENTS

A special thank you to Irma Davis, Edith Freund,
Dr. Bertina Hildreth, Mildred Johnson, Dr. Robert
Meredith, Willie Jean Morgan and Stella Pevsner for
reading and for being supportive to me during the
creation of this book.

And to my editor, Linda Zuckerman, my deep
thanks for hearing what I had to say, for her
objectivity in organizing materials in this book, and
for aiding me in clarifying certain issues.

To my agent, Julie Fallowfield, for feeling so sure
about my work—thanks.

Thanks also to the library system, interlibrary
loan, and to certain librarians in particular: Martha
Edmundson, Denton, Texas Public Library; Marge
Schildnecht, Elgin, Illinois Public Library; Mary Jo
Wagner, Dundee, Illinois Public Library.

And my deep appreciation goes to the Ragdale
Foundation for supplying my basic need, uninterrupted
time, to write the first draft of this book.

As I THINK back to the place of my youth in southeast Missouri, I remember a mother quail marching across the dirt road with all her little ones trailing in a neat row behind her. So did we children trail behind our country-bred parents, except our line was not always so straight.

My story is the memory of my people. Though they are characters I've created, they are patterned after people who were a part of my life. Some, such as Maggie Porter and Grandpa, are real. Some are blends of several people. Some I made up, but they are as real as the others, for all come out of my own culture.

Our house sat near a massive drainage ditch, cut through by the government to reclaim the bottomlands of the Mississippi. Being a strong girl in this distant time and era, and contrary to my dad's instructions, I rinsed my hair five times in clear rainwater from the barrel by the corner of the house, telling myself that the water, being used up so quickly, wouldn't have time to set and hatch mosquitoes. I hung upside down from tree limbs to gain a different view of my small world. To ease boredom, I sat on the front porch and counted all the boxcars on the train. Indeed, I did the things my characters do: I slopped hogs, hoed and picked cotton, hunted hens' nests, and picked wild berries and tiny wild grapes, so tart and tangy. I lay at the water's edge, making the little shiners that swam near the surface dart at a hand's swish. But I envied my brothers who, with their black friends, could muddy those waters catching fish, or who could shoot off firecrackers with our cousins. Often, refusing to be excluded because I was a girl, I sneaked through the woods soundlessly behind my brothers to witness their adventures, of which I now write. Wasn't I strong?

Why, as I walked the path to the outhouse early in the morning I didn't even flinch on being hit in the face by a newly woven spider's web. I just walked on, breathing in the clean air, as if no invisible thing could ever block my way. Of course I expected the dry spells, when dust covered every tree and blade of grass and nothing green and vibrant existed until there came a good rain, washing the world. But I wasn't prepared for the low roar of distant thunder that brought a flood, nor the cruel words among grown-ups that hit me full face.

This book is fiction, a blend of things that actually happened: floods, fires, retaliations. Each exposed us children to a wider view of the world, revealing prejudices that we poor white and black children, so closely bonded, had never experienced.

As I think back on it all, I see clearly the qualities in my brother that made me love him, and those of an old black man whom I dearly loved.

I share my loving and growing with you.      —B. R.

# Hiding
## Mr. McMulty

# 1

THE RAINS had stopped. The sun shone now in the late afternoon sky as Rass Whitley walked two miles of railroad track from school to front door. It wasn't easy to balance on the rails with his geography book in one hand, but he mastered it. At last, sitting down on the right-of-way in front of his house, he waited to grab the *Kansas City Star* the train conductor threw to the Whitleys each week. He would read the funnies before Sally, as he had both weeks during the rainy spell.

Looking through the massive cottonwood and catalpa trees in the front yard, he could hardly distinguish his two-story unpainted house from the outbuildings, including the great old slanting barn—except the barn was fenced off. The ramshackle house had two great ramshackle porches, where he could play without being in the mud on a rainy day. He could do leg hangs from the railings, swing high in the squeaky porch swing, or sit in a tilted straight-back chair and watch Mom in the willow rocker peeling pota-toes for supper. He could tease his sisters and wrestle a brother, if only that brother hadn't grown six inches in the last year. He was not allowed to play rough with the girls.

Before his older siblings had left home, Rass had been free to do whatever he pleased when out of school. Now he did farmwork, plus the tough homework of higher grades. But with fields so wet, this should be a free weekend. He wouldn't waste it memorizing states and capitals.

No train roared past, no spewing of exhaust, no paper.

He marched to the front steps and slammed his book down, but got no attention. His little sisters were all squatting watching Sally, who lay belly down on the porch, painting.

"You girls wouldn't even hear the train if it had come. I could've hopped that freight and took a hundred-mile trip to St. Louis and you'd not know it." They still watched Sally.

"Some kids ain't so lucky, to have that opportunity." He watched Sally a bit himself.

"Sally is," said Rosalee, the seven-year-old, a tall spike with a white tail of hair atop. "Who else in the whole world has a rich plantation owner like Mr. Preston giving her paints?"

"Where'd you get that big paper?" Rass demanded of Sally. It was very white. No folds. Perfectly smooth. "From Mr. Preston?"

"Mom brought it home for me from Raymond's store," Sally said, then added, "Watch out, Rass, I'm catching up on you fast." He lunged and she was up running.

"I can beat you cyphering and I can outrun you, too!" he shouted, though she was past the swing, curving around the end of the porch.

"She ain't claiming to be smarter, Rass. She means it's 'cause it's her tenth birthday and Mom got her this present!" shouted Rosalee.

Every year when the jonquils bloomed, Sally had her birthday and declared she was catching up on him. Rass had gotten no birthday gift when he'd turned eight, nor nine. None, ever, unless he counted that unexpected time he got frostbite, which happened on his tenth birthday, and Dad gave him a nickel stick of candy. No chance this year, for winter in southeast Missouri was warm. That's why they had early spring rains.

He continued chasing Sally around and around the porch. Finally he swung around the end post and cut her off. "You're still a year-and-a-half younger." He did a quick leap to avoid ruining her painting, then stopped to criticize. "It looks strange how you got fence posts all the same size marching along in a neat row."

She was not hearing one word. She said breathlessly to the little girls, "My picture's good 'cause I'm catching up on Rass."

The little girls believed her and Sally loved it. He thought to chase her again, but it had gotten attention only for her. He took a couple of deep breaths, then said, "Sally, you better share your paints! If she won't share, you little girls just go inside and don't watch her paint no more." He watched until Sally began painting flowers.

"Why are you painting flowers now? Why? Why?" her sisters asked.

"Why? Well, all these April showers are gonna bring lots of May flowers. This is to prove it."

"The rains brought mud, that's all," Rass snapped.

"And it's made the barn lot stink to high heaven. And—"

He would have gone on, but a familiar voice thundered, "Ground's too wet for plowing today!"

All the children jumped. Rass froze. Dad would probably chew him out for sassing Sally. Farm boys weren't supposed to want attention or anything, except at Christmastime.

"Yes, sir. It's wet, sir." Rass spoke as politely as if he was talking to his teacher or to Mr. McMulty, the best neighbor in the whole world. Both men Rass could talk to, and some fine words often came shining forth when he did.

Dad positioned himself at a porch post for support. As always, he wore a denim work jacket that he called his jumper, bib overalls, and straw hat, sun or no. Underneath that hat Dad's head was bald and white as a leghorn's egg. He was all farmer, a full man, more stomach than most. His farmer's tan on face, arms, and hands nearly covered his freckles and it hadn't left all winter. Those brown hands were clenched now into fists.

"Think you're old enough to help log trees, soon's the mud dries?"

"Yes, sir," Rass answered immediately, and then added, "and to get all I make off them five acres of new ground what we'll clear logging? So's I can learn the responsibilities of a farmer, just like L.G.?"

That's what Dad had said to Rass's older brother L.G. on his birthday.

Irritation grew in Dad's voice. "Rass, I ain't discussing such. My mind's heavy 'nough with real problems. You

4

know I ain't ever promised what you can make off'n five acres. Keep questioning instead of listening like a boy oughta do, I may never. L.G. listens. He'll be fourteen in three months; he's old enough to manage land."

Rass had watched Dad write L.G.'s agreement, saw Mom tuck it into cellophane along with Dad's rental contract and place both in the family Bible and snap the leather binding tight. L.G. had worn jeans ever since, while Rass wore his hand-me-down overalls, the side buttonholes too big from L.G.'s fast growing.

"L.G. deserved that agreement," Dad declared while moving so his face was in the shade the great cottonwood offered. The catalpa's shade overlapped, leaving just a splinter of sunshine right where Dad stood. In the sun Dad's eyes shone blue as cold steel. When they found shade they mellowed, but his words were still strong: "L.G.'s ready for marking his manhood, same's your older brothers was. Rass, you ain't about to be ready to be out on your own."

"I'm ready."

"No you ain't. All my boys been ready to plant at thirteen, but I got doubts you'll ever be a farmer. You waste time questioning instead of obeying me or the rules of the land, long set." He wasn't even looking at Rass anymore. His eyes were on Sally's painting.

"But none of them stuck to farming, and I will," Rass said.

Dad sometimes claimed he'd failed because none of his older boys had followed in his footsteps. Mom assured Dad that as soon as their sons spent a few years in the service, they'd all be back to what they knew best, unless they got wise to the fact that poor farmers always stayed poor.

"I'll follow in your footsteps," Rass said out loud. He'd do almost anything to win favor with Dad. He leaned against a porch post.

But Dad spoke only of L.G. "L.G.'ll farm. He'll not be a-going off to service, nuther." L.G., the oldest at home now, had grown almost as tall as Dad, and in other ways—like showing off and storytelling—had become a man overnight.

Rass scratched his back on the rough part of his post. "I'll do fine, too," he insisted. "Just give me five acres to manage. Or even four. Three?"

"You're too young! I don't mean to let you manage no land when you're still acting like a boy dreaming too high. It's tough times and these rains 'bout done me in. I cain't afford to take a solitary risk. You'd be questioning my ever' word, and still trying out new ways o' planting if you was in charge. And we'd be in trouble too tight to move! You hear?"

Rass, equally exasperated, pressed his tongue against his teeth, but finally said, "So I hear better ways at school! Ain't that why I'm going?" He pushed high up on the post, never reaching high enough to talk level with Dad. "In hard times I'd think you'd welcome better ways."

"Schoolteachers ain't farmers! Stop that stretching. Tallness don't cut no ice. It's following patterns learned from being a farmer's son what counts." Dad shook his head. "I swear you're the hardest kid I got to talk to. Look,

**6**

I give you the full care of Ole Jersey. You just see to it she's fed, milked, and pastured proper."

"And I'll get what comes out of her?" Rass asked, thinking of calves like the ones in Mr. Preston's herd Sally was painting right now.

"If that ain't a dumb question. See what I mean? I notice you been drinking plenty of what comes out of her." Then, with a raw laugh—which suggested Rass was a strange boy—Dad jumped off the porch and was gone back up the road, leaving boot prints in the front-yard mud, bigger than life.

Sally gave a great swirl with her paintbrush to finish off a frothy pail of milk right beneath a heifer. Rass watched while she drew a flat boy doing the milking. Was it supposed to be him? He refused to ask. He'd never ask another question of anyone. Never utter another new idea out loud. But when he was grown...

Then Sally, flinging her red hair about, was up and gushing, "Oh Rass, you're so lucky to be in charge of Ole Jersey. Come on, Rosalee, let's give him a back slapping!"

He dodged, but the little girls had also caught Sally's enthusiasm. Rosalee swatted and congratulated. Then four-year-old Chrissy, blond curls bouncing, put her marbles into her mouth to free her hands and joined in. When baby Marylu gooed and clapped, Rass was almost convinced something wonderful had happened, though already his job was milking. Dad never thanked him for it. Never used thank-you words, even for L.G. Rass would settle for attention.

Mom stepped out to the porch, wiping her hands on

the blue apron that covered her purple flowered dress. She always heard everything. "Sally, I like them flowers and them cows you painted. And Rass, I'll tell you this family couldn't make it through these hard times without the milk Ole Jersey gives us. She's a mighty fine animal."

Rass nodded. He'd grown to love that old heifer, too. But loving made no difference in the amount of milk she'd give down. Ole Jersey would dry up, the same as the next cow, if she was fixing to calf.

Mom went back to her work. He couldn't appeal to her about logging or tending five acres. Dad was law in this house.

Someday Dad would be old and shrunken—like Grandpa got to be and Dad had to build him a little one-room house. When Rass was younger, he had thought about being a man and the law in his home. Out of kindness he would give old Dad a house with two rooms. Then old Dad would be grateful and say, "Thanks; you're a good son. Always questioned a lot but, by gum, you turned out fine."

Little by little Rass had to let go such comforting thoughts. Truth was, just as Grandpa never admitted to being beholden to Dad, Dad stubbornly would never be beholden to Rass, nor anyone. Dad often told his brothers, Uncle Jake and Uncle Tut, "If I ever get old and cantankerous as Pa was, just take me out behind the barn and shoot me."

Rass never wished Dad dead, not even when he was raging mad at him. Squatting near his little sisters, he put arms about their shoulders. He'd been the one to find Grandpa dead in his little one-room house two years ago, saw those opened eyes that didn't see him. Saw that mouth that scolded, but often gave a note of liking him and frequently told him stories. Saw it gaping without a word. He'd closed the door, banged his head on it, until Dad came to gently lead him away.

People, like all living things, had to die. He knew that. But he'd never have a hand in it. He eased himself up, pushed back really tall against the porch post, and looked toward the sun, glad it had shone for a while today.

Sally said, "That's it, Rass, hold your head high. It's an honor to be responsible for a family's cow and see there's milk to drink." Sally could be so full of herself at times. "Milk'll one day help raise your little babies so's they'll get to be big and important people, living by the rules you set for 'em."

"What's so all-farred good about that?" It was awful to have Miss Sally Teacher trying to learn him something away from school. He was tempted to chase her around the porch again. Instead, he adjusted his galluses, those wide shoulder straps on his overalls, and said, "When I'm a father, I'm doing away with rules. I'll let my kids get their own ideas and govern themselves."

"You cain't do that!" Sally was shocked. The little girls clapped their hands over their mouths. Chrissy, now tongue-rolling three marbles in her mouth, was drooling to beat it.

Rass said, "Spit them marbles out before you swallow one." Chrissy took the idea at once. It was too much. "Dad's rules cause more heartaches than good!" He watched their shock as he, like Dad, jumped off the end of the porch.

Chrissy spit out two marbles and began to cry. Sally

furiously swung her painting to dry it. "Rass, you're being mean on purpose. God says there has to be laws! Newspapers is full of lawbreaker stories!..." Then came the roar of the train. Before Rass could blink, Sally was off the porch, slopping through the mud, racing to the right-of-way. Rass held the little girls back. "I'll see you get the funnies first," he consoled them. Three little blond heads nodded in agreement.

*A-ooo-ga! A-ooo-ga!*

Why, that was L.G. backing Dad's Chevy out of the car shed! No one ever questioned whose kid L.G. was. His eyes and freckles matched Dad's. He had Dad's real name, Leo Grover Whitley. Dad granted that to the baby who had looked most like him, but ordered everyone not to use it. L.G. wore his cap all the time, as Dad wore his hat, but L.G. smiled Mom's big smile.

Rass wasn't old enough to drive, and L.G. had no right to do it, either. Nor wave so grandly. Nor stick his red head out the window and boast, "I've been tuning this engine ever since I got home from school and now I'm taking it to the Browns'! We're gonna use their tools and *really* tune this baby. I'm staying the night. Dad said I could!"

Rass dashed for the slowed car as it turned from yard to road. "Stop!" he yelled. "I'm going, too. Sally, tell Mom I'm at the Browns' with L.G."

L.G. braked. But as Rass jumped on, the engine roared. The Chevy shot forward and Rass felt the impact. The spin whirled him away. L.G. shouted gleefully, "Dad says no riding the running board!"

Quickly Rass caught his balance, commanded his feet

to run. *Run!* His white hair caught high in the breeze. Hands stretched mightily. He'd catch the door handle. The fender. The trunk. Missed. Missed. *Missed!* He twisted abruptly. His feet took out for a shortcut down pasture. L.G. would have to take regular roads. The Browns lived the opposite side of Six Ditch, half a mile west. Rass would simply wade across.

He and the ditches were friends. They'd favored him with a place to wade or swim or fish, or to use as a shortcut to the Browns'. The government had dug these enormous drainage ditches nine years ago, in 1928, to reclaim swampland around Parma, Missouri, for farming. Like small rivers thirty feet wide bank to bank, these straight canals were dug every mile. They emptied far away into Castor, which emptied into the Mississippi at the floodgates. Their numbers let people know where they lived. Rass lived on Six Ditch.

His legs moved confidently in great elongated strides. Neither Sally nor L.G. could run so fast. He sped to the most shallow spot. Not that he could see the water, for dirt, excavated in the ditch's creation, was piled to bank either side, a caution against floods when the Mississippi rose. Slowing slightly, he ascended the levee-like ditch bank, then was fast scooting down the other side on the seat of his pants when he began pulling grass out by the roots to stop his speed. The water was really high! Halfway up the bank! Well over his head, even in this spot where dirt had drifted in.

A week ago he'd run across here hardly getting water in his boots. Now he'd need to strip and swim, but that wouldn't get his clothes to the other side. Luck always went in L.G.'s favor. Rass broke off a willow switch, threw it into the surging water in disgust. Hit right between two water snakes gliding by. He could've helped with that engine, pleased Dad all to pieces. He sighed. Why pretend? Dad would never give him permission to tinker with the Chevy. Rass watched the snakes.

Then he watched a crawdad building a mud chimney above the water line. Nothing could set back a crawdad— they always kept on going on. If Mr. McMulty were here, he'd have said such. Rass would have gotten his words confirmed. Those crawdads excavated for the longest.

The spot on the ditch bank where delicate ferns grew was ant country, owned and occupied by trillions of moving little specks. Uncle Tut, who preached part-time, said God was mindful of every feather on a sparrow, but Rass thought this many ants would leave even God a-wondering. Ants worked away, free as the wind, going wherever a kick carried them.

The growing sound of barking claimed Rass's attention. It was Ole Coalie, short hair black as new coal dropped from the train, tall and gangly though long past being a pup. He'd gone off seeking adventure like Rass. He came bounding up, licked Rass's face. Rass, in turn, rubbed the fur on Coalie's head real good. Together they started out for Mr. McMulty's, a man who would welcome them. A man without a mean bone in him. A friend who would always be there and would never die.

# 2

As Rass and Coalie approached the small shack sitting close to the road with only a tiny porch to separate private life from the comings and goings of the countryside, Rass called out, "Need any help?"

It was polite to ask. At that moment, Mr. McMulty, Nert's black sharecropper, was trying to loop a link of chain into a big hook attached to a rafter of his rotting front porch. He paused, then smiled a greeting more cheerful than the sun.

Rass knew that during the past two weeks of solid rain, Mr. McMulty had spent his cooped-up time carving dowels and the armrest of his porch swing. Such luxury of free time would end when this sun dried up the fields.

"It done, Rass. I welcomes yo' hep to rehang and try out my work." He glanced at some gathering clouds.

Instantly Rass pushed Coalie aside, dragged a straight chair to the right spot, jumped upon it, and slid the hook in easily. Feeling satisfied, he said, "Well, that does it. You're a genuine artist, Mr. McMulty. I bet Sally could never carve swirls and flowers like these. Can I try out this fancy porch swing to see if it swings as good as ourn, what don't have fancy hand-carved dowels and curved armrests?"

"Yep, my time be well spent." Mr. McMulty was most pleased. "And thanks for your compliment. Y'done a fine job hanging my swing, Rass. Since Miss Greene not be yhere yet to swing in it, and you being my best o'friend, I might let you be first to try it out. Thanks for your hep."

Rass knew Mr. McMulty never spoke to others about Miss Greene. The old man's eyes were as happy as if he really were a young person about to get married, instead of a short, old, bent-to-the-plow man, his overall legs rolled up four inches because of his shortness and another four to clear his work boots. Rass traced the beautiful carvings as he swung.

Answering as he'd been taught, Rass said, "I don't need no thanks. A boy's supposed to work." He motioned Mr. McMulty to come sit beside him.

They sat in silence for a while. Rass looked across the fields to his own house, then twisted about to see the Preston mansion's massive green lawns, its many flower beds with roses, iris, snowballs, cannas, and other flowers Rass couldn't name. The jonquils forming a border were in full bloom. Many trees, not common to southeast Missouri, had been planted as a buffer between the cotton gin, the hired men's quarters, and the mansion house.

What a difference between the rich and poor, Rass thought.

It was the way things were. The plantation had always been there, with sharecroppers' homes just a clod-throw away. Swinging, thinking, Rass wanted to cut the differ-ence, do things a new way, just once.

Getting right to what was bothering him, he said, "Mr. McMulty, I told you Dad's letting L.G. have his own five acres and he keep all he makes off it. Well, he's letting L.G. drive his Chevy, too! I'm getting closer to twelve every day and I cain't even ride the running board. L.G. boasts and laughs at me.... I'll skin him alive! I *will*!"

"Don't pay be vengeful, though things bad," Mr. McMulty said, putting his hand on Rass's shoulder. "You knows the Lord jest paving the way, when it look like we being slighted. You more lonely than mad. I knows that well. Best look to the earth a-waking up—it cheer yo' soul. Spring smells give me thoughts o' Miss Greene. Honey-suckle a-blooming!"

Mr. McMulty could always see the good when Rass felt down. Coalie, sitting at Rass's feet, moved backward and forward with the swing. Rass gently pushed him away.

"You a fine worker," Mr. McMulty went on. "I needs hep now with nailing my carved shelf up high outa reach o' yo' little sisters. A place to exhibit this fine little calf I carved for Miss Greene." He drew from his pocket a carved oak calf, perfect in every way: three inches high, a bull calf with sturdy neck, its feet playfully running.

"Looks exactly like the one Nert got when his prize heifer bred with Mr. Preston's fine bull!" Rass said. Nert was the landlord of the Whitleys and Mr. McMulty.

"I study it good," Mr. McMulty said, and smiled.

Rass followed him into the kitchen, placed a chair near the spot where he pointed. As Rass gathered up hammer and nails, he remembered how three years ago Dad had suggested that Nert hire Mr. McMulty, a single man, to sharecrop his swampiest land. Did Dad know then that Nert planned to cheat Mr. McMulty by keeping all the government parity money? Naw, nobody knew.

In order to control cotton prices during hard times, there was pay from the government for not planting cotton, called parity money. Nert contracted his land that produced hardly a thing to McMulty, declaring most of it as fallow to get the parity money, which they were to share. Everybody knew the old man got none. Instead, Nert's wife, Rose, gave McMulty carving tools for Christmas. Uncle Tut sharecropped Nert's land, too, and one of his fields lay fallow. Being a preacher, though, he got his share.

But Dad *rented* from Nert. Renters had their own say and could plant all in cotton. If it made good, it was far better money than the government offered. The Whitleys also had the woods, but the government knew nobody planted there. No temptation to call it fallow.

"This be my year, Rass," Mr. McMulty said, steadying the chair.

Rass wanted to believe that this was the year Mr. McMulty would be paid, but he knew Nert never let any cropper get ahead. "Miss Greene coming up soon?"

"I think it be soon, boy. Remember last year I tells you the good Lord whisper I not be slighted when Nert keep my share o' that parity money? Well, yo' Uncle Tut jest tell me this year President Roosevelt pass a new law. *Half* o' parity checks go to all contracted sharecroppers! I gets paid proper! Laws o' the land be a blessing, son."

Rass didn't argue. His mind was too staggered by the facts. The familiar naked furniture and walls. Sheets and bed covers strung tight and neat over hard springs of an iron double bed, like for married people. Plainness. The carved calf would help, but what of the cracks chinked with cotton and rags? Mr. McMulty had lots more idle land than Uncle Tut, and he could sure use the money. "How much money you gonna get?"

"Sh-h-h-h, not so loud! I cain't talk it. But I getting 'nough parity check to buy Nert's poorest soil where I lives! Don't talk it."

"Nert gonna sell it to you?" That was unbelievable.

"You must a-heard Nert say he gonna sell off this swampy land, soon's yo' daddy and yo' uncle Tut clear 'nough woods so's new ground can lie idle...till the stumps rot, o' course. Then Nert won't want me to share-crop no more. Don't matter. Least I be contracted with him this year, and plenty people witness his words." He looked out the window at two doves, whose attention went no further than each other. "Rose tell me her husband happy to be rid o' this ole swamp he letting her sell."

Mr. McMulty had known Rose Nert most of her life, since back when she was a sharecropper's daughter and before she became Nert's second wife. And Dad *was* logging a lot, so Mr. McMulty was not just imagining.

"If I was you, I'd be telling everyone!" Rass found it hard to speak with nails held in his mouth. Anyway, he was having a difficult time getting the small nails to hold the carved shelf to the wall and didn't want to pound harder, for fear he'd mar the carving.

"No, boy. Men might think a black man talk uppity, truth or no."

Rass removed the nails from his mouth and dropped his hands. "You mean lucky, not uppity. Well, I think it's good one of us got lucky. I'm glad for laws to make Nert be fair. Maggie Porter'll make him pay up, all right. She's a good sheriff, and if the law says so, she'll..."

Rass paused. Would Dad be jealous? Dad preached what everyone knew: Sharecropping never paid off. "Earn yourself a pair of mules," Dad always said to him. "Rent, use your head and plant well, be frugal, and one day you can become a landowner. Even if it be only a few acres like Jake has." Uncle Jake was younger than Dad, but had beat him in owning land.

"You're gonna be a land*owner*! And without never being no renter first!" Rass yelled, dropping nails as he danced about the room.

"You right, son! It do be my year. I see Miss Greene now, putting her crystal bowl handed down from her grandmama who was an honored slave right side this little carved calf on that safe shelf."

Rass scrounged around in the bucket of nails, pushing aside those so big they would crack the shelf. Finally he found four medium-sized nails. He got back up on the chair. *Kewack! Kewham!*

"I beholden for yo' hep, son. And yo' joy for me. Yo' day be coming, and I be there cheering. You got strong hands, good heart, too."

Rass laughed to make room for all his pleasure, losing two nails from his mouth again. Such talk was a song, whistling clean as a breeze around his face. Uncommon talk. Not real nor tough as Dad's man talk. Mr. McMulty handed Rass the dropped nails and laughed more.

Facts finally won over. Rass anchored the shelf and said, "But you ain't got no plow of your own, and this land's too sorry. I mean..."

Mr. McMulty's eyes were suddenly serious. "Way done paved, son. Our friend Dumas, what be the first black man to run a dredge on these ditches, let me watch and learn. When I owns this land, my nights gonna be spent using that dredge boat, digging a spur ditch to drain off this low swamp, make it fine land. Store's gonna credit plow and seeds!"

Mr. Dumas's dredge boat was enormous. And his work was fine. Rass would like to stay overnight at the Dumases' and have his friend Clever Dumas get permission for them to try to run that machine. Something L.G. could never do. But white boys never stayed the night with colored, nor the other way around.

Mr. McMulty placed the carved calf in the center of the fancy carved shelf. "Fine!" Rass said.

"Fine," Mr. McMulty agreed.

"Don't let L.G. help you run that dredge boat. You need help, I'm right here, even if it's dark. L.G. cain't stay awake like me."

"You be the one I ask, don't worry 'bout that none."

"L.G.'s staying over at the Browns'," Rass said. "But it's really my turn to stay. The Browns have fried yeast dough-nuts for breakfast."

Mr. McMulty's eyes were warm; his voice came gentle.

"Lord jest paving the way," he said again. "Yo gonna cotch up to L.G. one day. He not a bad boy. My pappy always tell me people be good if'n you scratch deep 'nough. I hast to remind myself that 'bout Nert. But if'n I don't believe Nert good deep inside, I forced to believe what'd be no good for me to believe. You understands, son?"

"I understand," Rass said, and felt better. Maybe he even liked L.G. a little. L.G. and he used to wrestle all the time. He'd just go to the Browns' and show L.G. that he didn't care about that old car.

Rass DIDN'T get to mess with the car, but he did get lucky.

Mrs. Brown handed her son Bill a loaf of fresh-baked yeasty bread when Rass and Bill left together. Maybe she meant Bill to share it at the Whitleys' table, but Bill wasted no time in tearing off one end and handing it to Rass. The smell rose, as only the smell of hot bread can, making eating the world's best pleasure. Bill pranced happily along, too. His hair, light, crisp, and curly, stood boldly out above his ears. He was a half year younger than Rass, built solid, a fine wrestler. He pushed Rass's shoulder, smiled in that way that surpassed words. Bill was deaf. Rass pushed him in turn and between great bites smiled back as best he could.

Bill, looking concerned, motioned a torn piece of bread toward the sky. The clouds were taking over, darkening the day to an early end, and the air was so humid you could wring it out like a dishrag. But neither of them bothered to run. They finished the bread long before they got home, then ran for a while to settle it down, allowing them room for plenty of Mom's supper of beans and potatoes. After supper Bill helped Rass do the night chores before they crashed into bed and tossed about with wonderfully full stomachs.

Toward morning Rass was having a grand dream of Ole Jersey's prize calf. When Dad objected to him owning it, Rass reasoned Dad into a corner until Dad finally began nodding and agreeing. It was a sorry thing to have to wake from a dream like that, but it was six o'clock. "Hey, Bill, wake up. Time to get dressed." Rass gave Bill a pull.

"Know what, Bill? 'Course I cain't pay for breeding Ole Jersey with Preston's bull like Nert did, but if I believe on it, it'll happen." Bill couldn't know what was said, but it always felt right to keep on talking. "Our pastures join, you know? However it happens, it'll start me a fine herd."

Rass smiled thinking of it. Bill smiled. So Rass kept right on daydreaming out loud as they walked downstairs to breakfast. The family was already eating at the long plank table covered with blue-checked oilcloth. Dad said, "Eat hearty, but soon's your belly's full, go get Ole Jersey relieved. Her bag's in a strut." He wiped his chin of his own breakfast crumbs, then added, "Come give me a hand with the logging soon's milking's done and Mrs. Brown has come for Bill."

Mom looked especially nice today, and Rass told her so. Her straw-colored hair was flowing down right into the browns and golds of her dress, making her young in spite of being thirty-eight. As Dad walked past her doing the dishes, he playfully patted her bottom. Rass and Bill exchanged looks, and Mom noticed. She said, "You boys get to the barn. I already sent your dog a-running. Blame thing's always in my way."

Mom said to Sally, "Fill the wash kettle," and to Rosalee, "Feed the chickens." Then she lifted baby Marylu to her hip and shooed all out the door, including Chrissy, whose mouth was still full of biscuit.

Rass took Bill to their chores, removing the slop bucket from the back porch on the way. He near tripped on a hen that had finished a dust bath in the dry space under the house, her feathers looking light as an erased picture. Then Bill kicked at that little dust bowl, and wheezed in delight as the dust covered him.

Shortly Bill was at his job and Rass had his head buried deep in Ole Jersey's flanks. While taking in her warmth and comfort as he milked, he dreamed again of the fine calf he'd get from her. Soon the strong white flow was finished, so he stripped out the last milk from the teats and set the filled pail out of kicking range. The sun was still shining, but stray raindrops pelted the snowy froth atop the milk. He looked to the sky for the rainbow, for rain and sun together assured it. Finding a small one, he waved to Bill, who was pushing at the pigs, his grunting sounds ordering them to share. The train whistled as it dashed through the morning, using its might to mark the trestle and make ready for a stop at the Preston plantation three-quarters of mile on past. Cows were shipped in to be bred with Preston's bull.

Sally was out on the right-of-way waving to the conductor. Raindrops came faster. Best get the milk to Mom and then get Ole Jersey into the barn. It was always a glad moment of the day, Mom welcoming the pail of milk as a gift, not exactly saying thank you, just saying how milk kept body and soul together during hard times. He hadn't taken two steps before Mom called from the back door, "Rass, don't let Bill tarry no longer with them hogs. Give me the milk. Take Bill to look under the corncrib for a hen's nest—" Her voice broke suddenly.

The air stood still.

Then she screamed in a voice of horror he'd never heard before, *"To the ditch bank! Lord God, kids, run! We'll all be dead!"*

Her words whirled Rass about to the direction she'd pointed, causing milk to spill from his pail in a great circular layer. A grunt came from him, wilder and louder than Bill's. Water was moving toward them from a break upstream in the ditch bank, as if it were a river formed in midair!

# 3

SCREAMS cut the world from all directions.

Where was Mom? The little kids! Bill doesn't hear the sound—got to save Bill!

Bill surely felt vibrations, for a wild cry came from him. Rass flailed Ole Jersey. Bill tried to herd the pigs, which scattered. Sally and Mom caught up the little girls till Rosalee froze in place. Cooperate, Rosalee! Bill dashed to Rosalee, snatched her up in strong arms, and swept her to safety on the ditch bank. A break upbank had caused the great gush, but that solid high mound of dirt was still the logical refuge.

Ole Jersey froze in place, too. The hogs, gone wild, tangled her feet. Rass had to save Ole Jersey! He hit her rump and shouted, "Move!" His focus switched to the great waters, only a quarter mile away, sweeping closer, the spill broadening. Oh no! Dad and the mules were caught in it! Dad mustn't be dead! Screams against death rose in his throat, but then came Dad's distant cry, "Save the mules!" Dad was alive, moving along in the waters, clinging to a tree.

The waters surged in, crashing down on Rass as he battled frenzied Ole Jersey, finally moving now toward the bank. Both he and his cow stumbled, then got up, to be felled again by hurling branches and roots. Just as they touched the ditch bank, a greater surge rushed in. It, like a river running parallel to the great ditch, covered the spot where they'd just been. Rising fast, it inched up to where Ole Jersey fell again, halfway to the top of the bank. She would not get up.

Dad's bellow was closer: "Save my mules! Hear me, save my mules!"

Just one more second. Have to get Ole Jersey a few feet higher. *Whump!* His cow kept her kneeling position, rolled her head, bellowed.

"Rass, dad-blame-it, save my mules!"

The mules fought to reach the bank. Dad was far behind. The tree limb he clutched, still attached to a tree, whipped violently. The flood, which had ripped trees from the ground as easily as it ripped the mules' reins from Dad's hands, seemed determined to bring tree and man into the current of the spill. Rass judged Dad had a tight hold, so glanced toward Mom. The girls. Bill. All mouths open, they stood in horrified silence, but on solid ground, away from the torrential spill.

"Obey me, Rass! *Save my mules!*"

Granting yet another second to pulling Ole Jersey to safety, for the family had to have milk to keep body and soul together, he willed time to stand still in accordance with Ole Jersey's stubbornness. But the air became more charged with sounds of disaster. Squirrels', coons', and foxes' shrieks mixed with squalls of cats, chickens, and piercing death squeals of hogs, worse than on butchering day. Underlying everything was the unreal roar of surging waters, the slippery sucking noise of the clay ditch bank. Noise ate away Rass's sanity as much as the raging waters ate away the trusted fortification. Again, Dad's calls punctured the roar.

The mules, drifting downstream, would soon be even with Rass, but at that frozen second in time, only Ole Jersey existed. "On your feet! Or else! Or else . . . I gotta get you to higher ground! Come on, *please*, so's I can get to Dad's mules." Rass's hands pulled and yanked.

Ole Jersey was a ton of solid, unmovable rock.

"Damn it! Move, you old bitch!" Rass cussed at the cow he loved.

Mom yelled, "Catch my laying hens! Let Jersey take care of herself. Grab my chickens right there at the edge. Toss 'em up to us."

A strange howling noise from Bill broke his terrible silence. Sally and the little girls' shouts were "Snowball!" "Ole Tom!"—calls for Rass's cat, the white one he let Chrissy claim, and L.G.'s yellow barn cat. Soaking wet, Ole Coalie dashed about, barking his head off.

"Our cats are drowning!"

"They're drowning!"

"Help! Save our cats! You can reach 'em, Rass! Bill!"

The cats swept past. The chickens swept past. Mom called her hens, "Cut-cut-cuti-cut, here chick, chick. Here chick, chick." Rass wailed, too; his wonderful mother had gone crazy. Her feed call could never get those crazed chickens to swim crossways against current.

Now the mules swept past. Rass was too paralyzed to reach out.

The waters were still rising! The horror would never end! The sky, dark as anger itself, a nightmare of birdcalls. Human shrieks held no more power than the animals' cries. All the sound of doom. Yet Rass refused it. "Come on, don't give up, old girl. You'll make it! You'll get us a fine new calf and..." Sweet talk was lost on her. He hit her flank with force enough to fell a tree. "Get up! Dad-nab-it, *move!*"

She rolled her head and bellowed more.

The family screams reached new highs as their house, the only home Rass had ever known, crumbled from its pilings. Not completely; the ground-floor walls splintered, collapsed inward. Fruit jars spilled from the smokehouse door as if from the neck of an exploding bomb. Grandpa's little one-room house, now used as a brooder house, floated away. Water spread into a wider stream, losing a bit of force, but the damage was done. Dad's calls got lost by screeching reports of that damage as the family dodged flying debris and glass.

"The windows and roof's all broke!"

"Beds downstairs is ruined. Boys' things upstairs are spared!"

"Lord, I do hope it ain't busted my good stove. Please God. Here, Bill, hold Marylu, I'm gonna catch my jars."

Dad's continuing shouts silenced their calls and penetrated Rass's pain. "Dad-blast-it, Rass, run for my mules!" The waters had washed Dad nearer as the force lessened, but he was still thirty feet out.

Rass called, "They've gone past, Dad. I cain't!"

"You can wade out to 'em, if you'll leave that damn cow and run down bank. Just grab the reins and help 'em to the ditch bank!"

"I'm going," Rass said, and started. But then waters churned, the tree spun, and Dad thrashed about. The branch was breaking loose. Dad was barely hanging on! He'd go under! *Dad couldn't swim!*

Rass dashed up the bank, calling, "Hang on, Dad, I'm coming." He needed to be L.G., a strong swimmer. He had never beat L.G. at swimming.

"Not me! Save my mules!" Dad was hardly audible above the ripping sound of tree limb, but his harshness forced Rass to glance at the mules, see their flailing heads sucked under by the surging waters, see them roll, their chains wrapping about them. If Dad lost his hold, he'd be next.

"I'm a-coming for *you!*" Rass yelled, and jumped in, not caring if Dad killed him for disobeying. His arms and legs churned in powerful strokes, as if he were indeed L.G. He surfaced in time to hear the final ripping as the branch broke free. Dad vanished below the water, so Rass dived under. He hated underwater. Not knowing to shut his eyes, he saw in those muddy waters strips of bark blend with long shadows of unknown things, swaying like threads. Nowhere did he see Dad. Air all gone.

Forcing his head above water, he looked about wildly. *"Save the mules!"*

Dad was still alive! Gasping in sweet air, he swam toward Dad's voice. Dad, still gripping the branch, was coughing and spitting. He hadn't let go! Dad had tumbled and rolled with that blamed old branch, but he'd held on. Then, knowing ten feet from land was still too far for a nonswimmer, Rass felt a force outside of himself move his arms and legs. A mighty push. He sent branch and Dad to the ditch bank!

With no energy left then to swim, or live, Rass went under.

His body moved with the current, like L.G. did so easily when they used to play in the ditches together. He was dead, he guessed. And it wasn't all that bad. But the sweetness left as his lungs swelled with pain and up he came, sucking in life-giving air. He found himself surrounded by tightly closed one-hundred-pound lard cans bobbing about like giant fishing corks. He grabbed one. It shot from his hands like a greased pig. The jolt forced his feet to sink toward bottom. Into the mud ... of the field! The field Rass had plowed, now a lifesaving cushion.

He pulled one foot from the mud; the other followed. Bobbing like the debris about him, grappling for support to hoist himself up to the ditch bank, he pulled young ash saplings out by the roots. There! He was out of the floodwaters. The family was cheering. The great drainage ditch's waters had found their level with the break. The surging current had stopped. How quickly the battle to save life was finished.

A few chickens and pigs were making it to the bank downstream where Dad was. His clothes tight to his skin, his hat gone, his swirl of red hair below white baldness matted down, Dad looked a pitiful figure. Exhausted and slipping in the mud, he moved upbank as Bill, Mom, and the kids ran to him, waving, calling cries of celebration.

Their joy cries seemed to make Dad powerful again. He caught up to Rass, pressed his hand, then pushed him along. Rass savored this strange feeling of Dad's touch and wished to please Dad forever. Dad never let go until they reached Mom, who cried and clutched Dad to her.

Dad, out of breath, spoke loud with passion, "Helen, you're a skinny, bony woman, your clothes is a mess, your purty blond hair is a-stringing, but I'm caught up in rapture just to have your head on my shoulder."

Rass, like Dad, was soaked and filthy. Also, he was out of breath, so he didn't even try to speak. Talk like that was as highly unnatural as Dad's touching him. It was as unnatural as Mom clinging to Dad now. At least Bill couldn't hear the words Dad used. Perhaps it was fitting to act like this in a crisis, but Dad and Mom had been married for twenty years and none of the older kids had ever mentioned such. Nor had Rass seen them embrace before. Mom ended the flowery talk soon enough, pushing Dad away so that the little kids could have their turns at claiming him. Then she did the most unnatural act of all. She enfolded Rass in her arms.

"Son, you're alive. Praise be to the Lord!"

She began to fuss over his scratches. He let her do it, the way he'd let her grease his neck with Vicks or lance a bad boil. He'd always trusted her healing touch, as did all the family and neighbors, especially men without womenfolk, Mr. McMulty in particular. Mom doctored them all with medicine from the Raleigh man. But these were touches of love. Mom kept touching bad scratches, saying, "I'll put Raleigh's carbo salve on this cut, son, but that one

I'd best cauterize first to assure a healing. A couple of stitches might be necessary."

Rass loved it. "Ouch, Mom, stop it. I ain't dying."

"Mommy...you ain't got no salve," Rosalee began. She, a thin seven-year-old mother herself, had baby Marylu astraddle her hip.

Bill came to inspect Rass, too, but Mom paid no mind to anyone else. Habit set by nineteen years of mothering said, "Rass, cauterizing won't hurt all that much. A boy's gotta stand a little pain in order to heal faster. There's always a light in the night. Think on the healing, not the pain." Then her eyes grew round with realization as Rosalee's words sank in. "I ain't got my medicine box!" Her lips went silent and her hands ceased to touch, and Rass realized their plight.

He moved away, looked across the fields to check if Mr. McMulty's house was still standing. It was and he said so, not caring if anyone heard, just caring that Mr. McMulty was safe. Suddenly, jerked about by Bill, who was pointing and making his happy sounds, Rass saw Grandpa's little house floating out to the edge of the floodwaters. It rested in the newly planted cotton field. Its brooder lights glowed. Rass gave Bill's shoulders a clasp and called, "See what Bill sees. The brooder hood's still a-shining."

The girls turned and gave a delighted yell. Sally said, in the light manner the farmers used when most all was lost and there was no use crying over spilt milk, "Daddy, you built Grandpa's little house so good, the baby chicks are saved!"

It was good to look away from dead animals and the house, whose broken boards and broken furnishings floated about, but reality called them back. Their plank table fully in view in the crushed lower floor, its blackened checkered oilcloth twisted and knotted, still held the blue crockery spoon holder and salt dish, a pound box of Watkins black pepper, a half jar of butter pickles, another of preserves.

"And we're alive and together!" Mom announced.

"We're muddy and wet, but we're alive and a-standing here on this ditch bank," Rass declared, and Dad took no issue with him at all.

The Whitleys and Bill, filled with thankfulness, laughed crazily. It lightened Rass's heart until he repeated the brag that was common among men at the pool hall, "No one and no thing can keep a good farmer down! We're made of barbed wire and steel spring!"

Little Chrissy, golden ringlets and tearstained face making her appear the most helpless of all, boldly and loudly agreed. "Yep, us farmers is used to taking the bad with the good." But this repeating of Dad's past words brought her too much attention. She blushed and quickly added, "I wonder where Snowball is."

The laughing stopped. Rass and all the others knew this little one would die without her pet. He reached for her. But on seeing everyone's concern, Chrissy clutched the back of Rosalee's dress, as if Rosalee were a woman grown, and began loudly crying. Finally she stuffed the dress-tail into her mouth for comfort, and her noise stopped. Bill had caught Mom's look of worry as she'd reached out to Chrissy. He made a sound of sorrow, put out his arm to steady Mom.

The children looked to Dad.

His voice firm, Dad said, "We've carried talk about far enough!" He gave Chrissy a gentle pat, then he looked from child to child, then his head kept turning until he saw his mules. His jaws clamped hard. The cords on his freckled neck stood out and his eyes blazed fire. He jerked Rass toward him. "I told you to save my mules," he bellowed. "My mules! I'll have to turn cropper now, without mules! How am I going to take care of your mother?"

Rass felt as old as the oaks as a deep knowledge arose from within. Dad would never see a light in the darkest hour, as did Mr. McMulty, or Bill. Still he tried some of Mr. McMulty's sort of talk. "Dad, the rain has stopped. Uncle Tut's a cropper, and he takes care of Aunt Crystal on little or nothing. None of us are dead. Things could be worse."

But nothing moved Dad.

Sally joined in, "Uncle Tut does some preaching on the side. Maybe you could get the call, Daddy, and..." Sally stopped talking, for Dad's breath had grown short and he slumped, down, down, until his knees rested in the mud. Out of his soul he cried, "Why? Why, Rass, didn't you let *me* drown?"

"But your life's worth more'n the mules!" Guilt flooded in to overwhelm Rass. "I'm sorry! I'm sorry. But wouldn't you a-saved me instead of mules?"

Mom said, " 'Course he'd a-saved you, Rass. You're his son. Didn't he set up three nights without sleep when you had pneumonia, watching your ever' move till your raging fever broke?" She paused, then whispered, "Whit, you're down and hope's gone, but I ask you to rise up and spare the boy."

Dad didn't rise from the mud. His head bent, his shoulders slumped, his body announced his deep despair.

"I'm sorry you got no mules," Rass said, his voice breaking. The moment for touch had come and gone.

Sally comforted, "Mr. McMulty will let us use his mules, Daddy."

Mom pulled Sally close. "Hush, child. Mr. McMulty don't own those mules. Nert's mules is sort of rented to Mr. McMulty, and they cost him the greater share of his crop earnings. So it will be with us now."

"I'm powerful sorry," Rass said again.

"No, Rass, don't cry," said Mom. "You're not to blame, and I'll not hear you say it. Had you grabbed hold of them mules, the waters' force would have drug you under, too. We'd have lost you, and your father, who you saved." She pushed stringy strands of hair behind her ears, gave the other children the eye, then bent to embrace their father in his grief.

Dad bolted upright at her touch, beat her away. "L.G. would have obeyed me! He'd have saved my mules!" He pushed all the kids aside and ran, crazed. "*I'll* save my mules! I'll not have no sissy boy, nor no flood do us in!"

Rass did not run after.

The mules lay in clear sight, though among the debris that had been thrown against the bank when the ditch emptied its belly to the level of the break. Water spread shallow and wide to a quarter of a mile. As Dad lifted broken tree parts and uprooted brush and flung them away, the girls cheered. He pulled the logging chains gently at first, then roughly when the chains resisted. All fell silent as the crushed, mutilated, mules were exposed. *Dead.*

Dad kicked at them and shouted, "Get up, you stupid, stubborn fools. Move! Dad blast it, do what I say! I got a crop to get planted!"

Rass said aloud softly, "I hate him."

"Don't say that!" Sally whispered. "God says honor your father!"

"He called me a sissy," Rass snapped at her. "At least I know when a mule is dead!"

"Shush," said Mom, who had heard. "Don't you see your father's not hisself? He'll come around. Thank heaven he ain't like that Tom Martin what walked out and left his wife and eight kids to starve when hard times hit. Your dad just worked longer, picked cotton by moonlight, so's we'd meet our debts. He's got a bad tongue, but don't take it to heart." She set Chrissy down and took Marylu. "A man's job means ever'thing to him. I declare he'd sooner lose his wife than his way to earn us a living. I stopped taking it personal long ago."

Rass turned away. Bill looked at him and reached out. Rass wanted to take his hand, but Chrissy and Rosalee were clinging to him, wailing, "Daddy's left the mules. He's gone! He'll never come back."

"He'll come back, if we pray," Sally said.

The sun was easing out again. Rass pulled the girls gently to him. "God's no help. He gives us sunshine one minute and a flood the next!"

"Rass!" Sally and Mom yelled in unison, shocked.

Then the gaping silence where their cries stopped was filled by a great bellow rising above all other ugly sounds. Rass thought for a minute it was from an angry God. But it came from the mouth of his prized Ole Jersey, that great giver he'd dreamed of breeding to Preston's bull.

He ran.

# 4

OH MERCY BE, Rass had not even saved Ole Jersey.

Making a last try to move, the cow had crashed down, inches from the water's edge. Her wild cries tore Rass's heart. One leg was clearly broken. She had bloody gashes all over. One teat was nearly severed. It flopped out to the side in the mud, hung only by a skin. There was no fairness or justice in the world! She would never give him a prize calf. Rass fell upon her and wept. How many times he'd washed the manure from those teats and talked to her gently as he'd milked! He cried forever.

Mom came over and pulled him loose. "You must kill Ole Jersey," she said quietly.

"No!" he cried. "I cain't kill her!"

He had grabbed snakes by their tails and popped off their heads with a whipping motion when no hoe was handy: copperheads, water moccasins, and spread adders. But kill Ole Jersey, that giver of sweet warm milk that kept body and soul together, even in the hardest of times?

"I won't!" he protested again.

Mom, standing solid, stern as when insisting a kid mind, flatly demanded, "Grab a club. Do it fast before the cow drowns and we cain't eat her. We gotta live on something. Till Whit gains control, you're the only man I got. Your arms are strong. Take on your duty. Sally, tote the little'uns outa sight!" And to the sky Mom cried, "God, I don't hate You no more for making it rain, nor bringing the flood. Now You got to help my boy do what he's got to do!"

"No. No! I won't. I cain't!"

The little girls had come closer and now watched in voiceless, wide-eyed wonder.

Mom said firmly, "It's natural for farmers to slaughter." Indeed, Dad slaughtered hogs. Mom had wrung chickens' necks in the name of food.

"But God says, *'Thou shalt not kill,'*" Sally said, and Rass loved her for it.

He pleaded, "I could make a strong splint for Ole Jersey's leg. You could sew her teat back on and sew up her cuts—please, Mom?"

Mom turned to answer Sally. *"Thou shalt not kill* gets altered by God hisself when there is necessity. Food's a necessity."

Ole Jersey could not be saved. Only death could stop her rising cries of pain.

Rass understood, as Dad had understood and explained to him about the time Uncle Tut had had to steal in order to have food to live. Rass reached for a club. Numb, he walked slowly toward his beloved cow. Then, dropping his club, he said to Mom, "I'd rather steal than kill."

"Rass, this is not the time for talk! To kill for food is God's will! Hurry! She must be bled properly, as the Bible says."

"Mom, let Ole Jersey live. Let me butcher a hog what's drowned." Ole Jersey's sounds in the background near blocked his words.

"We cain't butcher hogs what's died of unnatural cause!"

Rass knew she was right. Day laborers, nearing starvation, picked up chickens killed on the roads or coons found dead from trap injury, but good Baptists and Pentecosts went by the Scriptures.

"Drowning in a flood is natural!" Rass shouted. "Mom, I ain't even so much as wrung a chicken's neck!"

"The cow is gone, Rass. Now! Quick! Kill her afore she dies! Knock her out first so's she won't have to feel nothing. That's why we wring chickens' necks, so's it's quick."

"No!" Rass said again, but afraid he would hesitate, he picked up his club again, a thick stub of an oak branch, and looked into the big brown, crazed eyes of Ole Jersey... but then came her loudest bellow; he stopped midswing. Her dark mouth was beaded with the moisture of pain. He couldn't do it.

"Go on, Rass. The Lord is with you," Mom whispered.

He lifted the club and with all his might he steeled his soul and drove the club into the raging cow's skull. The impact hurt his arm, but he felt no pain. He felt nothing. Nothing!

Ole Jersey's eyes walled, a wild cry erupted, she fell to one side. Rass felt nothing.

"Finish the job, son. Cut the jugular. Bleed her properly."

"Bill, I'll need your knife." Rass reached a weak hand toward Bill's pocket as he spoke. Bill understood well enough what Rass was about. But Bill backed away, clutching his pocket tight. His green eyes seemed totally frightened and his hand rubbed quickly, roughly across the fuzz of his pale eyebrows. "Bill, I need you to help me," Rass said to him. "Ole Jersey's a big animal. I got her knocked out on the first try and I think she may be dead. But don't let me have to do it again. I ain't got no strength left in me. Please." Rass kept reaching.

Bill pushed him away with great force. Bill was strong and often wrestled with his brother Louie and won. Mostly he used his muscles for pleasing folk, like carrying wood for his mother or plowing and harrowing for his dad. Louie said once Bill decided to do a thing no one could stop him.

Sally said, "Use a broken fruit jar."

Everywhere were shards of broken jars and window glass, as if they came from a many-windowed mansion house. But Rass did not have to search for the right piece of glass, for there was Bill, reaching out beyond fear, deftly cutting Ole Jersey's jugular to let her bleed properly. Blood spurted against his arms and hands, and though he jumped back, his clothes were covered as red as the beets in the broken jars nearby.

Jersey's eyes were still open, milky and blank, but free of pain, free of life. Once again Rass knew what death meant. This time it was Bill who led him gently away.

Dad always said, "All farmers kill. Feelings have no place in it." Rass's three oldest brothers, men fifteen to nineteen, now gone from home, had killed their first hogs in the winter of their fifteenth years. "Only tender little kids hide their heads under pillows to snuffle out a hog's long squeal of death," Dad had said. Rass heard the squeal always. Since he was eight, after the squeal was over, he'd stood boldly to witness the butchering and carted fat to the big black kettle in the backyard for Mom to render out the lard. He knew Bill had done the same. But Mrs. Brown would probably never make Bill kill anything.

Bill had tried to drive the hogs to high ground, but hogs don't drive so well, nor run very fast. Did he feel he'd let the Whitleys' source of meat drown? Bill wiped his hands free of blood on the back side of his pants, then handed his knife over for the butchering.

"Thanks," Rass said.

"Sally, get out of here. This ain't for kids." Rass pushed her and the little girls toward some trees. That action made his queasiness sharp, and he escaped behind a tree to vomit. As soon as he could, he scolded Sally, as if he'd never taken that pause. "It ain't good for little ones to have to witness the cruelties of life."

"We heard you a-puking, Rass. Didn't we, Rosalee? Chrissy?" Chrissy hid behind Sally, but Rosalee nodded soberly.

Mom rubbed at the hollow in her neck. Her mouth closed tight. Again she brushed aside her hair. "Rass, give me Bill's pocketknife. I'll dress out the beef, so's we can move it to wherever we'll be a-going. You and Bill done your first killing of a loved animal. I ain't forcing you to butcher, too. That's too much for young boys."

But Rass began the butchering, just as he'd seen Dad do year after year. He said, "Mom, you never watched Dad butcher." With a quick draw of knife down the belly of the carcass, he split the skin. Bill peeled it back.

"I've watched my own daddy, like my boys has watched Whit," she answered. "I know it by heart. Killing's the hardest part. Hand me the knife."

Rass handed over Bill's fine knife, the envy of every boy in or around Parma. Mr. Brown had declared his youngest son needed to own something other boys could only yearn for.

"Mom, you don't have to butcher," Sally said. "We can fast for weeks and still not die. Indians has done it from time immoral."

Mom said sharply, "God meant animals to be eaten. Enough said. We're subject to His will. And your father's. You come back, Whit?"

Dad had returned. Though he didn't say he was sorry for not attending the slaughter, his face was wrung with sorrow. Dad never allowed butchering 'less he was in charge. Even now he put his knife next to Mom's, cutting quickly, deftly. When he did speak, Rass noticed his effort to sound in control again. "This ditch dump is alive with more rabbits than any one of you kids could chase down. Rass, take Bill and hep them little girls catch rabbits."

Rass ignored that. "Where was you?" he asked.

"Out walking the ditch down yonder, scanning the amount of damage, seeing if'n others needed help, or was handy to come help us."

Rass figured he'd not have vomited if he'd been able to go out alone, gaining time to recover from the shock. Dad could at least apologize for calling him a sissy. Instead, Dad's voice grew stronger as he kept talking. "We'll need a boat to get us outa here. None of our neighbors' houses been hit. Just ourn." Then came a spark of anger. "It's always been a sore point with me, and next time I ain't *renting* from no landlord what builds a house right on a ditch!" He paused to stand up straight and tall, as if he still had the right to call himself a renter.

Then Dad put a bloody hand up to shade his eyes and looked across the floodwaters, declaring, "Morning's still young. Thur'll be neighbors coming to fetch us soon, same as I'd do if they was the ones stranded."

Dad would. He'd always helped neighbors. When a husband was sick, he'd log and split extra wood for winter, or help with butchering, or fix flat tires or mend wagon beds.

"Mr. McMulty'll come. I know he will," Sally said.

"Why sure, they'll all be a-coming, and we'll get this house of ourn righted again before you know it. Any one of 'em will take us in, if'n it comes to it. Rass, you gonna chase down rabbits with these girls?"

Dad was trying to be cheerful, but Rass was still angry at Dad for calling him a sissy. Lots of grown-ups didn't respect kids, but that didn't make it right. Rass never answered. He just joined Bill, who was carrying meat to higher ground, and remained equally silent.

Sally stayed riveted to her spot. Twisting the long red pigtail she'd made of her hair this morning to the front of her, she chewed on it. Mom answered in Rass's stead. "The

**4 3**

boys is needed here to haul cut meat over to the grass. Let 'em be. Neither of 'em's boys no more. 'Tween the two, they done what had to be—they killed this cow."

"I figured 'twasn't you," was all Dad said.

"Well, you too scared or too proud to tell the boys thanks?" Mom said under her breath. If Dad heard, he did not respond. Then quickly her voice shifted. "We cain't be proud, nor picky. We gotta get our kids some place 'fore nightfall. And before you ask, I'd rather we stay homeless than stay at Tut's!"

"Tut's my brother."

"So's Jake."

Rass took the liver, which Dad handed him, and said, "Uncle Tut's eight kids and our six'd make fourteen kids in two bedrooms. Counting you and Mom it'd be sixteen."

Mom handed Bill the cow's heart. "If you wasn't always accusing Jake of acting uppity, we could look to him and Kate, Whit."

"I won't stand beholden to Jake!"

"Now, talking big ain't going to spare us none. Without no mules, you'll never get your own piece of land. We might as well face up to that and get on with living."

Surprisingly Dad agreed, then he added, "Now that Tut's got them matched bay horses give 'im by that man who got saved and went back to his mom in the city, it sure don't set right with me. Especially with my mules dead. We do got to go somers else. Tut's and our kids don't get along nohow. I'm feared that many kids'd cave in his place worse than ourn right here. Don't know where we'll go, but it sure won't be Jake's."

This time Mom handed Bill a bloody cut from the neck as she said, "Never has set right with me why a time waster and fast spender of other folks' money, as Tut is, is deserving of matched bays or anything!" Rass had heard this exchange many times. He knew what Dad would say.

"Helen! He's my brother. Brothers stick together. That's how families survive. You know that."

Rass thought how he and L.G. really used to stick together when they were little, and wondered if they'd ever again. "Uncle Jake's your brother, too," Rass reminded Dad just as Mom had.

"Rass is right, Whit. Don't be too pigheaded to say yes if Jake and Kate asks to take us in."

They were interrupted by a scream from Sally. "Someone's coming! Mr. McMulty! We can live with Mr. McMulty!" The little girls' screeches were a joyful echo.

Delighted, giving no thought to the fact that Sally had been the first to spot Mr. McMulty, Rass shouted, too. "His *is* the likeliest place for us! Him being just one. Altogether we'd not number as many as Uncle Tut's. Me and L.G. won't mind sleeping in the loft, like Tut's boys. Mom, you and Dad could sleep with the girls in the bedroom. That'd leave Mr. McMulty to sleep in his living room as always."

Mom was aghast. "Why, such cain't be thought on! I . . . I don't mean the loft. Nor parents and kids in the same room. It's just we cain't . . ." She paused. "Mr. McMulty abides by certain rules, or he gets a warning."

Dad looked up. "Boy, you know better'n talk like that! The Klan's on the move agin. They don't tolerate colored folk staying with whites, nor the other way around."

Rass knew about the Klan, and that he and Clever were not allowed to stay overnight. "Aren't things different in an *emergency?*" he asked, then said no more. He just watched Mr. McMulty direct that mule of Nert's into the flood-waters. First the water covered the mule's ankles, then knees, then up to its belly. It stayed belly depth all the rest of the trek.

"Yhere, Barney. Yhere, boy," Mr. McMulty said, and got the frightened mule to step up out of the water and move at an angle up the bank a bit. He dismounted with a leap, standing only slightly taller than the mule. Today his wispy gray hair looked like a half crown sliding off the back of his balding head, making his face appear long. No talk. Immediately, he reached out to touch all around. He gave Rass a hug when he pointed to the dead cow.

Sally said, "Her leg was broke."

"Bless yo' soul, boy, you done lost yo' cow *and* yo' home."

"And Dad's mules. I didn't save Dad's mules." Rass near cried.

Dad coughed a hollow metallic cough, signifying Rass to stop showing feelings. It wasn't a man's nor boy's place to cry.

Bill put out his arms and the old man embraced him, too, and said, "When I out walking Rose's dogs, I see this deaf boy traipsing home with Rass. I figure he swap places with L.G. for the night. Flood's a turrible thing for a boy to see and not be able to talk on. You all alive, though. Blessed Lord Jesus! What can I do to hep you, Whit?" He gently patted Bill and moved him aside, and took Marylu in his arms.

46

"Looks bad, Whit," Mr. McMulty continued before Dad could answer. "Looks bad. I come outa my barn when I hears the commotion, and I don't believe what I sees. First thing I knows yo' house been laid low. Number times I say to the Lord, 'Tell me it tain't so.' " His lips trembled as he wailed, "It gone Lord, gone! Gone for good. Killed not jest yo' mules, but most yo' livestock, too. Lord, Whit, what you gonna do? A man gotta have a house, food."

"Them's the facts," answered Dad.

"Baby chicks are alive," Rass said. "Coalie, too."

Sally added, "And we got meat, but we gotta take it somewheres. We cain't go to Uncle Jake's or Uncle Tut's. Mr. McMulty, can we come stay with you? It's an emergency."

Mr. McMulty quickly handed Marylu to Rosalee, then awkwardly bent forward, as if to search out his mule's rein. He found it, knotted and reknotted it. Still not looking up, he muttered, "Chile don't know what she a-saying." He turned to Sally. "Dotter, my place got a skimpy yard," he said quietly. "No place for chillun."

Sally's face held disbelief.

Rass, remembering the time a person first spoke to him of race, said to Sally, "Once John Henry Litikin told me Clever was colored and I was white and that's why we had to go to separate schools. Clever wouldn't come spend the night with me 'cause he couldn't sleep in a white boy's house. He said it couldn't be any other way." Just thinking about it made Rass angry. Then turning from Sally, he demanded, "Mr. McMulty? Dad? You explain it to Sally. Tell her friends cain't even help friends in bad times!"

Dad said nothing. Mr. McMulty looked away from

Rass and Sally and spoke just to Dad. "Preston plantation got extry croppers' shacks setting empty, on up the road, though it not likely Nert ask a favor of such a big landowner."

"No. Ever' landlord tends his own business. Ain't no need us second-guessing Nert," Dad said, then went back to butchering. He handed Rass a cut from the loin section to carry away to the grassy spot. Rass's and Bill's hands were as bloody as Mom's and Dad's.

Mr. McMulty nodded. "Nert sure has his say on *all* things. He not gwine bow down and beg from no big plantation owner, but he come up with something. He cain't stand lose you and yo' two boys as work hands. He do what he gotta do, like this boy yhere, killing his own milk cow. It gonna be the way Nert say. He the man o' power." He touched Rass.

"It ain't right," Rass said.

"All's us do what has to be, son, according to set rules. Nert the boss, boy, you got to know. Whit, want me to ride out for hep?"

"Maybe. Let me get all this meat cut up. If no one's come with a boat by then, I'll ride out with you, double."

"I hep by hanging that meat up off'n the ground." Mr. McMulty, acting as if this was no emergency, took a swirl of baling wire from the loop in his overalls and twisted a length back and forth until it broke off. Rass wiped blood, or tears, he didn't know which, from the corner of his eye. With a thrust of his shoulder, he hoisted the meat up while Mr. McMulty wired it to a willow branch.

"A bending willow holds up in a bad storm what'd

break a sturdy oak," the old man said, as if he were story-telling. With a little motioning, he had Bill helping tie, too.

Rass exploded. "We're not going to find a place to live!"

"Things look dark at times, I knows. But keep yo' eye on hope, boy, so's yo' ear hear no other kinda talk."

Sally was picking up large pieces of glass near the edge of the bank. With hands held away from her body, she carefully carried them through the debris and out by the ash trees. Rosalee and Chrissy carefully picked up smaller pieces and followed. Rass said, "We'll be picking up bits of glass here for years."

So Chrissy stopped and tried to pull a dirty plaid blanket from the water, slipped in the mud, cut her knee, that same knee that hadn't had time yet to scab over from the skin she'd gotten from jumping off the porch, like Rass, before the flood. She curled her hands about her knees and hid her face. Rass spotted a brown guinea egg there among the rubble and handed it to her, saying, "The guineas flew to safety in the brush on the right-of-way or ditch banks." Chrissy nodded and took the egg.

Mom handed Bill his knife, wiped the blood from her hands on the back of her pretty flowered dress, and took Marylu from Rosalee. "She's a-crying too hard. I best nurse her. You other kids run chase them rabbits now." She motioned, but Bill, turning away from the butchering to stare at trembling wild rabbits too scared to hide, shook his head no and sat down. The girls did, too.

They had often chased and killed rabbits that fled inward during great circular hay mowings. Rass caught short his breath. He *had* killed before. Why had he not remembered? It was what was done, one of the rules that governed farm life. Rabbits were welcome food. Ole Jersey was needed food. It was the way of things. And Clever not sleeping over was simply the way of things.

Rass sat down next to Bill, letting the meat from Ole Jersey swinging on the willow tops block his view.

# 5

RATHER THAN helping Dad kick mud over the butchering site, Rass watched Mr. McMulty take out his pocketknife and carve a simple willow whistle for the little girls. That's why, not long after the flood, the sounds on the ditch bank were "Twinkle, Twinkle, Little Star."

With quick, impatient strides, Dad moved to the highest point on the bank. Then, his hand shading his eyes, he scanned the horizon. "I cain't believe folks ain't coming. I oughta let our whereabouts be known with a holler. 'Nough time has lapsed so it'd show no signs of begging."

Rass admired Dad's talent at hollering. He pulled at Bill to watch. Hollering for help was much better than pretending all was well.

Setting his direction toward the Dumases, Dad cupped his hands and gave a *whoop*, louder than when done for pleasure or in competition. He repeated it toward Nert's. All waited for a responding holler.

"Pray for patience—the Lord gives us tests," Mom said solemnly.

Mr. McMulty moved to first one of the girls then the next, touched their heads. "The Lord do test us all."

No holler was returned, so Rass tried. He didn't project far. Dad, seeming to accept his neighbors' silence, took Mr. McMulty to see his dead mules. Rass and Bill went to the water to wash away blood from their hands and clothes. Then the men returned, with Mr. McMulty talking hope. "Don't worry. Nert gwine have to do something for youns, Whit."

Rass fell into step with them, saying, "Rich folks suffer out hard times, too. Nert cain't spare us men during this season of the year." Dad didn't correct Rass calling himself a man. Just nodded. Rass tried to catch the look in Dad's eyes, but Dad was looking to the skies. "Everybody's going be hit by the rains what brought this flood," Rass went on, "whether they're living too close to the ditch and got it bad like us, or just got all their early seeding washed out."

Mr. McMulty agreed. " 'Course most my land be sorry. Nert not gwine spend money on seed for replanting when he get more if mine lie fallow."

"I don't know if it works like that," Dad said, looking at Mr. McMulty. "I heard last week that the landlord cain't restate his claim for parity at this late date. I'm tempted to go with the Dumases to one of them farm meetings and find out if that's a fact." Rass remembered Mr. McMulty's plans for that parity.

At that moment great honking from Uncle Jake's Chevy filled the air. It pulled a wagon holding two boats. Whoops came from all windows. Uncle Tut was along, too, his head and arms out the windows, waving. The change was welcome.

Uncle Jake waved his panama hat and called, "Anyone hurt, Whit?"

"We're all alive," Dad answered.

"We'll get you outa there. Hang on."

The cheering got loud as Uncle Tut's and Uncle Jake's flat-bottom boats were pushed into the water. Uncle Tut, his bib overalls tight over his round and full form, jumped into one. When his two oldest sons, eleven and nine, got in, their weight almost overfilled the boat. Uncle Jake and Aunt Kate, a large woman of high, firm breast and wind-swept hair, got into the other. Closer, closer they came rowing, to the beat of Aunt Kate's yells, "Praise the Lord, you're all alive!" Mom answered in kind until finally the two women were together and embracing. Mom wept for the first time.

The uncles shook their heads and cried out, "Ain't it awful!"

Rass greeted his cousins, who saw only adventure.

"Sorry to come so late," Uncle Jake apologized. "We weren't hit. Wasn't till Tut asked me for boats I knowed anyone had been."

Dad wasn't answering. Uncle Jake's good luck was too much to acknowledge, Rass guessed, so he answered for Dad, "We're glad youns come."

Uncle Tut laughed as his boys ran down-ditch like little devils, jumping over a dented roasting pot, tossing a dead chicken into the air, throwing broken things around as if it were a free-for-all. Rass thought maybe Uncle Tut had hit rock bottom with his drinking so many times and got up again as a preacher and storyteller that his boys saw this crisis as normal.

Twice Mr. McMulty saved a boy from falling headfirst into the floodwaters. He got no thanks. So Aunt Kate took things in hand. "Tut, I left my boy home, like you oughta left your younguns with Crystal. I'll jist haul these wild boys back and let thur mommy take care of 'em. I'll drive Helen and the little'uns to our place. Helen, leave the salvaging to the men."

"We'll go and wash up, but Whit won't let us stay with youns," Rass heard Mom say.

"I know." Aunt Kate nodded. She went on talking, giving no attention to Tut's protest against her taking his boys. "I intend to enlist the church sisters, and other neighbors'll be a-coming, too." She motioned toward the water's far edge.

It was L.G. and Louie Brown in Dad's Chevy. Rass had never been so glad to see L.G. Right behind Dad's Chevy came three people on mules—Clever Dumas and two white day laborers, who pulled Louie and L.G. up to ride with them.

Aunt Kate asked, "Where's Nert? That man's never here when he's needed. He's an evil man if there ever was one. How he got Rose blind to that fact I'll never know. Evil begets evil."

The little girls clung to Mom and screamed, "L.G.'s coming!" Rass soft-talked them quiet and shooed them on toward Aunt Kate's boat. "Get in, don't jump. Be good and Mom'll let you touch L.G. in passing."

"Sure," said Aunt Kate. "We know it's important to count family in the middle of a crisis, but step quickly, Helen."

Mom hesitated, saying, "I cain't leave. Men need a

woman's eye on saving things. Lots of things a man'd throw away can be mended."

Sally nodded and said, "Mom, I'll stay. I know ever'-thing you've ever taught me."

Mom still looked concerned, but Dad gave her a push, saying firmly, "Helen, go tend our little girls. 'Sides, you'll be needed at the other end to unpack what gets saved. Sally's ever' bit as picky as you."

Mom reluctantly stepped into the boat.

Meanwhile Rass, half lifting, half shoving, got Uncle Tut's boys into the boat, then helped Aunt Kate in last. He and Bill pushed the boat out and away. It was so full it barely floated.

Tut called out, "Now you boys stop rocking Kate's boat!" Raymond stood and immediately rocked harder. Clever, riding single, was there bending from his mule and pushed Raymond back down. Aunt Kate swatted the boy good. Uncle Tut laughed and waved them on.

Soon the boat was even with L.G. He rode double, sitting still as stone, his mouth open in shock. The little girls reached up to touch him. Tut's boys acted as if they would toss Marylu to L.G., and she began to cry. So Clever turned his mule around and rode alongside Kate's boat to keep Tut's boys from further extending the touching art. Finally L.G. pulled his oily cap bill face forward, and waved them on. His usual good smile was missing as he came on toward the ditch bank.

Aunt Kate's sturdy rowing through the floodwaters was most serious. Soon her Chevy gobbled them all up and sped them away.

Uncle Tut thumped Rass on the head. "I'm glad me

and my family ain't rich, to get hated as much as Kate hates Nert. Some say it's no sin to be rich and point to good rich like Winters or Preston, but I say when folks gets riled all rich gets shoved into the same pile as Nert. That's why the Good Book says it's harder for a rich man to get through the eye of a little bitty ole needle than ever to get to heaven."

Rass let Uncle Tut's preaching rest on the world. His eyes were on L.G., a lost, red-haired, freckle-faced boy, not the talkative, muscled rival Rass knew. Finally Rass pulled him to the ground. It wasn't proper to hug as Sally did, or as Bill hugged Louie, even though he thought of it.

L.G. asked, "Nobody hurt?"

Rass kicked mud from the covered-over butchering scene.

"Not Ole Jersey?"

Rass nodded; tears came. Maybe they would have said things sincere, if Dad hadn't moved in then and greeted L.G. warmly, tears welling in *his* eyes, and led L.G. away.

Anyway, Clever had come checking on Rass and was asking about Ole Jersey. Clever, getting tall like L.G., though he was just a few months older than Rass, had hair curled tight to his head, like his father. His brown fingers were long and thin like his mother's side of the family. He gave Rass a warm slap on the shoulder, then explained, "Me and Pop was out till early hours at a farm union meeting in Sikeston and was sleeping in, when Pop gets a call for the dredge to repair a break in the ditch bank. I cain't believe it was near youns."

The day laborers had heard Dad's whoop, but offered

excuses for being late, too. "Before venturing out, we moved our families to the loft, in case water kept a-spreading and reacht our living quarters."

They shook hands with Dad, his brothers, and Mr. McMulty.

L.G. was back. "I told Dad I'd walk down-ditch to where most of the stuff what didn't stay in the house has drifted. Collecting and piling up good items is the first order. You wanna help?" Then L.G., in charge as usual, moved on. Rass, Clever, and even Sally followed. Eventually all the men set to work retrieving and stacking drifting things. The furniture, broken or pulled apart, clothes, pans, buckets, and lumber from the house was saved. Sally, thinking of Mom's instructions, insisted it could all be mended. L.G. agreed. "If I can fix Brown's truck, I can fix a broken drawer!"

I could, too, thought Rass, though he didn't say so out loud.

The morning was still overcast, and as Rass stretched for the first time, he saw the workers as if they were shaded figures in a horrible dream. A couple of men were bent picking up girls' muddy dresses, laying them on top of the lard cans. Others were at a tangled mess of clothes clustered about a sapling's trunk, and Mr. McMulty had set to racking the wood from the house. Rass wanted to remake this dream, as was his custom after waking from a bad one, but there'd be no waking up, and he was too tired to create.

The second time Rass paused to stand straight and stretch, the sun was burning its way through. So he scoured the horizon and shouted, "Nert! Nert! Here comes Nert!"

Instead of feeling fear, he had the silly thought that, for once, he'd beat Sally at spying someone. There was no mistaking Nert, a big bull of a man in his late fifties, a full head of gray hair, tanned, lined, hard face, sitting astride a big white horse. Dressed in brown corduroys, tan shirt, showing off like gentry. Stopping short of the bank, Nert remained out in the waters. "The county dredge crew'll be on the job to speed up the drainage, get this water settled out," he called to them. "In a week, my fields'll be workable. You okay?"

"We're all alive," Dad answered, deliberately calm before his landlord.

"His mules and livestock's gone. Whit's ruint!" Uncle Tut called.

Nert looked about and nodded. "My property is totally wrecked," he said.

"You got some place to put Whit's belongings, till we can have a house-raising?" Uncle Jake asked. "We're salvaging a good bit o' lumber."

Nert snapped, "There'll be no house-raising during planting season. Get Whit's stuff on dry ground. Use the cotton wagon and tarp by McMulty's." He paused. Nert was the real power, as Mr. McMulty had said. Nert added, "On second thought, Whit, pull your wagon out and use it. McMulty, you can pack your belongings in the cotton wagon. I'll be letting you go. Whit, move into that house." He said the last without change of voice. It stopped everybody dead.

Rass, looking toward Mr. McMulty, saw a fierce anger sweep the old man's countenance, but instantly he bowed his head. When his face was visible again, it held a blank, obedient look.

"No," Rass whispered. "No."

Mr. McMulty stood tall. " 'Bout my contract?"

Nert gave his head a jerk and said, "What contract?" Then he ordered, "Whit, you best come over later and sign a sharecropper's agreement, unless you got some way of getting yourself more mules. I'll give you Sunday off for settling in. Fields where you'll be living will be dry enough to work come Monday. Every hand's to be back to the plow immediately to offset flood losses." He looked at Rass and L.G. "And keep your boys outa school! Reseeding and planting's to be done on time."

"My mule?" asked Mr. McMulty.

"McMulty, don't waste my time. You can use *my* mule to get yourself outa here. I'll expect you moved and my wagon back by four."

Again Rass saw Mr. McMulty's anger almost surface, then recede. "I means my mule colt Miz Rose done give me."

"Rose don't give! Get my wagon back by four!" Nert was final.

Mr. McMulty's eyes did not agree. But he said, "Yasuh, I'll bring 'em back to thur own stalls on my place."

"*My* place. I own it! Don't talk back to me."

"When we gonna settle books, boss?" The accent on the word *boss*.

"I said at four! Move! Cain't have this on my mind. Gotta take Rose to Sikeston for an overnight." Nert fought his horse, prancing to his shouts. No more was said. Mr.

McMulty mounted the mule and eased out into the floodwaters. Clever mounted his mule and followed.

"Whit, I want that dead livestock buried before I get
back."

"What time'll that be tomarr?"

"Late! But do it today. You can get some mules from
my barn for dragging, if McMulty's using the others to
move." Nert turned his white horse and rode quickly back
through the waters.

Rass waited for someone to speak out, but all stood
silent until Nert hit dry land and galloped away in the
direction of his fine home hidden in a lovely grove.

"Dad, why didn't you tell him we cain't take Mr.
McMulty's house?" Rass demanded. Then he shouted toward slower-moving Mr. McMulty and Clever, who had
not yet cleared the water, "Mr. McMulty, don't let Nert
do this! Go tell Maggie Porter. You got a contract!"

"Nert's word was his contract," said Uncle Tut in the
manner of calling a fact. "Colored folks gets no paper
what'd stand up in court."

Rass could see by everyone's faces that it was true that
only white men had written legal contracts kept inside their
family Bibles, safe in God's hands against fire. Such knowledge drove Rass wild. He punched L.G., punched Louie,
and even swung at Bill. He would have hit Sally, too, if
she wasn't a girl. He hated these men! Didn't they realize
that the Whitleys' gaining a house meant Mr. McMulty
had nothing? He was hitting wildly.

"Rass! Stop showing out!" Dad hissed.

Uncle Tut, closest to Rass, grabbed him, stopped his

hitting, preached to him. "Cain't talk back to no landlord."

"Boy, don't you know there cain't be no backtalk to Nert?" someone said. "Your screaming'll be silenced by the pound of nails in your coffin."

"It drives the nail in tighter, if'n you protests." Curses followed.

"Dad, why're you letting people cuss in front of Sally? Why ain't everyone swearing against Nert depriving a man of his home with no notice?"

Dad exploded. "You acting up ain't just harming our family, Rass! We're a community here." His hand circled the land. "We got to stick together if any of us are gonna live. Cut it out, boy! Mind!"

It was L.G. and Louie who finally jerked Rass to one side, using their own scorching words to quiet him. "Hellfire, Rass, slow down."

"Shut your mouth, boy."

Rass grew silent, then it followed that all the men's tone sobered to mere reasoning. "Nert oughta took youns in," said a day laborer.

"For two cents I'd knock his ugly block off," said another so soberly all knew it was just a wish.

"His home's big enough," the first worker added, as if that made sense.

"We'd not set foot in that man's house," Dad declared, and Rass instantly felt close to Dad again.

Uncle Tut said, "Whit, ain't Nert's wife, Rose, one of Helen's girlhood friends, for God's sake?"

"Tut, remember you're a preacher. Stop taking the Lord's name in vain," Uncle Jake scolded as he got back to work. He paused to mutter, "Taking purty Rose to a party, he says! Rose hobnobbing with gentry, plantation owners. Staying overnight in Winters' mansion, I bet!"

Surprisingly L.G. joined in with equal heat. "Everyone knows Nert's just hoping to be a Preston or a Winters someday hisself." Some of the other helpers went back to the job at hand muttering likewise.

"Then Nert oughta let his wife give a mule colt to an old man what's tended her dogs for years!" Rass cried out to them, wanting them to stop and hear. "And all Nert says is, it ain't so. Nobody stopped 'im! I never stopped him! I hope every bridge they cross gets washed out, and they fall in, and Nert drowns!"

L.G. nodded. Rass loved him.

Dad grabbed Rass once again. "God can do with Nert whatever He pleases," he said harshly, then pushed Rass back to work.

Uncle Tut, to make sure Rass heard from him, as well, said, "You know colored folks got no stand in court. On account of the new law, Nert woulda let him go soon's planting was done anyway, so's to keep the whole parity check."

Uncle Jake added, "It's sad, Rass, but you gotta know we cain't make this black man none of our business, or you and your family'll be without a home. Now just stay quiet and let's get on with salvaging for youns what things we can."

"No!" Rass yelled. "We're not moving into Mr. Mc-Multy's house. I won't do it! I'll kill Nert first!"

Dad was there instantly, caught him in a grip-lock this

time. "Rass, I ain't letting you talk threats agin a landlord! Hold still. Settle down. Cut it out!"

Rass couldn't wiggle free; Dad was powerful.

"Then let Mr. McMulty live with us!"

At that there arose a general mumbling from everyone.

"Rass, we ain't in no place to give charity. We're beholden to *take* it, like Jake pointed out! We're down, *ruined*. This flood hitting us was real, cain't you see?" He smacked Rass's cheek hard.

Rass staggered from the blow of Dad's words and hand. He'd find a way. Had to!

The crowd grew quiet until Rass got his balance, then a day laborer offered, "My house cain't hold everybody, but I could put up one or two, till youns could find a place. That'd leave McMulty stay put." He bent back to the job. Day laborers seldom just stood as they talked.

"Mr. McMulty won't break up no one's family." L.G. was helping. "Rass is right, wishing what he did, but Nert's too mean to be killed off."

"Yes, Nert's mean!" Rass declared, then turning sarcastic, added, "Didn't you hear, Dad? Even your favorite son L.G. thinks that it's wrong what Nert did!"

"Obeying the rules society sets don't have a blame thing to do with what we think, nor what's right nor wrong. We mind the rules if'n we want to survive. Learn that, boys," was Dad's strange reply. The others were silent.

Rass's mind exploded with anger. So *silence* was their way! Okay, let them be silent. But he'd find his own way to change things. He set to work near Bill, who had seen all and would understand. So would Clever.

From time to time the rest of the morning Rass glanced across the water to see Clever help load McMulty's stove and heavy stuff. He almost believed Mr. McMulty would manage fine with good people like the Dumases to take him in. He held tight to that thought as he and Sally and Bill loaded the boat with things salvaged.

L.G. and Louie got to row belongings across the water, transfer them to the wagon hooked onto Dad's Chevy, then drive on to the McMulty place. Rass didn't even care anymore that L.G. drove Dad's Chevy. His mind had its mission.

# 6

As the day wore on, more neighbors, black and white, came to help salvage. The sky had lightened a bit by the time Aunt Kate and the church women brought food at one o'clock.

"You're doing great. Whitleys'll have a place to sleep by nightfall!" one church woman called out.

No one mentioned the place was McMulty's. But when Rass again cried out that fact, the black neighbors quietly said they'd better be getting on home. To shush Rass, L.G. allowed him and Bill to get in the boat to help deliver things. At McMulty's flies swarmed over the heaps of soiled clothes. Only white women helped Mom in the scrubbing of those salvaged clothes, bedding, dishes, and furniture. Never before had such a separation happened. A cut on Rass's finger smarted. He and Bill returned quickly to the wrecked house.

Somehow the smell there of dirt and mold from uprooted trees, too long in damp weather, was more tolerable. "I don't like it," Rass said to Bill, though he desperately needed someone to talk back.

They worked side by side till late that afternoon, when Sally spotted a news reporter and cameraman from the Malden paper—strangers coming to inquire and to take pictures. A boy was hanging along behind.

It was...yes, Shark! Such neat clothes and well-combed straight black hair could belong to no one but his best school friend, a town boy.

As soon as they got on dry land, Shark ran to Rass and gripped his arm. The reporter announced, "I heard floodgates broke on a Mississippi River tributary, but I never expected to see the likes of this. You folks got a place to go?"

"We're working on it," Dad answered. "What about them floodgates?"

"Last I heard, they're being fixed."

When Dad didn't respond, the cameraman spoke up. "We've come for pictures, not to interfere with your work. Hope you don't mind."

"When's a man's minding ever stopped anything?" Dad asked coldly, and went back to his work. The reporter never bothered Dad again, but he made notes of the talk that followed, worker to worker, as they removed blame from God and placed it on engineers.

At first Shark had seemed too shocked over Rass's loss to speak or move. But after saying, "Rass, this oughten ever happened to you. It's a great tragedy. I'll record it for history," he clicked his Box Brownie as often as the photographer clicked his huge camera. They took several pictures of the waters, of the house with men crawling into fallen rooms, and of others pulling the walls apart plank by plank to get at possessions. Everything—except what was in Rass and L.G.'s rooms upstairs—was wet and covered in mud, including Sally, who got into most of the pictures.

The newspeople stayed till near day's end and seemed surprised when a sole black man came to help. Rass wasn't surprised, for Mr. McMulty was always there to help or comfort, but now he seemed strange, too. His eyes were angry, yet his voice was soft.

"Whit, I apologizes that my friends hep *me*, 'stead of youns what needs it more."

Dad's grave answer was, "The mark weren't drawn by neither of us."

Mr. McMulty helped Dad hoist the library table into the boat. No words were spoken. Rass stared. Tell Dad the truth, Mr. McMulty. Tell him you're angry and you ain't letting us move into your house! Rass wanted to straight out tell Mr. McMulty how ashamed he was of what his family was doing. But only Sally talked. She thanked Mr. McMulty sweetly for all his help on the ditch dump earlier. She thanked him for his house. She thanked him for lifting her out of the wreckage she'd gotten wedged into while talking so much. Shark got a picture of that.

Finally Dad yelled, "That's about enough! No more picture taking of my girl. And I don't need pictures showing me up as being bad off."

The cameraman folded up his camera. "It'll be dark before long, anyway. Gotta get these pictures out. First time Parma's made national news since Ripley wrote Maggie Porter up in his *Believe It or Not* for being the only woman sheriff in the States."

Shark didn't move. "But Mr. Whitley, you *are* bad off," he said. "You've been hit hardest of any family around."

At that Dad promptly went to the willow tree, grabbed some beef, and declared, "Here. Here! *Here!* You men take this for hepping me out. It's too much for us to eat up before it's spoiled." He stuck some out toward Mr. Mc-Multy. "Go on, you take a good share, too."

Mr. McMulty shook his head. "Thanks, Whit, but I jest be going now." He touched Rass on the shoulder as he walked away. A good-bye-forever touch. Not knowing how to handle truth in the face of lies, Rass couldn't move.

The hungry day workers reached for the beef. It was a blessing to have most of Ole Jersey eaten by others, Rass thought. He asked Shark, "Would you mind dropping off some meat at the Dumases'? Mr. McMulty'll be there." Shark obliged and left with the newsmen, carrying the meat.

Dad looked extremely tired. "We'd all better quit," he said. "Gotta hep the womenfolk set the stove in place and tote this meat over so's we can grab a bite to eat 'fore we drop dead. Everybody's welcome."

He made Rass wait until the last boat, saying, "Cain't have you getting out of hand agin."

Just as they were leaving Dad and Rass both saw L.G.'s Ole Tom washed up to the ditch bank, dead. Dad nodded his okay for Rass to take time to bury it.

INSIDE MR. McMULTY'S house it seemed strange, not warm and welcoming. Mr. McMulty's wicker chair with the narrow, high carving table in front of it was gone. Every shave of wood, even his sawdust, had been swept out the door. L.G. and Louie were placing Mom's stove where Mr. McMulty's small black cookstove had been. All wrong! Mom was thanking them and telling how Dad had given her the stove the year the rains held off and he'd won highest cotton prices because of early planting and had paid for it in one fell swoop. Just a while back Rass had helped Mr. McMulty dismantle and high-polish then reseat his small stove in that same spot, for his bride.

He checked for the carved wood shelf he'd anchored yesterday. It was gone, and so was that perfectly carved little wooden calf.

Soon Mrs. Brown—using Mr. McMulty's firewood— was baking yeasty bread. Rass stayed as silent as Bill, who stood close by him. Mrs. Brown occasionally stopped to give both of them a hug. A most unusual thing.

Mom said, "Rass, don't be idle." She pointed as if counting to see if all belongings were there. "Us women has already placed my work cabinet, worktable, those four chairs, bench, and our eating table we took in a plank at a time. Can I trust you and Bill to seat my food-safe and use some wood chips to level it solid? This here floor's so warped. Get that done and I can set my blue pitcher on top of it out of reach of small hands." Gently she set to cleaning the mud and debris from her pitcher. "I cain't believe my ironing board got broke in half and this pitcher left with nary a chip. God is with us."

But not with Mr. McMulty, Rass thought bitterly.

Dad brought in the two rockers inherited from his grandparents and the oak library table from Mom's grandparents, a chest of drawers, and his and Mom's bed to fill up the living room, same as in the other house early this morning. Quickly the place was transformed from Mr. McMulty's to the Whitleys', as quickly as the Whitleys had changed from renters to sharecroppers, as Mr. McMulty from sharecropper to laborer.

Meanwhile, with Bill's help, Rass seated the safe in place.

"Thank y' boys, I'm beholden. Now that safe's got my whole kitchen restored." Mom placed her sparkling pitcher atop it.

L.G., to show off, put up and leveled the King heater. Rass got Bill to help carry in the sewing machine to the tiny bedroom where the girls would sleep. Sally was industriously driving nails into the wall for hanging clothes. Rass asked, "You ain't got no closets?"

"I ain't complaining. Everyone but you is trying to be good about things, Rass. All my art stuff and my painting of Mr. Preston's plantation is gone." She held back a sob. "We're accepting what has to be."

"Is Mr. McMulty accepting what has to be, too?" Rass shot back.

As if to ward off that fact, Mom began ordering. "Rass, get your and L.G.'s belongings to the loft. Your bedsteads and dry mattresses will have to stay downstairs for the girls. Girls' bones is soft. It won't hurt you boys none to sleep on the floor. Ain't no space up there for bedsteads, noways."

Rass tried to find his own way to shift into what had to be. He teased Sally, saying, "Careful! Don't hit your thumb a-whacking in them great big nails." Feeling better, he obeyed Mom, then felt ashamed as he moved his clothes to the attic. His had survived and lots of Sally's hadn't.

Afterward Mom ordered, "Rass, check the staples in the hundred-pound lard cans. If anything got wet, throw it out. If beans, wash 'em."

He struggled to open those tight lids. Rass hoped the shelled corn, which Mom would soak in lye and boil into hominy, was ruined, but it wasn't. "Everything's fine," he said.

"Thanks to providence, tight lids what was meant to keep out moths and mold has also kept out water. Last week I was worried and questioning the Lord about our short supply, but those cans being half empty made 'em float. The Lord does work in unusual ways."

"Mom," Rass said, "God made a flood happen, and that made us have to move into another man's house and ruin his life!"

"God's never stopped it raining on the good and bad alike, but it wasn't God what caused this," his mother answered firmly. "It was men what made weak floodgates and a man, Nert, what ousted our good neighbor. You got no cause to bewail the Lord." She put her hand on his shoulder, and her voice softened. "Now, you've done good work all day long. Take time off and get some sticks sharpened."

"A biscuit roast?" He couldn't believe Mom had reached so far for peace as to offer the family the sport of roasting golden braids of biscuit dough on the end of a stick! "Did Mrs. Brown save us her good light bread dough to roast?"

"Whatever are you thinking?" Mom replied, shocked. "I'm a-letting you kids roast liver."

"Not Ole Jersey's liver! I won't eat it!"

"*Beef* liver, Rass. It being the most perishable meat, it must be cooked tonight. Tell Whit to light a bonfire."

So, when helpers left at milking time, Dad lit the fire and said, "Rass, L.G.—string up some lanterns. We'll work into the night."

At the bonfire, set between the barn and outhouse, Sally declared, "I love liver. Rass, give me a sharp stick." The light shone rosy about her, making her pretty, even though he hated her words. He couldn't fight her. He'd only be stopped, but he did say, "Here, let me roast *your* liver," then laughed like mad.

Dad said, "I'm glad to see you've settled down, son."

Mom came out from the back porch with a bread bowl in hand. She interrupted their eating to say a long grace, itemizing all the things spared, finishing with, "And Lord, I thank thee for our youngest boy, who saved his father's life."

Rass gasped.

L.G. almost choked on the liver he'd eaten during the prayer. "What? How? I ain't heard a word!"

Rass, letting Sally tell most of it, noticed how she admired him. Then he added a thing Sally couldn't know, how he'd felt he was dead when underwater. Even L.G. was greatly impressed, and said so.

But Dad said bitterly, "Rass done me no favor. My mules is gone, and I'm sentenced to lick Nert's boots and act beholden to 'im. To watch whilst he ousts a friend and sets me in the good man's house, causing Rass here to rant and rave as if it was my fault." He stared into the fire. "I ain't beholden to Rass nor God—and don't try to shut me up, Helen! I cain't lie in the face of truth's gale. Get your Bible. I want to read my contract."

"It's gone. Sally looked and looked for it," Rass said with sadness, knowing the hurt this would cause Mom.

"Lord spare us," Mom cried.

Dad put his head down. "I wish I was dead!" he said. There was silence for a full minute. Then Dad ended the day with, "I'm tard. I know youns is tard. Finish eating and blow out the lanterns; it's time to bed down."

"Least you're alive to feel tired," Rass muttered.

Mom spoke with great solemnity. "Rass is right. Hard times is nothing. Catastrophe is nothing. Being alive with family's ever'thing. Children, your daddy's mouthed off, but what he means is it'll be even harder work for us to make it now, and he doubts he can manage. Whit, I wish you'd out-and-out ask the kids to help you through this hardest of times. At least Rass says what he means when he mouths off."

Dad pulled back away from the fire's light.

No one had words for such openness, but Mom's words comforted Rass. Mr. McMulty was alive, even if he was fired. And Dad was alive, even though now the mules were dead and he'd gone from renter to sharecropper and lost everything he'd worked for. . . .

The sight Rass saw next added a strong ray of hope. Snowball, looking grand in the most straggly way, marched into the light of the bonfire and went right to Chrissy. She cuddled him, then slept.

L.G. said, "I figure Ole Tom'll show up, too, sooner or

later." Rass kept his mouth tight closed. Dad sloshed water on the fire. Then L.G. helped Rass tromp the coals into ash and together they went inside. L.G. climbed to the loft, but Rass said, "If I'm gonna sleep on a bare floor, it'll be in the kitchen, what still smells like fresh bread."

The wood floor next to the stove was warm, just like when he'd visited with Mr. McMulty at mealtimes. A safe place to think freely.

He hadn't wanted Dad's mules dead. Nor Ole Jersey. Nor L.G.'s Ole Tom. (Someday, L.G. would pry the truth out.) Rass had wanted everything to stay alive. And it really wasn't his family's fault that Mr. McMulty...

Sleep and rest finally won out against Rass's aching heart.

But his dreams were of the flood, drowning pets and people in all the states' capitals as it roared its sweep across the United States map. Of Dad kicking Rass, who lay dead beside Ole Jersey. Then Rass came alive and was hacking away at death with Bill's sharp knife, and Dad came up and started hacking and hacking until he turned black and wasn't Dad at all, but Mr. McMulty...startling Rass awake. But exhaustion claimed him again, and into his dream flew Nert on a winged horse and ordered every colored person in the world to move. Move! *Move!* Rass grabbed Bill's and Dad's knives and with both hands began hacking at Nert, but the foot of the flying horse hit Rass in the mouth and...

Rass awoke between each nightmare. He was afraid to go back to sleep, so woke himself completely and created his dream in the manner he would have it: There was no flood. There was only the warm croon of Mr. McMulty, saying, " 'Course, my woman's waiting, Rass. She can cast a holy spell on people, rig them a ladder to greater glory, ever' rung based on forgiveness, hard work, and good will. Her skin glistens with sweat and tears equal, but oh, can she build a dream. Rass, don't pay to hold grudges, nor think on bad things. Think on nature. Sometimes we misses our turns 'cause we in the Lord's hands and He preparing a better way."

Those words, said with an assurance he yearned for, made it hard for Rass to keep his eyes open. He closed them, bidding Mr. McMulty of his memory and imagination to seat himself on that porch swing with its carved armrests. Then Rass put himself beside his friend and they moved back and forth. Back and forth. He let sweet pretense lead him to sleep.

# 7

Maybe it was the beginnings of another nightmare, or a sound in the night, or maybe it was that sleep had rested Rass's muscles and they resisted his pretense and the bare floor. Whatever, something made him abruptly awaken in the wee hours and leap up, charged.

The strangest determination comes in darkness, when fact and fantasy are not separated and you're not sure you're in a dream or out of it. And you need to go to the toilet.

Stealthily Rass tried to move out the door, but fumbled the handle of the screen door, which was on the opposite side from the handle at their old house. Outside, his eyes not fully accustomed to darkness, he dodged under mattress ticking and sheets on the clothesline and stumbled. His heart beat wildly, but it was just a sheet in a white heap on the ground, probably knocked down by the wind. The wind was high and there was little moonlight. Rass lifted the sheet to rehang it and heard groans.

"Mr. McMulty?!"

"Boy."

Mr. McMulty held a wadded white cloth to one leg. He groaned as he began to move. The crumpled cloth fell.

"Mr. McMulty! What happened to you?" Rass helped him stand.

"Ask no questions! No man gonna do me out of my land, my house, my mule, and then let the sweet night float by in a dance. Oh. Sorry, I takes a strip off'n yo' mama's sheet to stop blood." He took something from the hammer sling on the side of his overalls, a flashlight. In its dim light Rass could see a bloody raw wound the size of a baseball on Mr. McMulty's leg.

"I'll go wake Mom. You cain't wrap that sore without it's clean."

Mr. McMulty clutched his arm. "No! No! Be quiet! Need no noise of that pump, neither. It a loud primer. Get the rag wound tight. Stop the flow!"

Had the old man been in a fight? There was a noise of dogs howling in the distance.

Rass talked fast. "I'll fill this bucket with Mom's rinse water she saves for the next wash. Saves lots of pumping." He tried to be quiet, but the bucket hit the washboard and the soap that had been left in place.

Mr. McMulty, guessing the sound, ordered, "Lye soap be good disinfectant."

Rass, obliging, poured soapy water on the wound, then got up nerve to say, "I got to know what happened."

The old man flinched, said, "Sh-h-h. What you don't know you cain't tell no one, even if they holds you down and chokes you, and it likely gonna come to that."

"You know I'd not tell nobody nothing, but you gotta tell me."

"Quiet, boy. I ain't gotta do nothing, ever 'gin. Tear me more sheet! Hurry!"

"I'm tearing. I won't tell anyone. I'm in enough trouble not saving Dad's mules. You fight Nert 'cause he ousted you? We didn't wanta take your house, but I couldn't stop them." Rass was crying.

A softness returned to his old friend's voice. "I know, boy," he whispered. "Shush yo' crying. This poor light to wrop by. Here, you hold the light steady. I done in no time." His body contorted as he wound the bandage tight. "I gonna try control myself, not cry, neither." A sad joke. Then came a harsh laugh. "Mama told me control be born in me, but tonight I done lost control. All my life I control what I say, what I do, never let on I be hurt, even if I die. Not past age ten did I cry out to 'nother human being, 'cepting when yo' mama lanced that boil on my neck."

The bandage done, talk stopped. Rass held the light until the pant leg was in place and turned up eight inches to match the other.

"Where you gonna go? Stay with us—I won't tell."

"Thanks. It be fine, son. Jest hep me inside my barn. Soon's I rest a mite, I be gone." Suddenly he grabbed Rass's nightshirt; his voice changed. "Don't tell nobody. Understand?"

Rass promised, and Mr. McMulty seemed to settle back to being his loving self. Helping support him, Rass said, "You've a right to hide in your own barn."

The barn was pretty clean with its wide-open centerway

to catch the flow of air. One side was the stalls, which held two of Nert's mules that Mr. McMulty had used, and on the other was a slatted corncrib. Except for a boxed-in tool corner, the underside of the crib, and the tight under-eaves of the hayloft, the barn kept no secrets. Dust that collected one day was windswept away by the next morning.

"The corncrib be the best place, boy."

Rass got him there and draped a cotton sack and the remains of a sheet over him. "I sinking fast," the old man whispered. "Go back to bed like this be a dream, easy forgot. You wake, I be gone. Never been here." Dogs howled again as Rass went to the house. Ole Coalie mustn't get wind, howl back, and wake the girls! Rass fell asleep on the bare floor.

COME DAYLIGHT, he wasn't sure the terrible wound wasn't a dream. Stepping out the back door, he expected to see the banks of Six Ditch, but got instead a good view of the Preston cotton gins. It jolted him to wakefulness and reality. *There really had been a flood yesterday, and they really had moved into Mr. McMulty's house.* He must check if Mr. McMulty was still in the barn. First to the toilet, which had no latch—he'd fix that, give Mr. McMulty time to leave in case he'd just awakened.

Rass hammered noisily while the sun came up pink in the eastern sky that Sunday morning, outlining trees, barn, and the outhouse, making them into a pretty picture. A good omen, surprise beauty. Then he moved to the clothes-line and started taking down and folding the sheets so that Mom wouldn't notice one missing. That done, he saw

Mom standing in the doorway, watching. So he primed the pump long and loud in order to warn Mr. McMulty, as well as to wash himself.

Mom called, "Build a fire under the wash kettle 'fore you come in. Sally'll be doing wash early. I don't know what's found or what's lost forever, and won't till ever'-thing's washed. Then you can help Rosalee and Chrissy wash my saved jars. I gotta can the beef before it spoils."

"Mom, don't keep calling Ole Jersey *the beef*. And I ain't settling into no house what's not ourn!" Anyway, Mom would think her sheet lost if Sally did the laundry and he helped her take in dry sheets and add to the stack.

L.G. appeared in the doorway, too, and asked kindly, "Mom, what you want me to do first?" As he squeezed past, Mom answered, "Repair the door to my work cabinet and make a new drawer for the clothes chest to replace the one lost. And, Rass, like it or not, I want you to—"

Suddenly Dad was there. "Rass goes with me to survey damages," he said curtly.

What? Dad never had singled him out over L.G.

"Whit, you been out since daybreak! I need all hands this day Nert's give us to settle in. It's the Sabbath, but the ox's in the ditch, and God won't hold us accountable." Rass had often heard her use that scripture, which allowed for tending to emergencies even on the day of rest.

Dad ignored her. "L.G., be a hep to your mother! Rass, get gum boots on! Don't need a boat no more. Dredge worked through the night patching the break in the ditch bank. Water's gone down some and will be more by noon. Hurry! I'm taking out time to learn you a lesson."

What lesson? Was he to bury the mules? His parents believed to spare the rod spoils the child, but sometimes they just made him undo whatever he'd caused, no matter how hard, to set his brain to never do it again.

"I cain't bury mules," he said, but Dad was walking away toward their old place. (At least it was away from Mr. McMulty.) He pulled almost-dry boots from the pile of salvage and took off running. When he caught up, Dad cut toward Uncle Tut's.

"Dad, I know I oughten fight with Uncle Tut's boys. I won't. I don't need no lesson." Dad's only reply was to splash along in those floodwaters which, late yesterday, had stood a foot deep in the fields and now were calm and flat as a sheet of paper, ankle deep.

With a jerk of his clenched hand and saying, "Come," Dad changed directions again. He kept his determined walk. At the woods Dad turned onto the shortcut to Nert's, working his way through underbrush. Suddenly Rass knew. Mr. McMulty had left the barn, and Dad had found him. He braced himself to see his injured friend; his imagination and heart ran wild as he kept following. Ought to get a hold on himself. Mr. McMulty wouldn't have to tell anything, even if Dad choked him. Or would he? Rass wasn't sure he knew Mr. McMulty completely, anymore.

At the clearing where Nert's big white house sat private, with woods on three sides and imposing bay windows on both top and bottom floors, Dad pointed. "Tell me you didn't do that!"

At first Rass didn't understand. Then his eyes followed the wraparound porch with lattice railing to the entrance steps of the porch that led to the elegant entrance doors. He sucked in his breath. Hanging on that brass hook anchored at the roof just above the steps, the place where Rose Nert hung a big Christmas wreath each year, was Nert's prized calf—out of Preston's prize bull. Its eyes bulged, the tongue swelled out from the gaping mouth, the throat was slit across. Another slit downward. Entrails protruded. Blood puddled on porch and steps beneath.

"Dad, no! I couldn't! I never!"

"Never said you did. I'm asking. I know you could; you killed a cow yesterday, spite of your age. A dozen people witnessed you throw a fit, bad-mouth Nert, and threaten to kill him." Dad snapped Rass's gallus as he pulled him back a few feet. "We need to see, not be seen."

"Dad, I was in the kitchen, a-sleeping!"

"You tweren't inside early this morning. I heard noise, got up, and found you a-missing. I figured Ole Coalie had run off with a pack, and you was out getting 'em, so I went to hep, but what I hear ain't Ole Coalie. It's Nert's dogs howling enough to wake the countryside. So I come looking over here and found this. Where was y' in the wee hours afore dawn?"

"I . . . I went to the toilet. I didn't do this!" Rass had been so wrapped up in his worry in hiding Mr. McMulty, he'd let those dogs barking register only as usual night noises. Unclaimed dogs often roamed in the night.

"Ever'body knows what Ole Jersey meant to you. Ever'body knows what Nert's calf meant to him. Was you trying to settle the score even with Nert? If I gotta hep you out of it, you gotta answer me honest."

*Mr. McMulty had done this.* He had settled the score

even: His dream gone, Nert's dream gone. Fine mule colt, prized bull calf. Rass began fighting Dad, hitting him hard. "I *am* honest. You hate me!"

Dad grabbed his hands and held them tight. "Had to know, boy," he said quietly, "or I couldn't go hepping you one way or t'uther." Rass noticed Dad's touch. "Just 'member what your mouthing off caused me to consider. It tweren't you; now I know who 'twas."

Rass did not ask who. Dad let go his hands.

"I figure colored men has left Nert a sign in his front yard, same as I 'member the Klan leaving them a sign when I was a boy. Shore ain't no purty sight I brung you to. It's overstepping the line big. Let it be a lesson so's you don't ever go around speaking outa place again. Don't never associate with no one who's stepped outa line. I better not hear o' you threatening to kill no one, ever agin." Dad hit the trunk of a tree. "What'll Nert do 'bout this?"

"Nert'll call Maggie Porter. She'll come with her gun, I reckon," Rass said, calmer now.

"Oh, that'll happen first, all right." Dad strained to get the scene in full focus. "And she'll be questioning me. I oughta took Nert's mules to bury mine yesterday, but dag dang it, I was trying to save our stuff before the house caved in more. I cain't leave my dead mules lay longer. Best I use the mules Nert's rented to McMulty to drag mine away and bury 'em. You and L.G.'ll have to hep Helen."

Rass knew he must say something to keep Dad from the barn. "Right. If you took Nert's mules now, he'd see fresh tracks and think it was you killed his calf. So I'll run ahead and get the mules Mr. McMulty used."

He was stopped by the sound of a car motor coming

up the dirt access road on the far side of Nert's house. Sound ceased. Someone was going in the back door. Shortly those front doors opened wide and Nert stepped out onto the porch and let out a keen whistle. His wife's dogs shot out past his legs and began yelping and leaping at the hung calf.

"Nert wasn't supposed to be home for hours!" Rass whispered.

"Only one man coulda put them dogs inside. It's common knowledge McMulty tends Rose's dogs when thur gone," Dad responded. "He'll pay for stepping over the line. We better hightail it home, 'fore them dogs get *our* scent."

Dad drew Rass back into the woods and moved fast among trees, around brambles. Suddenly Rose's screams added to Nert's angry shouting. It gave them speed.

Surely Mr. McMulty was so far gone by this time, those angry dogs could never find him. (Would he kill them, too?) No one Rass knew had ever been so violent as to hang a calf, not even John Henry Litikin, who he'd once seen beat a horse with a tree limb to knock sense into it.

Dad cut clear from the woods then, to avoid open pasture, skirted up the ditch bank, where he walked along the grassy top as if surveying damages. Red and sweating, he spoke as if the trees might have eyes and ears. "A man has to watch his actions. Cain't have *my* doings causing a landlord's suspicions, so we might as well check things, like I told Helen we'd do."

Secrets and fears, as unpredictable as the spongy ground under Rass's feet. Violence done. Violence waiting.

Dad slipped and swore, then sidestepped to miss sinking into a water hole.

Rass did the same footwork, thinking how Rose had truly given Mr. McMulty that mule colt. But Nert had power on his side. "Dad, Mr. McMulty won't be able to get another sharecropping job, will he?"

"Course not, at this season. It's hard for a man without no sons to get a good job. I'm lucky I got you and L.G. . . ." Dad's voice sputtered to a stop as they got closer to their old home place and the sounds of dogs and shouts came from down-ditch.

Instantly, thinking his old friend was being chased, Rass shot toward the sounds, but stopped short. He wasn't sure what angry Mr. McMulty might do. What anyone might do. Even himself.

## 8

$\mathbb{T}$HOSE HOWLS came from two big black police dogs, which ran on ahead of their master, who also walked toward the Whitleys' old place. Rass and Dad quickly caught up to the great plantation owner, a man as old as Mr. McMulty, about fifty-five. His face was more rounded and lighter than a farmer's, his eyes sharp, keenly aware. He wore striped serge pants stretched tightly over his belly, a plain blue vest with a gold watch fob in the pocket—his usual dress. Except today Mr. Preston wore gum-rubber knee boots, not wing-tip shoes.

The dogs obediently quit barking and nipping at his command. Mr. Preston came right up and asked, "How's the welfare of your family, Whit? This is an awful thing. From what this paper says, it sounds bad. Very bad." Rass tried to look, but Mr. Preston handed the paper to Dad.

After a glance Dad said, "Paper don't show what happened."

Rass examined the paper's dark photographs as they walked down the ditch bank toward the house site. In one picture muddy Sally was being lifted up by Mr. McMulty.

Dad and Mr. Preston skirted around, while Rass jumped over the jagged ends of porch boards, great splintered beams not salvaged, and behind those, floorboards, undersides up, pithy and rotting. The flood pictures didn't show things rotting, like those potatoes over there and the sprouted onions in Rass's old seine, as if growing vegetables was its purpose. At some time in the future, he'd have to untangle his seine and mend it. The family'd need more fish now that their animals were gone.

"But all's well as could be expected, I reckon," he heard Dad say. "We got a few nicks and scratches, but none of us is bad hurt. Water's going down. My smokehouse's leveled, but I'll build another one day."

Chrissy's Kewpie doll floated about serenely with a chamber pot, parts of a dead chicken, and a child's underslip. Pungent smells and flies filled the air. In the picture, all such was muted background. In clear daylight was real destruction. Uprooted rosebushes wilted on limp muddy grass. Mom's garden seed packs lay in puddles.

They came sharply upon the house, its whole second floor intact, sitting there lopsided, no windowpanes, as if the little girls had built it and then given up and walked away, leaving it in a mud hole. Mr. Preston pointed at the old slanting barn, still standing. On its lowest side, through gaping cracks of rough lumber, the sun glistened on standing water. Another large puddle filled the foot-worn space beneath the tire swing in the catalpa. Trees that once shaded the back porch now seemed dark and dank, blocking out the sun entirely, their trunks black with mud and already spotted with fungi. Dad reached out a hand to slow Rass and he was glad, so afraid was he to see the bloated pigs and chickens.

Surprisingly, there were no carcasses at all. Just a chicken crate, broken from being overloaded.

"Who buried them?" Rass asked.

"No one. Word got passed fast to the hungry. Day laborers' wives will be canning hogs and chickens today," said Dad. He stopped, and then he made a sound that would have been a cry had Mr. Preston not been present. Rass pushed near Dad. There lay only the skeletons of Dad's mules.

"No! What...where did the meat go?" Rass squeaked the words.

Mr. Preston murmured, "Someone's cooking roast 'beef,' or making 'pork' sausage, like your dad said."

"People cain't do that!"

"People do some surprising things," said Mr. Preston, shaking his head.

Though he didn't wish to, Rass thought of what Mr. McMulty had done. When disaster hit it bounced, causing a cyclone, never ending. His anger flew at these multiple hits. "A limit has to be set somewheres, or people will be eating people!"

"That's been done, too," Mr. Preston said, rocking on his heels.

Dad had regained his composure. "When the last word's said, I guess we're all animals." He slapped his hat against his pants legs. "Well, this saves me having to bury 'em."

Rass descended the ditch bank and waded away, picking up things. Dad followed. Mr. Preston, atop the ditch bank, was hardly audible, but Rass heard him say, "All people are helpless until they're hungry or angry—then they act." He cleared his throat, looked at his watch, signaled his dogs, and headed back toward the bridge, then paused and called loudly, "Well, we can't have floodgates breaking and people made homeless. I'm angry about that. Is Sally handling this all right?"

Sally used to bring in good sweet milk from that cooling trough that now had the porch swing resting on it in the ripped-apart pump shed. "Sally's been a-wailing about a picture she made of your plantation. It was a pretty fine one and it got ruint." Rass lied a little about it being fine. "All her paints and art paper got ruint, too."

"Tell Sally I'll see she gets some new paints. She can count on it, if she'll promise to make that picture over again."

Mr. Preston left. He could have bought them a new house, but to offer such would embarrass both Dad and him. Rass understood. Rich and poor didn't mix. Sally was the only one who ever tried, and she was totally out of line.

"I'll tell Sally, and I'll see she gets this newspaper," Rass called after him, or else the proper thing would be to return the paper. Mr. Preston gave Sally the *St. Louis Post Dispatch* whenever he gave her rides home.

Townspeople arrived shortly, as should have been expected with waters going down. They came to question and shake their heads in disbelief at the destruction. Social politeness kept Dad from showing his anger about his prized mules being butchered. Having to greet people and answer all their questions kept Rass from getting back to check on Mr. McMulty.

Then out of the crowd came Shark, making his way toward him.

Rass pulled his friend to one side and away. Shark said, "I still cain't believe this flood has done this to you-all's place. Did you see they put one of my pictures in the paper? The one with Sally? Man, it's unbelievable. You never know!" That picture could only mean more trouble for Mr. McMulty, but Rass asked, "Shark, what you doing bringing your camera along again today?"

"Well," Shark said, "well..." He bent a dark head over the sight in his Box Brownie. "Mr. Aaral says none of the pictures in the paper ain't worth a fart in a windstorm."

"Our teacher said that?"

"Not exactly, but that's what he meant. He says I gotta record history as it is and not make it look like a sunset over a nice ocean."

"I thought the same thing."

"You did? You thought it looked like an ocean?"

"No, not that. You know I ain't never seen no ocean, Shark! The pictures sure don't tell the facts, that's what I meant. Somebody needs to tell the facts. Dad didn't even tell the facts to Mr. Preston."

Shark hesitated, then thrust the camera at Rass. "Want one free shot on my camera? Here. It's all set. Just look in here. Push this when you get a picture that tells facts."

Rass took the camera and walked to the skeletons of Dad's mules, lying there at the edge of the water with muddy foot-shaped holes in the ground all around, plus traces of the slaughtering. *Click!*

"Why'd you take a picture of them for?" Shark wanted to know.

"Just did." Rass handed back the camera. Though he dared not say it, another telling picture could be of the hung calf. Shark, a town boy, never knew hard times. Rass enjoyed that about him and he didn't want it to change. But now he needed to talk to Clever. If Mr. McMulty was safely gone, he'd just do that.

"I gotta get home, Shark. Mom has all kinds of work lined up for me. Anyways, I hear Dad a-calling."

"Yeah, sure. I forgot for a minute."

Actually it was big, husky Bud Mac, Shark's dad, calling. Bud Mac's pool hall was the seat of all gossip. Bud was saying to Dad, "Whit, I come to check on you and to tell you Maggie wants to talk to you in town." All action stopped.

"Yep, Nert called Maggie about his prize calf being hung on his front doorsteps," Bud Mac went on. Without looking at each other, Dad and Rass registered shock along with the crowd. "Soon's the operator at central called my pool hall, it started filling up with the curious. I need Shark home to help. Cain't have my wife tending bar, 'cept in an emergency."

Dad asked, "What's being said round and about?" The crowd quieted to hear Bud Mac's reply.

"Well, they're guessing that McMulty did it, 'cause he ain't at the Dumases'. I tried to sneak over to Nert's place for a look-see myself, but already Maggie's setting up a barricade. Had to walk back here as far as the trestle. Maggie's blocking cars. What you know, Whit?"

Word had spread too fast. Dad needed space. "We don't know nothing," Rass said quickly, remembering Dad's despair yesterday, afraid it might show again. Sightseers' faces lit with astonishment. They'd gotten more on this trip than they could have dreamed.

Dad's words came out grand. "I don't interfere with my landlord, ask anybody!" He even managed to look astonished. "Why does Maggie want to talk to *me*? I'm here with my boy, trying to salvage. I've lost all I own but my kids, and thur what counts. I'd never do no calf hanging. Go tell Maggie that."

"I'll give the sheriff your message," Bud Mac said, and pulled at Shark. "Come on, son, let's get back to town. Rass, you try getting your dad into town in one piece. I'll tell Maggie he's a-coming."

Rass would try no such thing. Dad shouted a final message for Bud Mac, then he crowed a bit to all listeners, as if he was his old happy, storytelling self. "Anyone what wants to say they helped bury my mules' bones, grab one of them shovels agin that tree yonder. Bones don't need be drug anywhere. We can bury 'em on the spot. Hurry up, for me and my boy needs to get on home. Helen'll have our dinners a-waiting."

Now that the entire countryside was on alert, Rass hoped Mr. McMulty was long gone.

## 9

IN A VERY TENSE manner Rass sang "Crawdad Hole" all the way home, to keep his mind off that calf hanging, to keep his determination up, and to keep his mouth shut. Dad joined in the song, playing it big. What would Dad do if he found Mr. McMulty? Would he turn him in?

Sally was outside washing muddy curtains. L.G. wasn't in sight.

Mom came out to greet Dad, her voice flat and hard. "Well, while you was punishing Rass, making him help bury your mules, our girls helped me use up the morning, as well. Fixing, cleaning, canning, and settling in. Since I wouldn't let L.G. drive your car without your say, he harnessed up the mules to go get them things Kate says she don't need no more. Ole Coalie follered him, and I let that be. I told him no use stopping at our old barn to hunt for his cat, it was drowned." So Dad had told Mom about Ole Tom.

Rass gasped for L.G.'s sake, then again because L.G.

had been inside McMulty's barn. He took off running. Dad snagged him back. "Dinner's a-waiting." Dad didn't respond to Mom, nor did she seem to expect it.

"Dinner ain't a-waiting," she said. "It ain't noontime. Beef's cooked for canning. We can use some for today's eating, I guess."

"I don't eat...beef," Rass mumbled, wondering why Dad wasn't telling about the mules being butchered and eaten, not just buried. Or that it was a calf hanging he'd taken Rass to see. Anyway, L.G. never kept secrets from Mom, so L.G. hadn't seen Mr. McMulty. Rass relaxed to hear Dad assure Mom, "No hurry. I gotta drive into town. You need anything?"

"What don't I need?" Dad followed Mom inside. "It's the Sabbath and there'll be no shopping," she continued. "Money's so scarce it takes deep planning."

Rass headed for the barn. Sally, bent over the washboard, straightened up, left her wash, and followed along. "Rass, I'm tard. I ain't had milk since breakfast yesterdy. God's flood forced me to tell Chrissy and Rosalee I hate milk. Now I'll go to hell. I gotta repent and tell the truth —we ain't ever having milk again. Did you build a box for the mules? Or put a marker on their graves? I wanted to, but I had to wash. Why'd God kill Dad's mules with a flood?"

Rass liked her for not blaming the death of the mules on him. He said gently, "The mules are taken care of. Now Sally, you cain't start hating God, 'cause you love God. You always have." Gosh, why'd she make him want to protect her? He'd never get to the barn.

Sally pulled a mattress cover off the line and he quickly helped her fold it. She said, "Mom says that rich men building dams and drainage ditches to become millionaire landlords brought on the flood. But Mr. Preston would never bring on no flood. Never!" She was about to cry.

Rass couldn't stand it. So to cheer her, he told how Mr. Preston was getting her new paints and added, for science's sake, "He and Mr. Winters by Sikeston has to build dams and things what nature cain't do, or we couldn't grow cotton and we'd all die. It's like Mom sewing us clothes, you see? Everyone's born naked. You wouldn'ta made it through winter having no clothes on. Clothes and dams has to be, or we're done."

"Rass, don't talk of nakedness. Go!"

Swatting off tall burdock weeds, he ran toward the barn. Ordinary talk concealed his knowledge of Mr. McMulty's deed. There was no reasoning for violence, as there was for clothes and dams.

As he feared, for there was no science to it, Mr. McMulty was there, hardly covered by the sack, looking as if he was dying, calling, "Water!"

"I'll be right back." Rass moved quickly, got a jar of priming water from the pump without Sally noticing. Mr. McMulty sipped from the jar, then apologized weakly, "None o' this be to my liking, son. Old man necessity set me right in the middle of this yhere barn, but left me without no tools to get out. I barely hide from L.G. and now I weak." He no longer sounded angry, so Rass's fear about that left.

"I cain't keep ever'one out of the barn," Rass said. "Dad

has to go talk to Maggie about the calf hanging. She'll come a-looking for you. I gotta hide you good."

No sooner had he said the words than he regretted it. Hiding a criminal was against the law. Much different from letting Mr. McMulty stay till he could rest and leave. To hide him would get his whole family in terrible trouble. Rass wanted to say that, but his hands began piling gunny sacks, loose corn, and a few hoes from the tool cabinet over his friend. "I'll get you some food," he said.

"No. Don't. Cain't have you hepping me no more. God done let me know I rebels in a wrong way. You not mixed up in it." Mr. McMulty sat up, drank more water, wiped his mouth. "I feels fine. Water done give me life." Pushing things aside, he stood, flexed his leg. "See how fine." He stopped short. "I hears someone coming. You go. I be gone, too."

Rass was out of the barn instantly. The sounds were made by tall, thin-as-a-pencil Rosalee clanging away on the tubs to entertain Marylu. She didn't talk much but was noisy when Sally allowed her to mother the little girls. Her hair, a shade lighter than Mom's, was bright in the sun.

Sally was explaining, "We have to make clothes to wear to keep us warm. We do it, and God blesses us."

"God's not blessing us! Chrissy and Marylu wants milk!" Rosalee emphasized that with a slap of the wash water. Chrissy splashed it, too; her curls bounced with the joyful impact. Marylu began to cry.

Rass was amazed how life went on if people were ignorant of another's crisis. Rosalee picked up and balanced Marylu on her thin hip, mother style. Baby legs locked tight, crying stopped, and baby hands clutched at eyes and mouth for more attention. Chrissy kept splashing. Sally wiped spray from her face. "God blessed Adam and Eve by giving them fig leaves. He gave us mothers who sew. Quit your splashing, Chrissy; I'm tard. Go play some'ers else!"

Chrissy ran toward the barn. She'd come back. How impossible to hide a man with a family the size of this.

"I ain't washed so much clothes in all my life. I wish nobody had invented them. I hate you, Rass, for mentioning that!" Sally gave him a fierce look, then let her long red hair swirl down over her eyes as she bent to the washboard. Soap. Scrub. Soap. Scrub. Soap. *Howl?* It was Chrissy howling as she came running back, toward the house.

"A man's in our barn. Mommy, Daddy, a man's in our barn!"

"No one's in the barn—I was just there. Ever'body's gone crazy!" Rass yelled so Mom and Dad could hear and bounded past Chrissy to check on Mr. McMulty.

Mr. McMulty was holding on to Bill Brown, directing him to the corncrib! Rass naturally should have expected Bill to show up today to check on things, after the horrible flood and move yesterday. Bill was always coming and going, causing his parents to have to search for him. He was excited, now, motioning and making his sounds.

Rass wished he could explain things to Bill. Instead he put his fingers to his lips and looked stern, then quickly ran out to yell, "It wasn't no man! It was Bill!"

Apparently he was heard, for neither parent came to check.

Rass gave Chrissy a quick hug, saying, "I didn't mean

you was crazy. It's true, Bill is a man." He dashed back to the barn.

Bill was coming out, but Rass ushered him right back into the barn. "I know you know something's wrong, but we cain't tell nobody. Right?" Bill wasn't understanding. So Rass tried different acting-outs of things, finally covering an ear of corn with a sheet to hide it, then put his fingers to his lips. But it was seeing Mr. McMulty making an effort to hide himself that caused a look of understanding to come to Bill. He held fingers to Rass's lips, then to Mr. McMulty's. It was sad Bill couldn't hear nor talk and therefore couldn't go to school, for he truly was smart. It almost made Rass feel guilty being glad Bill couldn't tell anybody even if he wanted.

The creak of wagon wheels announced L.G.'s return. Rass pulled Bill outside with him.

Mom and the girls rushed to see what Aunt Kate had given. Dad followed slowly. As Dad helped L.G. unhook the mules from the wagon, L.G. said, "Aunt Kate skipped church the first time in her life to get things sorted for us."

Rass quickly let that pass and offered to put the mules that Mr. McMulty rented from Nert in their stalls and feed them. And to make it all seem natural he added, "Hey, L.G., how's Dennis?" Dennis was Aunt Kate's only child.

"Save your jawing, Rass. You and Bill go ahead and feed the mules. I've done more than you today. Dad, is it okay if I go right back and stay with Dennis for a while? It's Sunday. Aunt Kate said I could." Dad nodded.

Rass was so relieved, he nodded approval grandly. L.G. had never admitted being undone at the sight of the flood damage. Usually he knew every loving thing that happened and was on top of it, smiling. It could be he was jealous Dad hadn't taken him this morning to survey the ruins. Then Rass saw the soaked bandana in L.G.'s pocket. "I'm sorry you lost Ole Tom," he said softly. L.G. turned away.

To stay clear of the girls and Mom, Dad moved near. Rass, slapping the mules toward barn, heard L.G. whisper to Dad, "As I come through town, Maggie was corraling last night's drunks. She told me she wants you in to see her."

Rass, waiting for Dad's reply, pretended to be occupied buttoning the sides and adjusting the galluses of L.G.'s old bib overalls he wore.

"Well, you done what you was told," Dad said. "I'll think on it."

When Rass and Bill had the mules moving again, L.G. was beside Rass, saying, "Don't tell Mom and the girls about Maggie. They got troubles enough, being forced out of our house, spending hours on a ditch bank, and having to settle down in a new place, all unexpected."

Rass felt a pang of guilt. He'd been so concerned for Mr. McMulty he hadn't even thought of his family's suffering. L.G. would never jeopardize his family's safety to hide out a criminal. Rass envied such goodness, but his mouth said, "You running off to play with Dennis's store-bought toys in the middle of a bad time?" Mr. McMulty was much worse off than the Whitleys, if L.G. only knew it. "You see anything of Mr. McMulty?" Rass added, pretending innocence.

"Not a sign. But he's on my mind. How could a good

man, what let me learn driving a car in his dirt-smooth pasture, a-done what he done?"

"You know what he done?" That slipped out too loud.

"Yeah, I know what he done. The whole town knows. That's why I'm going to visit Dennis. He may know something. He sits to one side playing like he don't hear a thing, but he hears plenty when Mrs. Dumas visits Aunt Kate.... Hey, how did *you* know? You been talking to Clever?"

Rass didn't tell L.G. that he and Dad had seen it all, for Dad had told him to keep quiet. "I heard it from Shark's dad. You know Dumas'd not hide Mr. McMulty."

"I know they *are* hiding him cause I read it on your face just now. Well, I ain't telling your secret, Rass, except maybe to Dennis." Right at the barn door, L.G. turned, waved to the family, and took off.

Bill fed the mules, while Rass warned Mr. McMulty. "You ain't safe. First Chrissy. Then L.G., who'd tell. And you know Dad never lets nothing get past him. I'll bring food so's you'll be strong enough to leave."

"First, not to raise concern, you best leave Billy here and hurry back to hep unload," Mr. McMulty said.

So Rass dashed out, and once in the kitchen, took some beef from the pot, put it in a cup, and hid it under his shirt. Timing it just right, he got the food back to Mr. McMulty unnoticed. As the old man ate, he said, "Son, food or no, I not going no place. I best be hid good. I knows my barn, ever' inch. There be one hiding place. Under this crib. I 'spects the space so narr a man cain't go under. When I uses the outhouse, I test it—it be fine. I gets weak, 'most got caught, 'cept there be Billy."

**100**

Rass whispered, "Bill will be cautious about not being seen near you, for he understands you need to hide. Mom says people what cain't use one sense gets real strong in others."

Mr. McMulty was up, moving toward the door of the crib as fast as his pain allowed. Bill was quick to help him. "I knows. I knows. Now I ask you to push me under. Feet first. No room to crawl, and I cain't wiggle. Laws, my leg's bad!"

All corncribs were four inches to a foot off the ground to keep down mold. Rass knew that underspace well, a dark dingy hole where rats nibbled as grain dropped through. A place a boy could slither during a tough game of hide-and-seek and never be found. Some hens hid nests there, and unaccounted eggs got exchanged for gum and ice cream in town.

Rass began moving some of the accumulated dirty straw that had wedged in front of the space and said, "It ain't a clean place to be."

"I knows a clean barn be dirty under the corncrib, where wind can't find no place to move. Don't matter, son. If'n you push my feet to the far wall now, please. I get out for necessaries when the land be clear. Won't need but one feeding a day. I be well and out o' here, hiding myself proper in a couple o' days."

Rass hesitated. "I cain't let you go where it ain't clean, or let you be hungry."

"Don't argue me none!" Mr. McMulty was sharp. "I better be hid right now, while ever'body looking at the stuff yo' Aunt Kate send over. Oh, lan', I sure do got a hurt leg."

Mr. McMulty finished the water and tried again. "I ready, boy. Hep me."

Rass worked, first behind and then in front of him until he was situated. Bill was watching closely.

A pained look came to Mr. McMulty's face, and he lay back for a moment's rest. "I payin'. I payin'. Don't worry I be hungry. They say, hunger makes a man mean." He chuckled. "Meanness done find its way. And a calf done rendered punishment, kicking my leg, making me have to hide 'stead o' running off free. The Lord need add no more to it. He know next time I stand up, it be a better way, son. Give me little minute."

"You made Nert pay. He deserved his comeuppance," Rass said.

"I knows that, son. He kick me out 'cause I cain't sign no written contract. His witnessed word 'sposed to stand in court. Not right he steal my parity check so's I don't get a cent. Keeping my mule colt what Rose, a girl I knows all the days of her life, done give me with thanks. But I the one what's a-running. Lan's, I do hates to go under."

"You thinking of the rats and spiders under there, ain't you?" Mr. McMulty would be all the way under, with no room to kick or swat.

Still resting, breathing heavy, Mr. McMulty said, "My oldest sister done scooted me, when I 'bout age nine and sound asleep, so my gaping mouth line up 'neath a spider dropping from the ceiling. I choke on it. Mama administered sister a deserved whaling, her older in years. I swore I never scare a chile. I sorry, son. Shove!"

Rass shoved and Mr. McMulty pulled. No go. Then

another pair of hands were helping. Bill's. No words needed. They got the old man to the far wall. If it hurt, Mr. McMulty never let out a sound.

Rass and Bill squirmed back out, grabbed pitchforks, and filled the opening with layers of old manure-soaked straw, which Rass had transferred. It didn't appear that the crib sat as high off the ground as it actually did. Bill's eyes approved all things. Maybe he didn't know about the hung calf, Rass thought, but he'd been there when Nert ordered Mr. McMulty to move. He'd witnessed Rass's old home demolished and saw that the Whitley family now lived in the McMulty house.

Ole Coalie came sniffing, and they pushed him aside. Rass took Bill's hand and called to Mom, "Bill's come to play. We'll be in the barn. We won't throw no fruit jars!" He and Bill would be as matched in deception as in wrestling.

Up in the barn loft, Bill pushed Rass into the mound of loose hay. The wrestle was about to begin. Rass quietly said to Bill, "Mr. McMulty felt hot. I think he's got a fever. I know the right thing'd be to turn him in, so Dr. Nitcheley can fix his leg. But I cain't do that. Him and all of us could hang!" He heard Dad say something to Mom. Rass rolled to his knees and crept to the loft opening and listened.

"I'll leave you and the girls to finish this—I'm taking the boys," Dad was saying.

"Rass's with Bill. It's the Sabbath, and kids need a free moment." Mom's voice.

"Rass has had his moment. We'll overtake L.G. easy. Be gone 'bout an hour." Dad explained nothing, just looked toward Rass in the barn loft and called, "Rass, tell Bill he's got to go home."

Rass did.

Once in the car, all Dad said was, "Calf hanging ain't my concern. I see no sense talking it to Helen. What she knows she'll spread. She's long on worry. Men have to hold a front for their wives. Mind you know that."

Overtaking L.G., Dad talked about the power of the law, while Rass thought of things to tell Maggie Porter and throw her off Mr. McMulty's track. That proved to be dumb thinking, for once in town, Dad announced, "L.G., I'm taking you along with me to the sheriff." Then he headed up Church Street and on past the church with its one stained-glass window. "Two sets o' ears better'n one. Rass, wait in the car and keep your ears open."

At first Rass was hurt. But quickly he had a better idea. In a minute he could be to the pool hall at the south end of Main Street, by cutting through in back of the butcher and hardware stores. "Three sets of ears, you mean," he said, "for I can wait in the pool hall. Shark's my friend. It's there I'll hear what everybody's thinking." He waited for approval, unable to breathe.

"Yes, I'd like to hear what sort o' talk is being bandied about," was Dad's reply. But he had to add, "Don't say nothing. Just listen and see if anyone's trying to involve me. Can you promise me that?"

"I promise that on a stack of Bibles," Rass said, and there he was, being trusted by Dad.

# 10

THE POOL HALL wasn't usually open on a Sunday. Aunt Kate and other church women had put a stop to that years ago. Hours were from eleven weekday mornings till customers went home at night. Saturday night, the big night, often lasted till daybreak. So Bud Mac Mozena wasn't actually closed when he'd opened for this calf-hanging crisis. As a community service, he would stay open till word of McMulty's capture.

Rass tried easing through the doorway but Big Red Revelsen shoved from behind, saying, "Go on in. Nobody's gonna bite you." Red was an all-muscle man, save for a stomach that hung over and almost hid his silver-dollar belt buckle. No boy would argue with Red. His name came from his hair and maybe from his flushed face. His truck and motorcycle were red, and his silver spoon ring held a big red pebble.

Lights, smoke, and the smell of beer inside made it like Saturday night, and some men, looking droop-eyed and drawn-faced, swore it was. With fields too wet to plow, every man who wasn't in church was there, most just country people, Rass could tell, in for the news.

Some agreed the calf hanging was animal for animal. "Nert took that fine mule colt Rose give McMulty; McMulty took away a calf Nert prized. Even up."

Pool shots slit the air as the room buzzed the gossip to a higher level. "I say it was a threat on Nert's life."

" 'Course it's a threat—what else could anyone call it? It was the same as McMulty spelling out to Nert, 'Next time, it'll be you!' "

Rass, forgetting to just listen, said, "A hung calf ain't no threat on Nert." Then he slipped over to other men, who debated the whereabouts of McMulty. Everyone was sure McMulty had done it.

"No other coloreds got no reason to threat a landlord. 'Course Nert asked for it, but all in all, Nert's still the boss." Big Red took bets on how long till McMulty was caught.

Red challenged his even bigger brother, Rooster, to a game. Rooster sighted down his pool stick and said, "Maggie done the dumbest thing, cutting down that calf 'fore any of us got a look-see. Coloreds say McMulty was too little a man to a-done it alone. But a body has to split down the middle what coloreds say and then shave a little off to get close to the truth." *Crack!* The balls danced around the table. "Good shot!" Rooster whooped and his chest expanded.

Next sighting and next comment came from Red. "Shore, he's capable o' doing that job all by his lonesome. A man what's mad is strong. Get me mad, you'll see my point. So I ain't splitting straws on nothing. He maybe had reason to be mad, like I say, but Nert's his boss. Don't matter what, a colored oughta stay in his place."

Rass, pretending to misunderstand, asked, "How could Mr. McMulty stay in his place when Nert kicked him out of it?"

"Smart mouth! Stop listening if you cain't keep quiet, kid. That calf was Nert's property that McMulty killed. Miss Esther'll get a vision where he's hiding, and we'll root him out."

Rass's heart sank. Miss Esther Love was the oldest of the two old sisters who ran the store right across from the school. Most farmers got regular needs at Raymond's, but if credit was hit too hard, they went to the Love sisters' higher-priced store for a second chance to charge their groceries.

"Nert's big mistake was hiring a colored day laborer."

"Mr. McMulty had a sharecropping contract! Nert swore—," Rass blurted out, then clamped his hand over his mouth.

"Hey, boy, you know words said to coloreds ain't holding!" Rooster dismissed Rass with a turn. "Better watch your mouth, Little Whit." He tucked his pool stick behind his back for a trick shot. "I bet McMulty's lit out for the Tennessee border to save his hide. And the Dumases' hides. There's some mean laws agin harboring a criminal."

"Naw," Big Red said. "Maggie already had the Dumas place searched inside and out. Found McMulty's belongings, but not him. Dumas claims the old man never even slept there. How about your daddy, boy?"

"He slept at our house...I mean, we all slept at Mr. McMulty's."

"Whit knows better than to harbor coloreds," Rooster said to the other men. "Maybe McMulty weren't at the Dumases' last night. On the other hand, maybe he was. Thur a tricky lot; that boy Clever puts on airs, talking like a city slicker." He eyed Rass. "Watch who you be friendly with, boy."

Rass knew Rooster meant Clever, but he said, "I ain't ashamed of my friend Shark," and walked toward Shark, who was serving bar.

Rooster laughed. "Smart-mouthed little snot, ain't he?" He kept on shooting.

Only Shark's head showed above the bar. He turned up the radio so "Pistol Packing Mama" blared out as he came around the bar to talk. His wraparound apron, a dirty gray, covered Sunday clothes. He explained to Rass that his ma thought he'd gone to church when he'd been out with his camera on the ditch bank.

"Mr. McMulty's hiding," Shark said. "He didn't ride off, 'cause I seen L.G. pass by with both mules hitched to youns' wagon."

"Where could he hide and not be found?"

"The old man sure wasn't at the Dumases' when I dropped off the meat yesterday at dusk." Shark, always with pocket money, saw every detective serial movie that hit Parma. "He musta gone directly to Nert's when he left the salvaging. Think somebody helped him hang that calf?"

"What?" was all the answer Rass gave.

"Well, I don't believe it was a one-man job. It don't

look good for youns. Some say Whit helped. Your dad home all night?"

So that's why Maggie was questioning Dad. "He was," Rass said.

"Maybe it *was* a one-man job! Some say the calf wasn't all that big," Shark shouted over the music just as "Pistol Packing Mama" ended.

"Could be." Rass's words came out loud in the silence. Men began easing toward the bar as if pulled by a slow-moving magnet.

Rass, who had promised to collect information, now would be asked to give it by men who thought he knew more. Two strong-breathed men, the kind Shark said drank for three days until the muscles of their stomachs stretched from bloating and their faces drooped from lack of food, leaned in. Thinking fast, Rass said, "Shark . . . that's an awful interesting camera."

Shark asked the men for their orders. The smell of beer grew stronger as Shark drew it, two glasses at a time, for all gathered. As he took their money, he talked on to Rass. "You want to try out my Box Brownie for a day? I'll let you. I'll even sell you some shots on it. Newsmen asked to see all my pictures since I sold 'em that one of Mr. McMulty helping Sally. Developed it themselves. I'll sell yours what recorded real history, if you'll take this roll to Miss Juanita to get it developed and pick up another roll of film for me?" Shark's mom hated Miss Esther Love and forbade Shark to enter the Love sisters' store. Miss Juanita was the "good" Love sister.

Rass was horrified. "I never took that picture to be in

papers! Sally would die, knowing people eat mule meat! So would every newspaper reader."

Once men knew it was only camera and mule-meat talk, most gave up on listening, took their beer, and moved to join the common talk in the air about finding McMulty. But skinny, filthy John Henry Litikin, who bragged he'd never been to school a day in his life, had a little trouble walking away. He announced after he swooped a beer head to the floor and downed the whole mug of beer, his Adam's apple dancing, "Maggie'll cotch McMulty rit quick, if'n she'd tawk to Miss Esther Love. Miss Esther knows who'd let a colored live wit 'im." He then had a coughing fit, his open mouth revealing rotting teeth. Rass wanted to run to the Love sisters' store, away from liquor, tobacco, sweat, lies.

Shark pounded John Henry's back and offered him water. John Henry knocked it to the floor, grabbed his friend's mug. His friend grabbed it back. "Hair, you ignorant ass, give me my beer! Ever'one knows Maggie's more interrested in mindin' Nert! Havin' dep'ties search all wagons, cars, and trains, when no white man's fool 'nough to give McMulty a ride! John Henry, you're a fool's fool, but you're right on Miss Esther."

A decent farmer whose one eye never focused, giving him a look apart, said, "Sheriff's got to do her duty by Nert, for he's a landowner. Her old man'd turn over in his grave if'n she didn't!"

"Nert threats to get help higher up if'n Maggie ain't got McMulty behind bars in a week. He'll do it, too, strong and set as Nert is," said a cropper.

Then another from over past Aught Ditch, whose name Rass never heard, said, "I'll be dad-blamed if I ain't hoping McMulty gets free. Nert's not worth all that much of the sheriff's trouble."

Another interrupted, "No cropper, what's got a woman and kids, is itching to be no dad-blamed hero. Whoever'd be fool enough to harbor McMulty will hang right alongside 'im. We all know that. Man, I wouldn't risk it."

Rass felt the cords on his neck leap tight. He needed air.

Outside he breathed deeply, stuck his hand in his pocket to feel Shark's money and film, then ran on to the Love sisters' store.

He was greeted, on entering, by Miss Esther's thin little condescending smile, almost a sneer, showing her crystal-white false teeth. She was a thin woman in every way, but hard-lined and strong and ruled the world. Her gray work sweater had mismatched buttons, some seashell, others bone. Rass asked for Miss Juanita. Miss Esther gave him the eye. "Juanita'll be 'long dreckly. She's napping. I always let my baby sister sleep in on Sundays. I don't dock her wages none for it."

Miss Juanita was all of seventy-five.

"But the sheriff come early this morning with fresh veal for me to parcel out to the needy and woke Juanita up. I didn't like Maggie rummaging through my food vouchers to see if anyone'd bought salve. Sly and foolish woman. What she oughta done was ask me straight out who killed that calf, and where that colored man's a-hiding out. I coulda saved her a lot of searching. I have the sixth sense."

Rass nodded. Keeping his eyes away from hers, he spotted a stack of salve, twenty-five cents each... be good for Mr. McMulty. Could he use Shark's money, instead of for film? His hand reached his pocket, tempted. That crazy old woman planted thoughts in his mind! He resisted. Then his elbow hit a stack of photography magazines, spilled them and the salve, too.

Miss Esther started picking them up. "Juanita's magazines! She's caused me more trouble than Daddy ever suspected. There ain't a worse curse than a mixed-up child rebelling, buying magazines like these."

Rass helped pick up the boxes of salve. He held the last box, examined it, then touched his own worst cut he'd got when the flood felled him in getting Old Jersey up the ditch bank. Suddenly Miss Esther's chatter stopped. "*Juanita!*" she screamed. "Come out here! I told you who I saw in my vision this morning. Well, here he stands! Turned to the side like he is, I see the same profile, though he be a boy, not a man! Visions is never one hundred percent. And he's bunged up—look!"

Miss Juanita's large, round face flushed as she came out buttoning the thin gray coat that was always part of her daytime costume, inside or out, winter or summer. "Rass?" she said, but her sister took over again.

"I told them colored people what come asking, I saw a man wearing overalls torn on one leg and a work shirt with rings of sweat under the arms and across the back. And I saw the profile of one what's harboring Nert's calf killer!" Miss Esther slapped the counter hard.

The salve dropped. Rass quickly stepped near Miss Juanita, a befriender of children in a way scarce among adults, slipped her the film and money, and whispered, "Shark's."

Juanita got the new film. "Sister, you oughten accuse Rass! You'll have people believing, when he did no sort." Then to Rass she said, "She'll forget. You wanted to buy some salve for your cuts?"

Rass looked at the floor.

She said, "I been a-wondering what to send to hep youns." She put a larger tin into his front pocket.

Deeply thankful, he could hardly mutter, "Thanks."

With her teeth again flashing like pearls in the sea of fine wrinkles, Miss Esther was near him, declaring, "I tell you, boy, it don't pay to harbor the enemy. My granny lost her fangers on her right hand for hiding out a Confederate soldier. Tried to close a door on a Union soldier who'd come a-searching, and *whack!*" Her skinny old hands made a cutting motion right in front of Rass's face. He bolted out the door.

Soon, back in front of the pool hall, he found L.G. sitting in the driver's seat of the Chevy, and Dad standing by the door arguing with his brothers. "I said I don't know McMulty's whereabouts! He wouldn't never show up to my place, me the one what took over his house."

Uncle Tut asked, "Why'd I have to find out from Jake that Maggie's grilling you? You know I'd come hep you, Whit, if'n you're in trouble. You're the oldest of us boys, but that don't mean we cain't hep. Is it 'cause I owe you twenty?" No song was in Uncle Tut's voice this time.

Uncle Jake's shoulders drooped. His panama hat was askew. Though his belly was round, he seemed miserably small. "That's right. We know you'd never hide nor hep McMulty if he hung Nert's calf. Would you?"

Dismissing them, Dad pushed into the car. "Sun hid its nose by ten this morning and ain't come out all day. Likely be more rain. Me and my boys better get on home." L.G. revved the motor and honked. But Miss Esther's words and those from the pool hall clung to Rass. He needed to give Shark his film, and to reason out what to report and what not. He said, "I'll walk," and waved them on. So L.G. and Dad sped off.

Quickly he got the film to Shark, then leaving the street of stores and post office, Rass took the gravel main street past the house where teachers roomed, the simple white clapboard church, the school, and on past a row of small houses, some no more than two rooms, then past the one large home, which had thirteen rooms, two balconies, and in which the prettiest girl in his class lived. Then he was in country. If days would bring investigation, the nights ought not be wasted. Mr. McMulty must escape at night, the minute he was well enough to travel. He'd harbor him till then.

Darn fields were so plowed there wasn't enough birds nor animals to allow good thinking. He cut to the railroad track. Right-of-ways had snakes, bugs, rabbits, and all sorts of bushes filled with the daily changes of growing. He still couldn't think. He'd heard too much for reasoning. As he cut across field to McMulty's place, Ole Coalie found him and loped alongside.

Suddenly Rass stubbed his toe. He walked on, still trying to get his mind going in spite of the smarting pain...then reason did break through! He turned back, picked up the rectangular object, and scraped the dry mud from it. "It's Mom's Bible. Look! Look!" Rass wiped the leather clean with his shirttail, held it up to Ole Coalie and the world. "Mom's Bible ain't ruined! This latch has kept it closed tight! Down Coalie, down."

But Ole Coalie couldn't stay out of the action. Anyway, Rass got it open. The pages showed no signs of water except for some stains just around the edge of the leaves. The genealogy sheet didn't have any ink smears but what he could read through. "It's got to be a sign that things'll go good from now on," Rass said, then gave Ole Coalie the biggest hug ever. In turn, he got a lavish face licking. "It's a good sign, all right! Here's Dad's contract with Nert. Wait'll Dad sees this!" Rass took off running. He knew for sure it'd make Mom happy.

When he toted his find into the house, placed it on the oak library table that had come down with this Bible straight from Mom's ancestors, and opened it up to Dad's contract, Dad really got excited. "Helen, come see what our boy has found! Hurry in here! You're sure going to be happy 'bout this. It's something we thought was gone."

Mom came in from the kitchen and stood amazed.

Dad kept right on talking, the prettiest talk Rass ever heard. "I thought it was plumb washed away. But my boy has found it."

"Sure did, Dad. That snap sure kept it tight and dry." Rass's nerves had been strung so tight and his mind had been closed so firmly, now both were free! "It's a good omen. A fine omen!"

"Right! You've done something I never ever expected. Them mules may be dead, but you've found Helen's Bible what holds my contract still in cellophane, dry as a bone. Even a sinner like me takes this as a good omen. Let Maggie come investigating all she wants. Let Nert go mouth off that I'm a cropper what has to obey his orders! I got a written contract here what's signed, sealed, and'll stand up in any court of law. I'm a renter for this whole year of 1937! I'm my own boss!"

Dad was so happy he was prancing. Mom had a tough time getting the Bible from him. Dad did keep the contract in his hand, pecked Rass on the head with it, shouted out to all the kids, "This is my boy! This is my boy what checks things when he stubs his toe on 'em. My boy who knows enough to scrape off a little mud to see what it is he's found!"

Rass grabbed Sally, swung her around, gave the little girls a turn, told L.G. his agreement on the five acres was in there, too.

"Course it is!"

He swung L.G. around. All was an embrace to the good omen, and to his own fine mind that had been smart enough to find it. Finally, when they all wound down, Mom read a few scriptures about if only in this life one has hope.

And Rass worked well with his family till nightfall. As soon as the girls had Dad almost revved up to storytelling, Rass announced he had to go to the toilet. He tended Mr.

McMulty's needs, shared with him the joy of his find, then he quieted. Mr. McMulty had had no protection of a contract, and there was the planned search and Miss Esther's forecast.

"But I got some salve to put on your leg." Rass fished it out of his pocket.

"Ain't up to it being unwrapped and wrapped agin, son."

"But...you're okay, ain't you?"

McMulty sounded weak, but still insisted. "No salve now. Tamarr I be able to stand and fix my wound most proper."

"Mr. McMulty, you don't know how glad I am to hear that! No man alive ought to stay hid in a place where he cain't even turn over." He returned the salve to his pocket. Something didn't feel right.

# 11

RASS SLEPT in the loft, tossing and turning all night long. Then dawn's light came seeping in under the eaves to the music of Ole Coalie's howling, which made Rass jump, crack his head on a roof rafter, and come sharply awake. Need to check Mr. McMulty! Should get dressed before Dad or Mom wake up! Scrunching low, he moved to the roof center, a place high enough to stand. Ole Coalie's howls made good cover, but Mom shushed the dog. Dang! In the old house stairs led right to the front door, making it easy sneaking in or out to fill a need. Now he'd have to wait till Mom got decently dressed before he went down the ladder.

A chair scraped the floor. Mom, pulling her clothes from the back of it. He gave her time to pull her dress over her head, shake it down, and smooth out the skirt. He remembered learning her sounds and ways when he was little and could come and go as he pleased through the living room where his parents slept. He waited. She's turning a damper in the stovepipe. Building a fire in the kitchen stove. She's dressed. Go!

Ah, no, another chair scraping in the living room. A thud of shoes. Dad's noises. If he didn't get down there before Dad went to the barn, Mr. McMulty would be without food and other necessities. Rass shot to the ladder, let the rattling of pans and teakettle be noises to descend by. Raced past Dad. But Mom, removing a lid from a can and scooping out lard with her fingers, grabbed his gallus with her clean hand. "Where you going so fast? We need to settle 'bout you getting to school on time." She put lard into the cast iron skillet, for gravy, then another dab into a big rectangular baking pan atop the stove to melt.

Dad moved into her space, stood too near, blocked her work. "Hold it, Helen. I aim to do as Nert says and have my boys skip school today. Let Nert think I'm trying to please him, even if I ain't. Fact is, I need *all* hands. Keep the girls home, too. Threatening rain's held off. McMulty's fields are dry enough to work, and we got to make hay while the sun shines, as the saying goes. Them's my words."

The next noise was Mom mixing biscuit dough, becoming lightning itself, slapping and banging, her face growing red. Between forefinger and thumb she squeezed small amounts of dough to size, sopped the tops of the biscuits in the melted lard, flipped them over, nestled their bottoms onto the greased pan, and shoved them into the oven. In fifteen minutes they were browned to a golden hue, and Rass had hot biscuits out to Mr. McMulty, putting strength into his muscles. A good beginning to the day!

In the middle of his own breakfast came a call that made baby Marylu come crawling to Rass as fast as she could. She had no use for Uncle Tut, who tickled her unmercifully. Rass picked her up and stroked her. She was the sweet pet of the whole family. Squeezing her, rubbing her back, or patting her little head made his life lighten.

Uncle Tut's bigness filled the doorway, his overalls stiff with soil and the smell of yesterday's sweat. "Nert says he wants Rass far away from Jake's cropper; 'course he means Clever. Says all ground over here's to be worked first. He's counting your old house area and the wet grounds around as fallow to claim his government parity check."

L.G.'s face went white. "My five acres ain't gonna lay fallow!"

Dad's face was an angry red. "He's rushing it. I don't aim to sign no sharecropping contract with Nert! L.G.'ll replant his acres."

Uncle Tut grabbed a biscuit. Rass pushed him the rest of his gravy. Dad raved on.

"Nert don't need to think that 'cause he furnishes the mules he can tell my boys which fields to work! He's always ordered McMulty around, but not me! He ain't calling my rented land fallow so's he can end up not sharing the check with me, as he done McMulty! I'll rent mules. I got my own say. My contract says I'm a renter."

"Thanks to me what found it," Rass reminded him, and squeezed Marylu tight as he waited for Dad's confirming praise. Tut reached for another biscuit.

Mom snapped, "Breakfast is over. Girls, get off to school." Then came Dad's hiss.

"Nert's got to honor *my* renter's contract, till January first! Thanks goes to Rass getting it back to me, safe and sound." Rass brimmed with pride. "And it'll hold up in a court of law."

" 'Cause you're white," said Uncle Tut.

"Right, I ain't black!" snapped Dad sarcastically, and stretched out his hands for inspection. The little kids examined them just to be sure he hadn't changed color overnight.

But it made no sense. Rass asked, "If it's on paper, what difference would your color make in court?"

"This ain't no time for such questions! As far as you're concerned, this contract is about who gives you orders, me or Nert. Well, I give the orders to *my* family." To prove it, Dad's face became hard, he stood tall, and started giving orders. "Rass, you can jest go work that field next to the Dumases'! Don't let Nert stop you. L.G., come hep me pull Pa's little house closer over so Helen can care for them brooding chicks proper."

"Girls, I said get off to school," Mom whispered.

"Sally, take Rosalee and Chrissy to the edge of the waters!" Dad gave conflicting orders. "Little'uns can hep clear trash what's washed in. Them's my words, Helen! My word's all I got anymore, dad-nab-it!" He pounded the table, rattling the dishes.

So it had come to that—his sisters doing field work, Rass a full hand, him and L.G. out of school for the rest of their lives. Dad's voice held power, as did Nert's.

And Mr. McMulty hid in a spider's cove.

THE LACK of noise in plowed fields made them a fine place for thinking up escapes for Mr. McMulty. An occasional call of a morning bird greeting the world at seven o'clock didn't distract. Turning old bleached soil into a rich new earth for the sprouting of new shoots counted. Rass set his plow deep into the packed soil. The force of his arms held the plow there, causing the dirt to rise over the plow's curve to the surface and become loose black topsoil. Nert's mule pulled the plow along. Rass enjoyed making his field different from those unplowed, or even those already green with young sprouts. Soaking up the sun, he found goodness in nature the way Mr. McMulty always had. But as he neared the trees at the end row, he could smell the soured weeds of the flood-kill across the way, so he quickly turned the plow into the next row, against wind.

But the smell had done him in. Throughout the morning he looked up to see if Nert was coming to chase him off the field Dad had assigned. Or if Maggie was coming with her posse to round up all the family to be hanged. Or if the sun would surface or the rains would come. Or, on the saving side, if Clever was plowing yet. Mr. Dumas was the sole cropper working a small section of Uncle Jake's land part-time, when he was not on the dredge boat. Uncle Jake was a kind landlord, giving the Dumases options on work time and on what to plant. He had never expected twelve-year-old Clever to be a full work hand.

Indeed, Rass saw Sheriff Maggie Porter's truck and other sheriffs' cars from the towns of Malden and Bernie zooming up and down the road. All that action, thriving and humming on the smell of blood, sure meant time was a-narrowing. He sensed their need to make 1937 the year small towns banded together, caught a real criminal, and strung him up. Felt it in his bones. It made him want to bolt from the reins that held him. It made him too nervous to plow a straight row.

Morning dragged on. Clever never showed in Uncle Jake's field. Maybe the sheriffs had rounded up all black men, killed them all, as in times when a slave rebelled. By noon Rass was wiped out by tiredness, too tense to eat or listen to Mom tell Dad how Uncle Tut had brought his whole family over on a load of straw to fill mattresses, but actually had come to eat their precious canned beef.

They'd left 'cause Maggie had stopped to snoop.

"Maggie give this place an okay, found no one hiding out," Mom said. "But it must've miffed Nert, 'cause he come riding over on his big white horse charging through the barn, loping around the lot, circling the house, till I was ready to die."

"Did he have his dogs?" Rass managed to ask.

"No. Why, no. Why'd you ask that?"

"Just thinking Ole Coalie don't need to go messing with Nert's big dogs."

L.G. said, "I took Ole Coalie over to our old place out of Mom's earshot."

Family noises, family smiles of approval, then Dad giving the family orders. "Make ever' minute count—it ain't raining. Get moving!" Rass choked with guilt, ate Mr. McMulty's needed food, and got back to the fields.

A million escape plans came and went as the afternoon grew long, and hunger for something, anything, got Rass's stomach begging for food. He stopped the plow to rest, but wanted to die.

Then he heard, "Haw Willie, haw!" That was Clever's

call! Clever, a speck on the flat and massive horizon, plowing Uncle Jake's field! Feeling new life, Rass set his plow in and headed down-row, plowing and plowing till they got even. He threw plow lines over his head and ran, not waiting for the end row, not caring if Dad or Nert or the whole world saw him. "Clever, you ain't dead!"

Clever, tall for twelve, and with springy steps, came galloping across field, calling greetings. "Course I ain't dead."

"Where you been? I never saw hide nor hair of you all day."

"I was in school," Clever said.

Of course! Just because Dad had kept Rass home, he'd thought the whole world had stopped school, too. His mind didn't work right when worrying.

"You hear anything about Mr. McMulty?" he asked.

"Wasn't at our place all that long," Clever said. Then they settled in, crumbled dirt clods, as Clever told that Preacher Bloodworth said "a man's witnessed words is a contract." Also Nert had to record his croppers on the government contract to get parity. With proper protest it would stand in court. "Preacher Bloodworth says no honor's to be paid a man a-rising hisself in the world on stolen money."

"Nert stole money? Tell Maggie Porter! Let's get him jailed."

"Never giving Mr. McMulty his share of the parity check last year is stealing, ain't it? But Nert don't see it like that."

"Oh. Just like he's planning to steal parity from L.G., only Dad won't allow it. We'll tell Mr. McMulty to go to court!"

"Cain't tell him nothing when he's missing." Clever's face showed a tightness, then he added, "Besides, someone's got to vouch for his word in court—he's colored."

"Well, so are you." Rass suddenly saw why Nert hadn't *rented* to a colored man. Nert knew all along he could keep the whole parity check.

Clever said nothing for the longest time. Finally, "You don't think Mr. McMulty's the one who hung Nert's calf, do you? That'd not set well in court if he tried to get heard about his broken contract."

"The whole countryside thinks he done it," said Rass.

" 'Cause he's colored. They even afraid of me sometimes 'cause I'm colored," Clever said, and they grew silent.

Then Rass asked, "Do you think Mr. McMulty did it?"

Clever nodded. "He did it. Colored or not. Sheriff keeps asking us where he is. We don't know. I swear on my soul. After we moved in his things, I took a walk with Zeltha. When I got back, he was gone."

"Zeltha? You got a girlfriend? Gosh, even L.G. ain't got a girlfriend." Rass shot that out fast before Clever decided to ask what he thought.

"I hope he's took off to Arkansas." Clever looked at him, then added, "You know where he is! I can tell by the look in your eyes."

Rass's impulse was to tell Clever all, but he said, "I'm . . . I'm just thinking of all them sheriffs' cars zooming around like they're chasing a rabbit on the run. Noisying out my thoughts. There's nothing so open as a new plowed field, and I seen and heard every one of 'em. I know Mr. McMulty's got to be somewheres. But he ought to be a-living in his own house, a-sleeping on a nice straw mattress, instead of me."

"Yeah, the law's acting like he killed a person, not a calf," said Clever.

Rass nodded. Then he said, "I cain't stop a-grieving. We live in his house!"

"Now, you got to stop a-grieving over that. Weren't youns' fault. All colored people knows the power ain't with youns. Don't think on it," Clever said kindly. "Got to stop, or it'll kill you."

"I cain't stop thinking on it. He's my friend. Besides, whenever I try to stop thinking on something, I start thinking harder about what it is I'm trying not to think on." Tears came to his eyes.

Clever snapped a finger. "If you was colored you could. Colored people always keep on keeping on. My mama tell me, 'Think on something else,' I just switch over, like this." *Snap!* "Nothing to it."

Rass's hungry belly answered with a growl. He smiled and shoved Clever. "I already done it. I'm thinking on food."

"Hey! Don't shove me, Rass. Mr. Nert think we fighting." He pointed to a white horse on the horizon, and the howl of dogs sealed it.

"Nert's coming! He's coming after me!" Rass gasped and didn't know whether to run or stand still.

"No. Likely it's me. We still under question. Maggie Porter says McMulty cain't be in Arkansas, says he was hurt bad, lost blood, and is too crippled to make it far without no ride." Clever threw a hard clod of the clay soil.

"The blood could have been from the calf! Or a bloody nose or something. They don't know it was Mr. McMulty's blood," Rass insisted.

"Time to act jolly," Clever said. "Play dumb, Rass. *I* don't know nothing."

The dogs reached Rass first and sniffed him round about. He moved away, started running back to his plow. Nert caught up, his riding crop raised. Clever yelled, "I told you, get back behind your plow, boy!"

"Get back to *your* plow, boy!" Nert whirled toward Clever.

Clever flipped the reins and called out, "Gee, Willie, gee!"

Pacing alongside on that beautiful horse, Nert hurried Rass back, then demanded, "What you discussing with Jake's cropper?"

"Schoolwork. I hate missing school. Clever ain't good in math," Rass lied. He had no idea how Clever did, but the whole country, even Nert, must know Rass had won every ciphering match in Parma Elementary.

"You're lying. He tell you where McMulty's hiding out? Speak up!" The riding crop was just above Rass's head.

"He's in Arkansas. Clever's folks think so."

"I think you're still lying. Tell me, was you and your daddy standing at the clearing by the woods the morning I found my calf hung?"

Rass didn't have to think. He just nodded.

Nert was clearly surprised. "Well, shoot me in the head, I guess you ain't lying. I can always tell. Your daddy didn't have the sense to own up to Maggie what I knew for a fact—he lied to her face! And Maggie tells me your mama and brother swore you was both home all that night." They were near the plow; Nert's horse pranced around, disturbing the evenly plowed ground. "Was you?"

"Yes sir, I was." Rass breathed hot under Nert's piercing stare. Quickly he unknotted the reins, looped them over his shoulder.

"Tell me straight, boy. Your daddy hiding McMulty?"

"No sir, he ain't." Rass kept eye contact, for he knew that was the truth. He added, "Dad's dead set against hiding a criminal."

Nert believed.

"Tomorrow, soon's I get this contract business settled with Whit, you work where I say. Right now, bite that plow in. Get ground covered or I'll personally keep you out of school the rest of this year. Your mother and the law be damned! Her telling Maggie Porter I'm breaking the law keeping you outa school! Well, there's going to be some deputies helping Maggie *do her duty* to a law that concerns me and my property!"

"Yes, sir!" Rass forced the plow point in, never looking up to see Nert leave. He tried to switch his mind and think on light things, like Clever could do so easily. Mr. McMulty would surely find some light things to think on, too. He'd know how to keep on keeping on.

# 12

BILL BROWN came very early the next morning. So when all were to leave for the fields, Dad told Rass, "Get Bill pointed toward home, and you start disking." First, of course, Rass and Bill cared for Mr. McMulty, Bill's help welcome—but not his sounds, as he pointed to Mr. McMulty's leg.

"Bill, we ain't got no time for talking. You feel awfully hot, Mr. McMulty. You sick?" Rass asked, then tried to feed him.

Mr. McMulty pushed the food away. "There be times when man need talking more'n he need food. My leg not feeling so good—'fraid it getting no better fast. But most 'portant, I needs talk. I thinks till life got no meaning. Thoughts gotta have words." He took just a sip of the water Bill offered. "I wishes I undo my crime, and I cain't."

Rass remembered how when he felt down Mr. McMulty shared talk of the smells of good wet ground in spring, or of ripe oats in summer, overripe peaches in fall, damp leaves in winter. Or of good sounds, or pleasant happenings. He motioned Bill to stand guard, and granted Mr. McMulty time to talk by asking, "You been thinking 'bout sounds and smells?"

"Mostly I jest think how Nert no good, how he plumb rotten doing me in, and I not sorry one bit I stands up to him. My mind keep spinning like that, too worried to work good. My soul ache. I gives myself up for privilege of talking to Preacher Bloodworth one hour. That man all soul, all the time." He lay back against the crib.

"Your mind's thinking good. Nert did cheat you. Ever'one's got a right to fight their enemy. Now eat your food."

Mr. McMulty pushed the food away again, then surprised Rass by saying, "It be taxing living with an ear to yo' family. I not able to holler when Whit sound like yo' enemy. I glad when you find that Bible. It settle Whit a bit. You such a good boy."

That caught Rass off guard. He hadn't thought his family was so loud. "I cain't never please Dad for long. He'll be hollering again soon enough, telling me to keep my mouth shut. But I cain't spend my life not saying a word and still stand up for what's right, can I? Can you?"

"My own daddy never laid a hand on me in anger," Mr. McMulty said. "Never! Papa not be a loud nor fighting man, though he long preached I gotta stand up for myself—never let down on that principle one time. I never yell at Papa. He too good." Mr. McMulty ate a bite. "All my life I gone 'bout in pleasing ways. You and yo' daddy be my friends. I longs to speak out in yo' behalf, jest as I longs to cry out agin Nert."

Bill was making noises. Rass worried the girls were up and out, but the old man seemed not to notice.

"Papa live 'mong good people," he went on. "So I always figger, like Papa, I cast my bread upon the water and . . . That be my trouble right now, son—nothing good come back from a man like Nert. I hear Preacher Bloodworth know the way to stand tall and still not displease. I needs the man."

"I'll find him for you, I promise. You gotta go back under. Just you think on how Dad was happy when I found the Bible and his contract."

"I hears." The old man seemed faint. Rass whispered, "I wish I could go find you a contract. Oh, Mr. McMulty, you oughten thought Nert's words'd be binding in court!" He clamped his hands over his mouth. "I'm sorry."

"No apology, son. Standing up to truth always be hurtful. I hates Nert letting me see kindness don't always bring kindness, like Papa taught. I pleases Miz Rose caring for her dogs and she be grateful. Even Nert never got me to no point I couldn't swallow . . . till the flood." The old man suddenly seemed to pick up energy. His eyes got too bright.

Rass reached to steady him. "Mr. McMulty, I got to hide you, *now*."

"Some folk say Rose use me, running her dogs ever' day, but . . . this be secret, boy—you know that mule colt Nert give her that she don't hanker to? Well, she give it to me 'cause she know her husband ain't a kind man and she know my dream. I know her since she a little girl. She say 'cause I take good care o' her dogs, that colt be mine. I feeds it when I goes there to feed her dogs. Next year that little mule be big 'nough to plow my own land." For a moment he looked proud, tried to rise. Fell.

"Mr. McMulty, you ain't feeling addled, are you?" Rass helped him into position. "You know Nert done said Rose cain't give you nothing."

"Sorry, son. Mind don't stay straight. It be a puzzlement if'n Papa call fine what I done standing up to Nert, or if'n he say I best be punished, wipe my slate clean. I needs Preacher Bloodworth."

Rass had to motion to Bill to stay on guard, for he'd come checking the delay. Then Rass kicked at some of the old straw he'd removed from the opening and said, "I know. It's like it's wrong me harboring you, yet it's right. I wish none of this happened." He tried to shove, but Mr. McMulty wouldn't budge.

"All folks wish bad don't happen, but it do." He looked Rass in the eye. "It swaller my faith up, this fear. I got to ride fear—a scared man don't pray so well."

Was that sound Maggie Porter's truck? Standing there in the barn's great center opening Rass scanned the horizon. It was dangerous to stay out in the open so long, but it was most impolite to stop his friend's talk.

"Preacher Bloodworth says a man o' pure faith be ready for God's will. I 'members old family tales of long hidings during slave times, what led to freedom. They sustains me. Hiding out be standing up to evil powers—I thinks that till day got no timing to it."

Rass again tried to easily guide Mr. McMulty under. "You bothered by rats? Spiders?"

"No. No, boy. I hears 'em, once, then I hears a cat attack."

So Snowball had turned barn cat! Rass was relieved.

"My old head weary." His voice drooped. "Scoot me under, boy." Rass had felt like that when things seemed hopeless. Gently he shoved Mr. McMulty back into the hole. He was wringing with sweat by the time he and Bill got the opening resealed with the smelly old straw. Then the truck arrived. It wasn't Maggie's truck; it was Bill's folks come looking for him. Rass said to them, "It's a bonus, being kept home from school, to have Bill's company. I'm gonna teach him to disk, if that's okay." Mr. Brown couldn't turn it down.

Luck continued. They passed Clever going to school, and Rass asked, "Could you get Preacher Bloodworth to stop by our place?"

"Why?" Clever's look was one of great curiosity.

Rass thought quickly. "Dad needs to talk about parity checks. Nert thinks he can change his fallow-land place from Mr. McMulty's land to ourn." He was pleased by his own quick answer.

Work got done much easier with Bill along. It didn't rain, but the air was heavy, misty. Noon hour back at the house was spent talking about Bill, and how L.G. could move the brooder house and set it on blocks for Mom while she and Dad went to town for groceries.

Then Dad said, "Rass, you and Bill take time outa the field to watch the little'uns. If it rains, keep 'em inside. We're taking Sally to learn the shopping ways of a frugal woman."

Sally gloated, and Rass acted real put out until they left. Then he set Rosalee and Chrissy to pretending they were Mom rocking baby Marylu to sleep. "After that, bake me a hundred mud pies. I'll play I'm Dad at work in the barn." Happily they accepted that great responsibility. Rass and Bill ran to the barn.

Rass yelled. "We're here!" The answer coming back sounded faraway. Bill helped pull Mr. McMulty out, pointed at the bandage, and got as response, "Mighty close in there. Slep' most o' the morning. Fever put me under. Men searching wake me up. Fever put me under."

"Your head's hot. I'll get a cloth."

Mr. McMulty was sick. No time for food. Must keep him calm and get help. "Just think on this barn's good sounds and smells. Nothing bad. Just good, okay? I'll be right back."

Mr. McMulty's eyes seemed to take pleasure in memory as he said, "Even the smells of sweaty mules brings me moments of old satisfaction, knowing me and my team put in a fruitful day doing duty to the land we tills."

Rass got the wet rag and soothed his friend's brow, afraid he was going to pass out. Got to keep him talking. "I learned the smells of seasons from you, Mr. McMulty. I think on 'em, too." Actually he smelled a rotten smell. He hoped there wasn't a dead rat left by Snowball under the crib. "And Bill can smell right good, too, just like me. We can smell popcorn a block away from the movies, or a rotten egg three days after it's broke. Just name something, and I'll tell you if I can smell it."

"I loves work sounds and smells, too—the rattling of harness of my own mule, smell of the good leather as I mends it. Folks' sounds and nature sounds, they's what I longs for." He seemed free of pain now, as he talked on.

"Them grass squealing sounds yo' brother make do fall somewheres between—no music o' life to it a'tall. Bill's sounds be fine—he needs 'em. No talk be turrible."

"I know," Rass said with great feeling, his hand still stroking. When there was no one to talk to about Dad or L.G., there had always been Mr. McMulty. "I feel awful when I have to keep my mouth shut. It must be hard for Bill, too." He looked more fully at Mr. McMulty, and gasped. The blue work shirt was ringed with sweat under arms and across the back. Miss Esther's words flooded him, bringing the pulse in his temples to a roar.

Bill moved in closer, refusing to guard any longer. He began sniffing the air and making concerned sounds. Next he was tugging at the bandage.

Rass bent to unbind it. "Your leg's real hot—you need a doctor. Cain't waste no more time by cover talk!"

"Cain't do that, son. I speaks my word on it."

"I know we cain't let the doctor know where you're hiding. L.G. heard that Nert stationed Deputy Big Red Revelsen in front of the doctor's office."

"I too weak to fight Big Red. I not going nowheres today."

Bill was helping pull off the excessive bandage. A smell hit and Rass felt like vomiting. "I need to stop and go check on the little girls. I gotta use the salve this time, no ifs, ands, or buts about it." He got up, forced the round box out of his pocket, and handed it to Mr. McMulty. Before he could leave, Bill ripped away the entire bandage; cloth dangling in hand, he began dancing in anxiety, pointing.

"Blood poisoning! It's setting in, Mr. McMulty! Bill

smelled it. He knew!" The little girls totally left Rass's mind. He saw only the infected wound, the bloody marks going out from it.

Mr. McMulty raised himself to see. "Oh, Lord! Oh, sweet Jesus!"

"We got to tell Mom, soon's she gets home." Rass moved away from the smell, relieved to think of Mom's help.

"Not yo' mama, son. You knows it not good Helen and Whit know 'bout me; they get arrested for sho. It be you who operate! Get hot ashes and yo' daddy's straight-edge razor. Do same as yo' Mom do when she lance that boil on my neck. Cut out the 'fection. I heps you along."

Rass knew about boils. Mom had lanced a boil on his arm. Mrs. Brown had lanced one on Bill's leg, with Mom's help. And Rass knew he mustn't involve Dad or Mom in the hiding. He said sadly, "I know." Bill pointed again at the wound and made more sounds. Rass shook his head. "But Mr. McMulty, I cain't operate. Don't ask me to. I got to get help." Even Bill walked toward the barn opening, pointing toward the house.

"Got to hurry, son. I be dead in two day of blood poisoning. You go for hep, I be dead tonight. Billy be yo' hep. He know what we doing." Bill walked back. He seemed to know, all right. "Ever' minute Billy be here he putting two and two together. He come checking. No one else know where I hide; they be searching, not finding. But he know even on first day. It *was* him what smelled blood poison. You two boys—"

"No. No! I can't do it."

"You a big boy, Rass. You kill a cow. You can use a razor like you use Bill's knife. Don't think it be me. Think on pretty sounds and smells and jest carve away all the 'fection, till there be only clean raw flesh. Bring me wood chip to bite on, hoe handle to grip."

"I cain't! I cain't cut you. It'd take so long, we'd get caught. Anyways, I gotta go mind the little girls." Bill stayed near Mr. McMulty, as Rass ran. Marylu was asleep and there were seven mud pies. He found the hoe handle, paused. "Good. Just ninety-three to go." At the wash kettle he scooped up two big, curled wood chips, filled one with hot ashes. "I've got to do it," he said to himself to take energy from talk, but when he got to Mr. McMulty, all he could say was, "It'll hurt you. You'll kick if I cut."

"Billy gotta hold me down, son. Make him understand that."

Reaching toward Bill's pocket, Rass said, "I didn't get Dad's straight-edge razor. He'd kill me. Bill, I got to use your pocketknife, and you got to hold Mr. McMulty down tight! Okay? Okay?" Bill handed his fancy knife to Rass. Rass cleaned its blade with some ashes, and again declared, "Bill cain't understand. I cain't cut!"

"Farmer's got to cut. Got to butcher. You be good farm boy, Rass. You seen your daddy put a knife into a bloated cow."

"I never saw Dad let gas out of a bloated cow. I lied when I said I did. L.G. just told me 'bout that!"

Rass compelled himself to stop. He had to do it. Mom had taught that when gangrene set in, abscess must be cut away and the wound sterilized and left to heal inside out.

On the other hand, one jerk from Mr. McMulty and a bad cut could happen, and he'd bleed to death. Rass flung himself down across Mr. McMulty, pinning his arms, locking his feet to immobilize the legs. Then he jumped up and ordered Bill, "You see what I done? Now you hold him down like that! Do it!"

Bill backed away, alarm in his eyes.

"He won't hold you down," Rass said. "We need some whiskey. You don't happen to have a bottle hid in the barn like Uncle Tut, do you, Mr. McMulty? It'd knock you out cold."

"No, son, I don't. Wish I did. I never took on that nasty habit."

"Me neither," said Rass. Once Raymond gave him a swig of Uncle Tut's brandy found in Tut's barn. First came sweetness to his tongue, then a tingle in his throat, then sparks of fire bit at his nose and he was running for clear clean air and space to breathe. "Bill ain't gonna help, and Louie says he never changes his mind once he's set on a thing."

"Change his mind, or I be dead," said Mr. McMulty, putting the clean wood chip in his mouth and grabbing for the hoe handle.

Rass nodded and waved the knife toward the wound as he tried to think. Instantly Bill caught his intent and pinned Mr. McMulty, pressed his shoulders hard against the old man's hands gripping the stick. One leg put a lock on Mr. McMulty's good leg, his other foot held down the foot of the injured leg, and his body went across thighs and abdomen in a death lock.

Rass told Mr. McMulty what once the man had told him. "Whatever you love best, think on it!" He raised Bill's knife and made a quick small first cut. Blood and pus came out. Mr. McMulty's body quivered, but he was bearing the pain. Rass wiped it clear and made another cut, deep, which caused McMulty to jerk, as if he wanted to bolt upright. Bill forced the hold. Rass again needed to vomit. He had to stop, and did.

"Keep going, boy. Trim till it be clean. Put the chip back in my mouth. I a-holding."

Rass obeyed, turned his back to the old man's face, and cut and cut and cut as if it weren't a man's leg. His beating heart would surely interfere with his hand's motion, but somehow it worked separately. Hurt leaked from his soul. Groans came from both Bill and Mr. McMulty, until he'd removed all the rotted area. He gave one last scrape to make sure it was all gone. Mr. McMulty's body went rigid, then limp. Bill let go and moved to outside the barn opening, but didn't leave. Nor did Rass.

Thoughts of Mom's doctoring came and went as Rass finished the job of searing the open, clean wound with hot ashes, and filled the crater with carbolated salve. Bill stood guard. The strong odor of carbolic acid smothered the smell of rotting flesh. Finally, as he tore up the remains of the sheet he'd used the night he'd found Mr. McMulty, Rass motioned for Bill to come help. Together they finished the dressing.

"Bill, I know Dad'd say I done wrong, but I couldn't help it. I had to save him. I'm proud you held together and helped me. You didn't faint, nor vomit, like I done after I cut Ole Jersey. Mom always says life's lessons take aholt. I guess they did with me. Now we got to get Mr. McMulty back in his safe place. Ready?"

"Sis Greene!" It was Mr. McMulty's voice.

"Look, Bill, he's coming around! He's going to be just fine. He can get well and go off to Arkansas, and no one needs know it at all."

Bill kept pointing at Mr. McMulty, whose eyes were glazed over, but Mr. McMulty kept talking.

"See her, Rass? Bill? That be Sis Greene, sitting there on that old gray wagon bed, her feet springing with energy where they dangle."

Rass said, "She's right purty."

"Sis Greene's eyes still aglow with dreams, purty a thing as God ever created. Soon's I make it a-sharecropping, soon's I save my share of the parity checks, soon's I gets my acres..."

"...you gonna go back to Arkansas and claim her. That's right nice, Mr. McMulty." Rass kept smoothing the binding on the leg as he talked. "I knew you weren't ready to die."

Mr. McMulty's talking stopped, but in another minute he stirred a bit and asked, "Son, it be over?"

"It is. You gonna be all right. You're alive and doing fine." Rass smiled, and Bill smiled and made happy sounds.

"I had a dream when I under."

"I know," said Rass.

"I dreams my mama cast a curing spell on me, and preaches such goodness to me, and I ain't but a boy in my dream."

"That ain't what you dreamed!" Rass said, then changed it quickly. " 'Course it was," he said, lying like anything. At that moment Rass thought he and Bill were about as all right as boys could get. *They'd saved Mr. McMulty.*

"Here, let us get you into the corncrib. It's been searched through a million times. They know you ain't there. We don't have to put you back under and worry 'bout you a-lying in filth no more! I just cain't put you back in that ole hole and you so sick."

They got him in the crib and covered him over with a cotton sack and put a layer of corn over that, except for his face. "There now, everyone'll think it's the pile of corn that's forever been searched!" Quickly they cleared the area of evidence and Rass moved out to the entranceway and slung his arms high in triumph.

Bill understood their success and laid into Rass, right there. *Whump!* Rass was down. Then he was up, hitting Bill full-body, like a bale of hay falling on him from the hay wagon, laying him tight to the ground, smothering him, but just for a second. Bill resisted well. He was stronger than Rass, but obviously had no intention of proving it, just wrestled Rass over and over in a gleeful way. Rass rolled with him till he was finally on top, lying across Bill, hearing the rush of Bill's heart, knowing it matched his own, and for a couple of seconds they both rested as if by agreement. A bug crawled across Rass's sweating face. He felt its tracks and then suddenly Bill was alive and moving again, nostrils hissing.

Rass held his pin, demanding, "Say uncle and I'll let you up. Say it. Say it! We ain't got much time."

Bill grunted back, then pumped muscles full force, and Rass was off, leaping quickly, as if he'd gotten up with his own power, saying, "You never will say uncle, so I won. I pinned you long enough. I can tote a heavier cotton sack than L.G. I'm strong, like you. I really am." Bill was smiling, laughing. Rass let chuckles flow from him, too, until they exploded like popcorn in the machine at the harvest-time carnival.

"We gotta cut this out, for you got to go home," Rass said, and washed off Bill's knife and gave it back to him. Their eyes met. Bill took off, running.

Rass saw Dad's Chevy in the distance, and said to the corncrib, "I figure Mom went to town for more'n groceries. She's making Maggie enforce the law about us going to school. And maybe, by now, Clever's got ahold of Preacher Bloodworth. Wouldn't that be fine, too?"

Mr. McMulty didn't answer.

# 13

HAVING FALLEN ASLEEP fully dressed, Rass was down the ladder and out front before L.G. next morning. Uncle Jake, Aunt Kate, and Dennis had stopped by bright and early to beat the rain, bringing with them a sense of joy, as always. Dennis was a sharing sort, and in age right between L.G. and Rass. Thin and snowy-haired, tall like his mother, he bounded out of their Chevy, showing off a new spy box with black powder for taking real fingerprints. He'd gotten it, as he got all his stuff, by mail order.

Dennis whispered, "Where's L.G.? We gotta fingerprint your barn to see if Mr. McMulty's hiding out there like my dad and Miss Esther believes. I got 'em to come early to give a surprise they've got for Sally. It's for her breakfast, so we got time to do our sleuthing."

"Ain't gonna work. You forget this is Mr. McMulty's home and his fingerprints are going to be ever'where?" For a second, Dennis looked crushed, but then Rass said, "We can just play at fingerprint taking."

All that was settled before short, fat Uncle Jake had time to hop nimbly out the other side of the car, looking perfect in his striped shirt and panama hat. He stood now right in the middle of the pink tones of sunrise. Aunt Kate stayed put. But her big, lovable smile still lit up the morning. Dad motioned them in to breakfast.

Aunt Kate handed Rass a very large goose egg. "That ain't for you, Rass. That big egg's a surprise for Sally, my proof thur's still dinosaurs."

The girls were all tumbling out the door, followed by Mom. Sally gasped, grabbed the egg from Rass, and held it with great care. Aunt Kate warned, "Now don't you think to go hatching it, girl. You're lucky it's still whole. At the church supper I was hoping to see youns at, I turned my back and Tut's two oldest started playing catch with it."

Mom moved close to the car window to talk with Aunt Kate. Dad and Uncle Jake discussed fields. Rass stayed near to see why they'd really come so early. It wasn't to humor Dennis, nor to share a big egg with Sally.

"Well, how're youns doing, Helen? Whit?" Aunt Kate went on, "Settled in yet? I'm glad the sheriff's not suspecting you folks of hiding out McMulty like lots of folks do, having heard Miss Esther."

"Miss Esther Love makes news when there ain't none," Mom said. She gave a toss of her hand to dismiss the idea.

Jake said, "Nert come right in the middle of our eating church supper to ask if'n anyone'd missed food from smokehouses, or any chickens or pigs. Then he announced he'd upped his reward to five hundred dollars!"

Dad whistled. Mom gasped. Unheard-of money! Five

hundred dollars could buy a new Model A Ford or maybe a new Ford V8. Could even pay for a small house!

Dad swelled with anger. "Ridiculous! Don't Nert know if'n anyone saw the old man, they'd already a-turned him in, five hundred dollars or no? They'd have to, to preserve thur own self and family. A man what done what our old neighbor done has to stand up to the consequences. He's stepped outa line. No one'd risk hiding him."

Rass inspected the fingerprint powder, his heart pounding.

Aunt Kate said, "I told Nert, if'n I knowed I'd keep shut about it. He oughta use his money building up his herd. Girls, I brung y'—" The little girls swarmed the car. Uncle Jake grabbed Chrissy, tickled her, swung her around a few times till her ringlets shook, and then set her down to wobble off. "Nert's getting paid back for mistreating ever' colored man that's ever worked for 'im," he said. "Tickles me he's getting paid back, but Whit, some tough men are of another mind."

"Who?" Rass asked. "There ain't no Klan around here."

"Oh, day laborers, who've got no one else to hate, and uppity small farmers who're trying to feel more uppity. Who else?" said Uncle Jake. "But it's possible they'd take the law in thur own hands."

"They couldn't," Rass blurted out. "They're not like the Klan."

Dad shushed him. Aunt Kate immediately handed a sucker to baby Marylu and big jawbreakers to Chrissy and Rosalee. She paused to tease Rass and L.G. by inviting them to smell the bag. Rass didn't like this change of subject, no matter how nice. L.G. declared they were too old for candy treats. "That's only for Christmas or cotton picking season."

Aunt Kate gave them each a jawbreaker anyway. "To even it, this big one's for my favorite son, what won't get it till he's inside this car. Dennis!" All the kids but Rass chased after the car, hands waving, cheeks bulging; Chrissy was many feet behind, drooling colorful spittle like mad. Rass ran in the other direction, toward the barn.

Suddenly Dad and L.G. were behind him, snagging him.

"Where you running so fast, boy?" Dad asked.

"Rass, you gotta tell us."

"Just to the barn. I gotta go, bad."

L.G.'s eyes questioned.

Dad said, "Then use the outhouse. The door's wide open." Dad stopped. He grabbed Rass. "Where's he hiding out? I've always taught you to tell me truth!"

Rass's mouth refused to open. He'd die and never be loved by Dad, but he couldn't turn in Mr. McMulty.

Dad looked disgusted. "Go on! *Git!* Me and L.G.'ll search the barn. I thought no man in his right mind would harbor Mr. McMulty, but then I forgot how you're always with ideas of your own. Smarting off. The reward upped to five hundred dollars, Miss Esther'll talk this place into a swarming beehive. I'll haul 'im out myself!" *Swat!* Dad slapped Rass hard across the shoulders.

Rass ran for the outhouse, hidden by weeds and small poplar trees near the barn.

Though its door was wide open, behind that door on the outside stood Mr. McMulty! As Rass cautiously closed the door he made his body conceal the short man, who instantly moved a couple of feet in among tall burdock plants. Mr. McMulty didn't look so sick this morning. Once inside the toilet, Rass whispered through the cracks, "I oughta moved you last night. Glad to see you up walking."

"Barely, son, but my fever gone down. Couldn't a-gone nowhere last night. Lord sets the time to all things."

"Dad and L.G.'s searching. They'll leave no space unturned."

"I hears all," Mr. McMulty whispered back. "The egg and candy gone keep yo' family busy. I make it under crib fine." Not thinking that Mr. McMulty couldn't see him, Rass quickly nodded, pulled his galluses over his shoulders, and ran to Dad and L.G.

Dad filled the air with "What's that cotton sack doing in the corn pile?" He grabbed the sack and threw it into an empty corner. "If I find out you're aiding a man what's wanted by our landlord, I'll thrash you till you're half your size! You know what you'd be a-branging on this family?" Dad ranted on, but the barn was empty. L.G. pulled his cap bill to one side, sidled over to Rass, and whispered, "I'm glad we never found nothing."

Rass set his mind on fate's help. What if Jake's family wasn't loud talkers, or hadn't stayed outside while Mr. McMulty sneaked out of the barn? And what if he and Bill hadn't operated on that injury? Of all the good things he'd done in his whole life—milking Ole Jersey, hoeing and picking cotton, plowing, hunting hens' nests, playing with sisters when Mom needed, or mudding waters to catch catfish with Clever—doing surgery so Mr. McMulty could walk from the barn was the best.

As Mom fixed breakfast, she declared, "Rass wouldn't know how to hide out a person, even if he was tempted."

Dad, calmer, reasoned as how she was right.

Rass just sat behind the cookstove, that favorite spot in Mr. McMulty's kitchen, noisily sucking a big old jaw-breaker, thinking. Something needed to be fair and he needed to deal with someone his own size. Finally he suggested, "Mom, scramble the goose egg so everyone can share a taste."

As expected, Sally threw a fit. Mom said, "Kids, come eat, so's to be off to school."

Rass sat down beside Sally and punched her in the ribs for not sharing. "Sally, that's as selfish as not letting anyone look at that *Primitive Art* book you hauled back from Mr. Preston last night. You gonna share that gallon of molasses he give you, too, or eat it all yourself?" Someday, once Mr. McMulty was safe gone, he'd pick cotton long and hard and earn money enough to buy a hundred books, ten gallons of molasses, and geese enough to keep all his kin in huge eggs forever.

Mom seated herself and said grace, ending with, "We accept the lot thou has dealt us as a test of our faithfulness, Lord. And please, Lord, settle my nerves by helping my children settle their quarrel!"

Sally said, "I'm not quarreling. My things are mine." She jabbed Rass hard in the ribs with her elbow as she whipped together molasses and lard to smear on her breakfast biscuits. Around and around her fork went, making a golden copper mass that grew to an unbelievably high plateful. Heaping it on her biscuits, she gobbled them down as if there'd never be another opportunity. Before the flood, Sally had shared. Rass waited for her to fill up so he could get the rest for Mr. McMulty. After the fourth biscuit Sally attempted to leave.

But Dad ordered, "Clean your plate!"

A goodly amount of gagging followed until finally Sally won out and Dad said she didn't have to eat any more of her splendid creation. Sally moved toward the slop can, plate in hand, but Rass grabbed it to forestall the dumping. "Never, never waste good food!" he said to her in his best Sally voice. "Next time don't let your eyes be bigger than your stomach! Sally, you've got Mom's nerves raw to bleeding. She cain't hold up under this much longer."

"You mean your nerves," said Sally, but let him take her plate.

"Thanks, Rass," Mom said. "All my kids is so wasteful. Youns all got to realize there's little left around here to fill bellies. And Whit, making Tut's bunch welcome three or four times a week's too much. I put up with it before the flood, but our circumstances has changed."

"Tut's my family," said Dad firmly.

"Well, family ought to know better! Tut's excuse next'll be they've come to check on us, 'cause of all the searching of our place. Look what it saves him in food bills! Look what it's costing us! Least Jake and Kate ate before they come. We cain't afford company of no kind, let alone on a regular eating basis. We had to buy more at the store on credit than we can possibly pay off come fall."

Mr. McMulty was an extra mouth, but Tut's gang was ten extra mouths. Rass put back one biscuit from his pocket. On the other hand, giving Sally's leftovers to Mr. McMulty wouldn't make his family starve.

"Helen, company dinner's a gift given and taken without thought of being beholden in any way," Dad said. "My kin's my kin and they'll always stick by me. Jake's used up some of my morning and is spoiling kids with candy, but he come to warn me. I won't turn Tut out, neither. I always pay my bills. We may go naked, but I always pay my bills."

"I wouldn't bank on it," Mom said, and then to Sally, "Get the dishes washed!" Rass figured he'd be next, and was. Mom bellowed, "Rass, soon's you're done eating Sally's leftovers, haul in the wood. Right after school, split up the rest and rank it neatly inside the back porch. I'm taking no chances running outa dry wood if it comes another rain."

Dad did say as he went out the door, "L.G., if'n it don't rain again today, more fields'll be dry enough to work. If it does, we'll pull stumps. It burns me to say it, but all of y' git to school!"

Mom questioned where Rass was going with Sally's leftovers. "Why, I'm sharing 'em with Ole Coalie." He smiled just to prove he wasn't lying, but he was lying awful. He squelched that by reasoning that he *had* to feed Mr. McMulty, for strength to help him leave.

"Well, then feed Coalie. Maybe it'll cut out his whining."

Rass obeyed, but once Mom was out of sight, he retrieved the plate of food and ran to Mr. McMulty, who truly enjoyed the rest of Sally's concoction.

School went fine, too, though Mr. Aaral allowed talk of the search for Mr. McMulty, and everybody whispered it around all day. Talk of five hundred dollars sure kept kids' minds off studies! There came a light rain during class time, but none during recess or lunch.

Later, swinging the ax, Rass watched bright yellow wood chips form a golden layer over the old bleached-gray ones. It was like new hope piling up. He shared that in his mind with Mr. McMulty, the man on whom the reward stood high at five hundred dollars.

# 14

THE GIRLS watched and adored Rass's power as he split, then chopped, huge blocks of wood. He hoped Mr. McMulty heard all their happy talk. Luck remained with Rass. Mom came outside singing, "A Log in a Hole in the Bottom of the Sea," then announced, "I made us a fine ginger cake using Sally's big goose egg."

Sally screeched, but Mom went happily on. "I used your sorghum molasses, added lard, a little flour, baking powder, and plenty of ginger, and got your favorite cake! Come see."

Rass whooped and laid down his ax. And happy talk had its way. Sally swept up Marylu; the other girls joined hands. Mom, smiling, led the way. "It seems so long since we had us a cake. Oughta be near done by now. It's a celebration for Rass's kind deed."

Mom probably referred to his cutting wood. Whatever, the girls congratulated him with a few slaps, and Mom whispered, "You know, this celebration is really for Maggie making Whit and Nert let you kids go to school. Maggie told me she remembered how much school meant to you. I'm proud, son." Nearing the house, she said to all, "Youns can look and smell, but not one bite of cake till your daddy and L.G. get back in from stump pulling. Won't be long. They'll come in good and hungry."

Then came the distant bark of dogs. Rass froze. Bloodhounds! The making of his nightmares. But then he looked. "It's just Uncle Tut's hounds!" Life was always fun and feasting and fighting when Tut's bunch came. This time he would show the boys who was boss. They'd not be allowed in the barn at all.

Mom looked to the heavens and said, "Lord, we could do with less of Tut and Crystal. Rass, be sure it's them?" The wagon, a piece away, held several people fitting the sizes and shapes of Uncle Tut's bunch.

"It's them all right," Rass said, and the little girls went dashing about, here and there, like fireflies. Sally kept pointing at the distant wagon, screaming, "Thelma's a-coming. I get to tell Uncle Tut's bunch we're having cake!" She was cockily preening back and forth when Mom snagged her and pushed the lot of her kids toward the house.

Inside, the good smells of baking left everyone obedient to Mom.

She peeked into the oven then, grabbing stove rag from apron string, she pulled the cake out. They stared at it, inhaled the aroma. Finally Mom looked at each of them and said, "Now you all understand I ain't a begrudging woman. I enjoy company, the right kind, and I ain't selfish. I've thought to ask Kate over for a ginger cake thank-you for all the help she's given, especially for the spices when mine got ruint. But I won't have my nice cake eaten by Tut and his sponging lot!"

"Mom...," Rass began.

"No! They ain't eating us out of house and home this time! I know what it is to be down-and-out and I know the Good Book says be compassionate, but there comes a time when enough's enough." She picked up a butcher knife and hacked away with mighty strokes at that freshly baked sorghum cake spiced heavy with ginger. The girls danced and spun like tops.

"See, the wildness has started already! Now settle down. My kids will act like humans, not animals! Here, all of you! Eat a big piece!"

"Make mine real big," Rass said. "I've worked hard chopping wood."

Mom dished and served, and bemoaned the fact that Dad and L.G. hadn't come in yet. Rass's piece was big enough to save plenty for Mr. McMulty. As he dashed out the door, Mom set into the remainder herself.

He told Mr. McMulty of Mom's doings and how she'd reached the last straw, just as Sally had reached the last straw with little sisters fingering her book. Then he added, "Just as you reached the last straw with Nert doing you in, treating you with no respect."

Between mouthfuls of that delicious cake, Mr. Mc-Multy replied, "I knows, son. There comes a time in all people's lives when they got to stand up for thurselves! I ain't regretting that. I jest needs to find a better way o' doing it. I will, if'n the Lord let me live long enough."

Rass raced back inside. He hadn't even been missed. The cake was mostly gone, and Mom was still talking. "Now, I must get grease in the frying pan hot so's I can fry sliced mush left over from breakfast." She had the grease hot by the time Uncle Tut and his lot appeared.

They were adorned in brand new store-bought clothes, hair matted, at least what could be seen of it. The three oldest boys had new straw hats jammed down on their heads, leaving only noses visible to tell who was which. Uncle Tut got down, helped his wife and daughter down. "We cain't stay too long. Just come to jaw with Whit 'bout Miss Esther's talk."

"Whit and L.G.'s pulling stumps," Mom said. "Thur a-trying to manage and make every minute count."

"When's he getting back?"

"Since when has a husband told his wife how long he'll be gone?" Mom answered with a shrug.

Uncle Tut pushed his family toward the house. "Helen, don't go fixing nothing fancy for us."

Crystal said proudly, "I been managing real good." She was a fat woman in a large orange-flowered dress, hair blond-streaked and cut off straight, even with the middle of her ears. She sat down heavily on a cane-bottomed chair, pushed Thelma forward for her new dress to be admired.

"Our food bill at the store was so skimpy this month, we bought clothes, and Lord knows these kids has growed and needed 'em. Why, I caught Raymond swiping his daddy's long-handled underwear last winter, and they weren't sticking all that much down over his shoe tops. I wouldn't a-noticed if'n his overalls hadn't been at high water."

Raymond was the oldest, named for the store owner, a church member, who in response excused Tut's debt. "What's that good smell?"

"We're having fried mush, that's all," Rass said, and shot a look for Mom's approval. Mom in turn shot a look toward the kids and said to them, "Eat sparing. Our food stock's a-waning fast."

Aunt Crystal said, "Feed your family beans. Beans blows up their bellies and give 'em a sense of fullness. Hardworking never-winning men like Tut and Whit needs beans at the end of a long day."

Rass spoke to Tut's kids to stay off Mom. "If youns is set on staying long after eating, your games better be guessing games, for you're not going no further than the back porch in your fancy clothes."

Crystal bristled. The kids declared staying put was boring.

"I was hoping nobody had something to hide," said Uncle Tut.

"Nobody's hiding nothing, no matter Miss Esther's talk. Search the barn inside and out if you've got a mind to," Mom said as she set about washing the blackened bread pan she'd used to bake the cake.

Tut, trying to soothe his wife, said, "Didn't come to search, but I do refuse to let my kids settle in and eat fried mush while the spicy smell of cake's a-hanging in the air. You kids get back in the wagon." It was as close to showing hurt feelings as Uncle Tut ever got.

His kids crammed in mush, in spite of orders.

Raymond said, "We cain't leave till Uncle Whit gets home, so's you can talk to 'im."

Uncle Tut nodded to that and said, "He's my brother. We'll wait...outside, the rains come or no. New clothes or no, Rass." An adult had spoken. There was no way Rass's words would stop the boys.

Uncle Tut and Aunt Crystal sat on the stoop, fingering through *Primitive Art*, while their kids ran wild in the yard. Sally, playing with Thelma, forgot the art book she had been studying every spare moment.

Rass tried to pick a fight with Raymond, who headed for the barn. "There'll be no more jumping off the roof to see who can jump furthest. Someone's sure to get their neck broke. And none of you boys is to throw Mom's fruit jars in the mule's stall just to hear the bang. Mom says so. No going near the barn! I'll pin the first who tries."

Raymond pushed Rass, grabbed a jar, and took off running. His brothers followed.

Rass called as he ran, too. "You boys stay outa the barn. Stop! The boogeyman's in there!" The two youngest stopped. Raymond led the others at fast speed. They climbed the ladder easy as spiders.

Uncle Tut laughed and whooped.

Things weren't boring to the kids any longer. Loud talk. The hounds, barking, nipping, swarming around, paused at the spot where Mr. McMulty lay hidden and barked as if they'd treed an animal. No telling what would have happened if right then there hadn't been the roar of the Revelsens' truck, and not two but four sheriff's deputies swarmed the place. It was Rooster, Big Red, and that man who'd come with Big Red before, plus another man Rass didn't know.

*Crash! Bang! Crash!* The sound of breaking glass cut

all talk as Raymond tossed a fruit jar from the barn loft. His laughter was as loud as Uncle Tut's, who never put much value on his or others' belongings.

Then, suddenly, without a pause Uncle Tut ran toward the barn entrance, screaming, "I want you kids all out here! Watch your step! A one of you get a cut foot and I'll blister all your butts. Breaking up Helen's jars when she's told you not to! It's drizzling already, but Rass, you ought to get this glass picked up good, a'fore someone gets thur feet cut to shreds! You deputies better stand back, you cain't trust my boys to mind on first order. If they throw another jar, you'll likely get your heads split open."

The men pulled back and stood there admiring and muttering how Uncle Tut was a forceful, fine father. Uncle Tut soaked in the praise, and as his boys passed him, he swatted their bottoms and said, "Didn't I tell you a million times if'n you don't mind, the law'd be onto you?"

Rass rushed to stand guard by the barn entrance, but there was no need—Uncle Tut had all the deputies jawing. "Well, you men gonna lock my boys up or not?" he demanded.

Rooster drug out his handcuffs to go along with the game, but Big Red drawled, "Maybe not this time, but I give these boys one last warning—obey your pappy, or youns'll be setting behind bars!"

Rass was pleased to see Raymond especially cowering low and clinging to Uncle Tut's jacket.

"Rass, that goes double for you," Big Red said. "Get that glass picked up by tomarr. Soon's daylight hits, we'll come a-checking. Guess we'll hold off a search. If Mc-

Multy come back here, these boys woulda found him."
The deputies turned back to their truck, joking, laughing.

Uncle Tut in a friendly way leaned on the truck window and said, "Thanks for learning my boys. If'n I can be any hep in turn, say so."

"Sorry about busting in like this," the driver said. "Red saw the Whitley girl toting in a gallon of molasses for someone. That's all."

Sally cried out, "Mr. Preston give it to me, 'cause his wife won't eat that old-fashioned stuff, but his wife don't know what a good cake Mom can make of it!" She clamped her hand over her mouth. The little girls mimicked her, even cousin Thelma.

"Ever'body's wrong once in thur lives," Uncle Tut said to the deputies, following his words with a good chuckle. "I can testify to you that Helen used them mo-lasses for baking cake. Just sniff the smell a-hanging. Rest easy about Whit, too. Though he lets his girl tote in some big book that'll put learning in her head, Whit's as good a father as me. He sure ain't hiding out no one on the run. Nope! Since he was a little bitty boy, he ain't been that dumb." He waved the men on, went back to the stoop, and looked again at the art book with his wife. The kids on the small porch out of the drizzle went back to screaming and fighting. Rass raked up glass, and tried to figure out whether Uncle Tut knew Mr. McMulty was in the barn or not. The trouble was, if he did know, he wouldn't let his shirttail hit him until he spread the news. Uncle Tut couldn't hold information like ordinary folk.

Dad and L.G. came home after a bit. Uncle Tut walked

out to meet and greet. "Whit, you have someone hiding in your barn, like I heard on the wind? I'm the last person what gets told if'n you're in trouble."

"Heck, no, we don't," said L.G. "Just come on and take a look yourself." Rass was stunned. To keep luck from running out completely, he thought to join in, bluffing.

"Go ahead," he said.

Instead Uncle Tut hee-hawed, called his barking dogs, and began forcing kids into the wagon to stay out of trouble. "We gotta go. We've plumb waited out the drizzle on this porch."

Dad looked aggravated, but remembered his manners. "Come on in the house. Have a bite to eat."

"No, we cain't do that, Whit! I guess Helen's had some cause to be antsy and nervous about her jars. We don't take no offense. We'll be as good a kin to you as always. I'll see Crystal don't go acting hateful in any ways towards Helen. Crystal's ever' bit as forgiving in her heart as me—ain't you, hon? We'd best be a-going." He didn't say a word about the cake. Just acted like it was about broken jars. Rass was amazed.

"Now, looka here! Helen's my wife. She's not to be faulted on all things!" Dad said, and Mom, standing in the doorway, gasped at the compliment. "L.G., get the mules in their stall."

"I'll go feed the mules and let L.G. eat," Rass said quickly. As Uncle Tut's gang loaded into the wagon, Rass felt free to do that chore. Time was running out.

Mr. McMulty had heard all and said, "Could be Tut was doing what come natural, playacting to ward off deputies. Could be the Lord done use Tut as a vehicle to save me and yo' family, him being a family member and a preacher." He chuckled. "Tut may not be so good at what he do, preaching or farming, but the messes he make doing it be mighty impressive."

"That's right. Now you think you can walk about tonight, long enough to escape? You oughten hide under the crib and you so sick." They paused and listened to Uncle Tut's gang noisily taking leave. When the baying of Tut's hounds got lost on the wind, they again discussed plans of escape, each showing the other how their plan couldn't work, until Rass suggested moving him to Dumas's dredge boat after dark, that very night.

"Rass, you best go in now. Luck do run out, talk is about, time moving swift, and I needs be moving, too. Oh, Lord, I do. But I needs a bit o' rest first. Yes, son, we got to act tonight, though I hoped to see Preacher Bloodworth first."

Rass nodded. Luck was gone. Sally overheard so many things at school, and it'd not be long until someone smart as she got wise. To stall such, when he got inside, he said to her, "You're ignorant of life."

She was driving small nails into the wall. "Not ignorant. I'm an artist, hanging a picture so I can go to sleep looking at it." Such a little girl, thinking only of a beautiful picture. Really ignorant of life, all right. But he let Sally enjoy her moment. She and the rest of the family were within the shadow of the gallows.

# 15

R ASS DIDN'T accidentally fall asleep this time. Waiting bravely till sleep claimed his family, he slipped quietly down the ladder to go get Bill. At first, hunkering low, Rass went slowly out into the muggy night, across the yard, into the field. Then, in spite of the heavy air, the thin moon, and hardly any visible stars, with a leap like a wild rabbit he sped across pasture to that place where the ditch waters were again getting shallow. He felt his way in the familiar path, up and over the ditch bank. In the process of crossing the ditch, his boots filled with water, but he didn't care. He just kept on moving, his mind only on how he could he wake Bill without waking the rest of the Browns.

Tossing a wood chip through Bill's open window automatically made the curtains open and Bill's head pop out. Rass motioned with his hand and mouthed, "Come." Curtains fell back. Seconds later, there was Bill, fully dressed, climbing outside.

There was hardly enough starlight to see each other as

they journeyed back to the barn by regular roads. For the oddly comforting sound of his own voice, Rass talked about how both Uncle Jake and Uncle Tut had come a-warning, and even how he had lied to Mom. "That's something what lays heavy on my mind, but I won't have to do it again, once you and me get Mr. McMulty to Clever's dad's dredge boat. He'll be safe there. I figure we can put him on a cotton sack and tote him across pasture and leave no trail. I'll walk you back by the road."

Of course Bill didn't hear, but it didn't matter. The night deepened, pouring in its welcome dark cover, as the two successfully carried out the plan. Bill grasped the regular shoulder strap of the cotton sack and Rass knotted the other end and tied it fast to his overalls. Mr. McMulty climbed into the middle of this hammock and clung tightly all the way to the dredge boat. A few stubbed toes in the darkness, near spills, sounds from wild scurries of animals, but not a flaw! No other human knew the happenings of the night.

The dredge was a big flat box housing a motor. A cabin on top held the driver's seat and gears for controlling a crane. Mr. McMulty squeezed in back of the seat.

"See if you can get Mr. Dumas to take this dredge boat all the way to the Mississippi then downriver, out of the state!" Rass said to him.

Mr. McMulty sighed. "This boat be owned by the state o' Missouri. It cain't leave these ole ditches." Rass groaned. No sense dreaming.

But Mr. McMulty assured him, "I gonna make it, son.

I in God's care, I see that clear on this dark night. Move went fine."

"I'll see you first thing, on the way to school," Rass said, then Mr. McMulty said good-bye to Bill. "You fine, brave boys. Lord smiling when He look on youns tonight." He gave Bill's hand a quick squeeze, and Rass's too.

At Bill's window Rass whispered, "Thanks. But you cain't go back to the dredge or it'll raise questions. Okay?"

Bill grunted.

On his way home a sharp, cool wind stole Rass's breath away. It spun him around and around in the darkness, making the world dizzy, tickling him like bubbles of soda pop hitting his nose. Mr. McMulty in the good care of black friends! The threat of punishment lifted from his family! Mr. Dumas would get help from Preacher Bloodworth! On this dark, dark night the sigh of wind past Rass's ears made it feel like the opening of morning glories to a bright day. Happily he sped home, trooped through the living room, past his parents' bed, aiming for the ladder.

Dad woke. Then demanded, in the darkness, "Rass, you hiding out McMulty?"

"Course he's not," said Mom, awake now, too. Her shoulders drooped like a wounded bird.

"I had to make a late trip to the outhouse. I got troubles."

Mom said, "I seen you dancing about this morning. I better give you some herb tea." Tea would taste dreadful, make Rass puke, but he agreed. What with L.G. always saying he talked too much, wouldn't it be nice if L.G.

could witness just how tight he kept his mouth shut now? Being quiet paid off best at times. He knew.

"I'm sleepy," he said, and climbed to the loft.

WHEN HE AWOKE Mom was talking full steam at the breakfast table, demanding they move to another state. "My people was a moving people, staying at a place when they prospered, and when times got bad they moved on. Ain't right to live in another's house, Whit!"

Moving seemed a perfect idea. Rass thought quickly. He'd build a box underneath the wagon, stop by the dredge, pick up Mr. McMulty, and take him off to Arkansas, with no one the wiser.

"We ain't moving nowhere," Dad said. "I ain't the moving kind. A man don't question nothing when his own needs a roof over thur heads! Woman, I've had it!" Furiously, Dad grabbed some biscuits and left.

Soon Rass was letting the wind at his back rush him to school, hearing its whisper that Mom knew he was hiding out Mr. McMulty. She always told the merits of her ancestors when she needed courage.

At school amid the talk of calf killing, which led to talk of the Klan and colored people, Rass made no comments. When the colored vote was brought up, he asked Mr. Aaral why neither Mr. McMulty nor the Dumases ever voted. Mr. Aaral said, "If you grew up on stories of how your grandpappy was lynched for voting, would you?"

Did talk like this go on at the colored school? Rass wondered about Clever's ancestors. Did colored folks fight for a man just because he was colored?

Late in the day, when Rass and L.G. trudged home from plowing and Dad brought the girls in from after-school brush clearing, Mom said, "I give Big Red and Rooster Revelsen what for, coming again searching my house, as well as the barn!" All were too tired to comfort her.

After supper she sat in her rocker and told more ancestor stories. L.G. climbed the ladder for bed, saying he'd gotten in late all this week, what with having to fix another truck for a neighbor. But Rass respectfully sat at her feet by his sisters, listening to stories he'd heard time and again.

The girls fell asleep, but were awakened by Dad blasting out, "Helen, stop stewing so! I searched this place good. If'n we expect to amount to a hill o' beans and keep our kids alive, we gotta stay put and work hard, not run away. Ancestors don't matter! It's how we get along in our community and with our boss what matters." He sent the girls scurrying off to their room. "And take the baby with you!"

"Rass, come sleep on the floor by me," begged Chrissy, tears streaming.

Rass unlatched her hands from his gallus. "Dad just yells when he's worried," he said, and sent Ole Coalie in with her. He'd never get married or have kids. He'd stay single, do as he pleased, and amount to something all on his own.

As he climbed the ladder he heard Dad soothingly apologize to Mom, "I know buttering up the facts gives you peace, Helen, but..."

"Ouch!" Rass stubbed his toe, missed a rung, regained his balance. Then, just as his head rose to ceiling level, he glimpsed a light outside. His hands let go; he dropped to the floor. Such was forbidden once bedtime was called— no exceptions. He raced to the door.

"A cross is burning over at the Dumases'!" he whispered loudly to his parents. The Klan must have found Mr. McMulty in the dredge!

# 16

DAD AND MOM were there at once, beside him.

"Let's go," said Rass, putting on his denim jumper, the short coat, a breaker against the night air. The wind had risen. Dad held him back.

"Sh-h-h-h!" said Mom. "You got the dog awake already."

"Let me be!" whispered Rass. "I ain't going to let them torture the Dumases. Clever's my friend!" He'd heard talk about the Ku Klux Klan's tortures at the pool hall and in Mr. Aaral's explainings at school. "Turn loose of me. I got to go!"

"Nope! It ain't like that, son. You don't understand the Klan. Crosses are burned as *warnings*." Dad's voice held a resigned tone. "Get on up to bed. I seen too much of this when I was a boy. The Klan's just trying to get Dumas to talk, thinking he knows whur McMulty's hid. Dumases are okay, but they're foolish hiding out a criminal."

"Sh-h-h-h, Whit, you'll wake the little'uns. Rass, get to bed."

Rass moved again to leave for the Dumas house, but Dad blocked the doorway. "I ain't giving you no choice in this matter, boy. And I'm bigger and stronger than you. Mind you think on that."

Reluctantly, Rass went up to the loft. But as the night wore on and he lay there fully clothed and wide awake, next to sleeping L.G., he thought perhaps it was just a warning as Dad said. Maybe they hadn't found Mr. McMulty and weren't hanging the Dumases along with him. But what of the tales of the Klan's torturing and then parading the tortured person for the town to behold? He'd overheard it time and again at the pool hall. Thoughts of those tales hit his mind and exploded. "I ain't letting them do that to my friends, a warning or no!" he whispered to the dark.

He slipped down the ladder, stealthily. Maybe Bill had gone back to the dredge today and had been spotted by the Klan. Maybe Mr. McMulty had escaped. *He had to know.* It had been his idea to move Mr. McMulty to the dredge. He'd be responsible if anything happened to him or the Dumases. As he got to the bottom of the ladder Ole Coalie eased in alongside him. "Good dog," Rass whispered, patting him as they moved out the door.

Dad sprang out after Rass, yanked him to a stop.

"I oughta whup you for disobeying," he said furiously. "Don't go interfering! The Klan rides interferers out of town astraddle a rail, joggling 'em in such a way they pass out from the pain! I know people it's happened to, and them people thought they could hep. Don't pay to go butting around in the name of friendship and rile the Klan's suspicions!"

Mom sat up in bed. "Rass, obey your father. You're not going. I forbid it!"

She was up and following. She had called so loudly she woke the girls. L.G. could sleep through anything, but the girls spilled from their beds and ran to join Rass witnessing the glaring cross-shaped flame. It made the whole night sky seem lighter. A new moon was rising. Chrissy was saying, "Ah-h-h," as if enjoying something very pretty. But Rass told her, "No! It's bad. Smell the wood! Hear the cry of the scared animals? Those are bad sounds and smells of the Klan!"

For a long time Chrissy hugged Ole Coalie in silence. Finally she begged to go inside. Sally and Rosalee each grabbed a hand and took her in.

Shortly Dad made Rass go in, too. The girls hadn't gone to bed, but cowered in the middle of the room, holding each other, crying. Mom and Dad came in. Mom lit the lamp and said, "See what you've caused, Rass, wanting to go?"

"I still want to spend the night with Clever," he whispered.

"You cain't," Mom said. "Clever's your friend, I know, but it just cain't be done, Rass."

"I think you oughtn't to go near the Klan. They could kill you," sobbing Sally said with authority.

"We'd not be the Whitleys without you, Rass," said Rosalee.

"Come on, you can sleep in our bedroom right 'side

Ole Coalie," Chrissy said, and gripped Rass's hand tight. "Snowball's sleeping with me." He let her lead him a little way toward their room, then he jerked loose and turned sharply at the ladder to go up it again. At his jerk Chrissy and the other girls suddenly ran back to Dad.

Mom moved the lamp to a safer spot and Dad immediately assured his daughters there was nothing to worry about. Rass hung onto his perch to watch and listen. Soon Dad chuckled, the signal that a story was about to come. He placed the lamp in the center of that great oak library table, left by Mom's ancestors, seated himself in the woven willow chair, a gift from his own ancestors, and twisted around just a bit so as to pull Chrissy onto his knee. With a twinkle in his eye, he began, "Did I ever tell you that I had a dog once what crowed? Yep, other people needed a rooster, but not us...."

As Rass hung there he understood why his dad, his Uncle Tut, and all the men around were such good storytellers. Storytelling spared them from dark truths they could not change, made truth wait for the morning air. Rass felt the chill of it already. He left the ladder, huddled in close with the little girls, and when they were all finally sent again to their room, he allowed Chrissy to lead him there, too.

For Chrissy's sake, he propped a straight-back chair under the door handle to make the room safe from intruders. Then he settled down on a pallet, as her guard, in that little square of moonlight right beneath the window.

But he did not sleep. As night wore on and all the sounds cleared the way for him, he loosened the screen.

His toe hung on the torn blanket binding, causing him to stumble in his haste, but finally he was outside and on his way, the girls none the wiser.

Fast he raced across the pasture to the ditch and was over its bank and down away to the dredge boat. He heard *moaning*. Then in the light of the new moon, he saw Mr. Dumas, tarred and feathered. The work of the Klan. A pillowcase of feathers emptied on top of sweeps of hot tar. There sat Clever, his head bowed, his hands slowly moving, his cry a keening above his father's anguish, the most hopeless sound Rass had ever heard. This was the sight Dad had wanted to spare him. Clever trying to peel tar off his indecently stripped father.

Rass's thinking being more acute than his friend's, he said, "Get him into the water, Clever! Gotta get tar in water so's it'll peel. In and out fast. If'n it hardens too much, it'll take the skin right off with it." Together they got Mr. Dumas into the water.

"Enough! Don't let it get too hard. Quick, let's lift him out." Clever helped do that. Rass began peeling. Clever couldn't stop crying, but he peeled, too.

Clever croaked, "I cain't stop all my thoughts no more, Rass."

"I know. I know," Rass whispered back.

Then came a voice from close by in the water, "Boys, I believe I be able to help, too."

In time they heard the story. "Dumas finds me in his dredge," Mr. McMulty said. "Comes back late tonight to feed me. We hears horses and the talk-noise of two men. Dumas lower me into the water. When they ask, he won't tell where I be, so's they does this to 'im!" Mr. McMulty's voice rose in anguish. "It be all my fault. Cain't have others pay my price! I turns myself in."

"No. That ain't right," said Rass. Clever agreed, and even amid his groans Mr. Dumas agreed, too.

So, on the same cotton sack used earlier to transport and to cover Mr. McMulty, Rass and Clever took Mr. Dumas home to his wife's care. When she opened the door the light in her hand accented her dark brown face, deeply modeled in shadows. The face changed by a silent scream as long narrow fingers reached out to touch and measure the burns on her husband's body. "I shoulda made him stay inside! I shoulda gone with him!" she cried.

Embers at the core of the charred, fallen cross in the front yard shone red.

Clever motioned Rass to leave his dad in his mom's care. So the two of them returned to the dredge and transported Mr. McMulty back to the Whitleys' barn. It was best that Clever leave at once and not see the hiding place. Bill mustn't know, either.

First Rass redressed the wet wound, but for the sake of time and of raw fear, he shoved his friend back under in wet clothes. Two hours had passed. It was time for bed.

Dad didn't awake, but L.G. woke enough to whisper, "They wouldna searched our house today if you'd kept your mouth shut in the pool hall. And Big Red and Rooster wouldna volunteered to be deputies."

"I know," he said.

"Go to sleep," L.G. said, and obeyed his own command.

Rass didn't notice. He lay there at full attention, as if he were in the classroom feeling new meaning come into Mr. Aaral's words in school yesterday. "Crime always runs high where there's a class system. The Klan targets people who don't live, think, or look as they do. Not just Negroes, but Jews and Catholics. The Klan takes law into their own hands. Until everyone has a say in court, you children need to know the Klan'll be part of your lives. Any questions?"

Rass felt hot tar hit his own skin. He had plenty of questions.

# 17

THERE'D BEEN no hard rain by Friday, and Dad wanted them to get in two hours' work before school. Rass tended Mr. McMulty, then was harnessing the mules when he heard a noise and thought L.G. had returned for something, or maybe Dad was coming to bawl him out for being late. Then out from the poplar saplings stepped a stocky, bearded colored man, who said, "Rass Whitley? My name's Bloodworth." The preacher stuck out a hand.

Rass hesitated. This man was famous. All colored people followed his counsel. Surely he'd been called to help Mr. Dumas and had come to include Mr. McMulty. Rass shook his hand. The clasp was strong, friendly. Should he speak, or wait? He saw a twinkle in the man's eye and realized he had timed his arrival. "How nice you're using a mule. Never get yourself a tractor. You'd lose the fun of being so close to the soil. Hard work'd get done too fast."

"Yeah." Rass welcomed the lightness. "I sure couldn't stand that."

Preacher Bloodworth laughed heartily. "An old tractor

just rusts and needs parts, while a fine mule gets stronger the more you work it. It'd be a crime to even think about a tractor."

Rass waited. Serious talk would come creeping in sideways, making conversation unnecessarily long, but such was custom. The man's countenance changed. Small talk was over. "But I didn't come here to sell tractors or mules," he said.

"I know."

"Clever says to tell you things will be all right. Thanks to your quick thinking, his daddy be back to work. We honor you, Rass Whitley."

"I'm glad. I'm glad." Rass tried to express his relief and his pleasure at being appreciated, but words didn't quite do it.

"Miss Esther's words to colored folks checking on McMulty's whereabouts are, 'The place to look's the Whitleys'.' Everybody in the county's asking me 'bout that. I hear your daddy even got questions on parity checks. He wondering 'bout not following Nert's orders to plant on this land? Or Nert thinking he can collect a check on the flooded place instead?"

His tone was still light, cheerful. Feeling relaxed, Rass played back to him light and cheerful, dancing again round and about the real issues. "I'm just a boy. You'd best talk to a man. If I tell what you tell, then everybody in the county would hold an opinion on it." Rass went inside the barn and pointed. "You could tell it to the corn there."

"Why, sure I can. Ain't ever had the chance to convert any corn before. It won't take me long."

Rass left, because it was the proper thing to do. He fooled around with the harness until the drizzle stopped. He was almost ready to leave for the field when he saw Dad heading in. He ran to the barn entrance and said, "Dad's a-coming. Tell 'im you held me up talking about parity checks, please. Dad don't know about Mr. Mc-Multy."

Soon as Dad got there, Preacher Bloodworth introduced himself and after a moment informed him, "Nert can't declare your flooded land fallow instead of listed acres on his application, or he's subject to legal action."

Dad sounded off about that so loudly, Preacher Bloodworth began to instruct him on passive resistance. He quoted words of the Farmers Union and words of Gandhi. "Any harassment of landlord or even the law is best handled by these methods," he ended.

Dad didn't resist Preacher Bloodworth as he had city-bred and educated Mr. Aaral, Rass noticed. The minister was a man who'd once been a sharecropper, who knew the soil. Dad's voice took on a new, aggravated tone. "I'm much obliged to hear of this passive re-sistance and I'm obliged to leave Nert to the law.... Rain's holding off; my boy's got field work to do before school. Rass, get moving!"

Preacher Bloodworth took his leave along with Dad. Rass followed, wondering if this revered preacher had set in motion plans to remove Mr. McMulty. Mr. Dumas would carry scars for life, just because the Klan suspected him of harboring. If they caught Mr. McMulty here tonight, Dad could be lynched. Those weren't words thrown around in a history class, stretched out and repeated just to get Mr. Aaral going in order to delay an expected test. Preacher Bloodworth had spoken lightly, calmly, but his business was serious. Rass would do whatever the man suggested—as soon as Mr. McMulty had the opportunity to say what that was.

The sun was giving forth its full morning light when Dad set Rass to work the field next to L.G. They plowed along just rows apart, feeling a closeness in those expanded acres of plowed and waiting-to-be-plowed fields. At one point L.G. said, "I've never asked no questions, and I've let Mom believe the talk about how Mr. McMulty escaped to Arkansas. You gonna tell me if he's hid at Clever's or not?"

Rass's mind was on passive resistance. "He's not at Clever's."

As his plow broke down hard dirt into fertile particles, his mind broke down fear into manageable steps. He wasn't too surprised that L.G. knew Mr. McMulty was still around. Most people believed that. But why hadn't L.G. fought to know more?

"L.G., maybe Mr. McMulty hid on the railroad's right-of-way grounds alongside the tracks, escaped in a boxcar with the bums, and got lost among 'em?"

"He couldn't hop a freight with an injured leg. Trains are being searched. You're lying. Dumases *are* harboring him. Don't matter to me. I just want deputies to stop searching our place and worrying Mom and scaring the girls." L.G. sank his plow deep as it'd go, straining his muscles. Then, apparently feeling the power that brought, he continued, serious, "I'm real concerned about Mom."

"L.G., maybe you can do something about crazy Miss Esther's gossip," Rass said, hoping to put a challenge into L.G.

But school was just school that day. No challenges met.

When Rass got home, his mind remained on passive resistance while having his snack of cold biscuits, lard, and sugar. Passive meant not fighting. He watched Mom as she plopped a skillet into the stale dishwater. Grease floated on the swells. She looked worn-out.

"I'll scour this heavy old bean pot outside with some ashes," he offered, and removed it from the stack of dirty pans and canning jars yet to be done. She seemed pleased. Rass stopped at the reservoir, that metal container built into the stove for heating water. "I'll take some hot water to clean it proper." He got it and took off.

First he gave the bean leavings to Mr. McMulty, then scoured the pot with a little of the water, and used the rest to dress the wound. While he did that, the old man told him the passive plan that Preacher Bloodworth had offered.

Rass laughed with relief, then took off to do his plowing. High imagining wasn't always crazy! Clever and friends should dig a grave in the black people's cemetery and cover it over good, so as not to be noticed. Then it would be noticed, and folks would think Mr. McMulty had died and been secretly buried so as not to reveal the harborer. The war would be over! With no one searching, Mr. McMulty would have time to heal good. Then, disguised as a bum, he could hop a freight and head for Arkansas. Wait till he told Clever, who'd soon be doing after-school plowing, too.

Rass heard Bill's sounds, looked up, and saw him coming across the field to visit. He'd likely come daily now, being concerned for Mr. McMulty. Bill had a tender heart.

Hey, Bill was someone really good at shoveling. Bill helped his dad and brother shovel around stumps that needed to be pulled. But would he understand them digging a fake grave? He'd think Mr. McMulty was really dead, especially since he no longer was in the dredge boat. There were some things not easy to explain by acting them out.

Bill followed along as Rass plowed. Just to keep his thoughts moving, too, Rass said, "You see, I plan on us digging a grave so's ever'one thinks Mr. McMulty's dead, then they'll stop coming, searching. Just think on it. You might want to help, soon's it gets dark."

He said no more, wondering how he could possibly get Bill to understand. A good idea had to hit. The sun came out from behind the clouds—the threat of rain was gone. Rass never slowed in his work. Dad was too riled, trying to please Nert about his boys' short workday, to allow him a rest time, but when Clever took an end-row rest and came over to walk along, Rass told him all. Of course, he gave Preacher Bloodworth the rightful credit for the idea.

Clever was jubilant, which made Bill happy as well.

All the rest of the afternoon, though still on tenterhooks, eyes and ears always alert to cars and trucks, Rass felt light and eager, no longer powerless. He, Bill, and Clever had a grave to dig. Digging a grave was something boys could do.

Black clouds took over the sky till it looked like night.

With weather playing such games, Dad waved them in for supper early, and Bill left for home.

Sally greeted Rass and Dad at the door, embraced Dad, and cried out, "The sky got so dark that Mr. Preston give us girls a ride home from school. He's taking his bull to show at the New Madrid County Fair tomarr and he says I oughta take my picture of his plantation to the fair, too! Can I, Daddy? Can I, please?"

Dad's attitude even softened for a minute. He appreciated when his family was praised. "It's most uncommon for so rich a man to show interest in my kid," he said. "But you cain't go. I ain't agin having my daughter's painting being shown, but I got no time nor means to get you there, Sally. It's too long a trip with me thinking the transmission's going on the car."

"Oh, Daddy, please! L.G. can fix our car. I can take some of Billy Gene Huges's pictures, too, if that'd make it important enough."

Dad's voice rose. "Leave anybody else outa this. We're working the fields seven days a week from daylight till dark. Time's been lost to the flood, to food shopping, and to schooling, since your mother got in her word with Maggie! Even if I had money for gas, you ain't going. Don't aggravate me no more about it." He sat down to his meal.

Sally, crushed, went away to cry instead of eat. Mom was determined to finish some ironing before she sat down. She used both hands to lift a flatiron from the cookstove then, barely making it back to the blanket on the worktable, she let the iron down with a plop and said, "Folks keep aggravating me plenty, too, Whit, coming prowling around this place scaring the little girls. It's wearing me out having to chase them off. Least my boys has noticed my strain."

"That does it!" declared Dad. "I'm driving into town right now to tell Maggie Porter I've had about enough. It's making you act up something awful, Helen. Turning on my kin, even." Dad grabbed the lantern for a backyard light, and soon L.G. was cranking the Chevy, declaring he was going along with Dad. No mention or concern for the transmission.

Rass smiled to himself. Only Mom and the rain to get past now.

From the wood yard, he gathered up an armload of wood, careful to make familiar noises, then marched to the back porch and dumped it with a clatter. Next he picked two buckets off a shelf and noisily went back outside to the pump, letting the pump's sucking, squeaking noise work him up to his next playacting job. Buckets filled to overflowing, he sloshed his way back into the kitchen, across the worn linoleum to the stove, and filled the reservoir, saying, "The reservoir's full."

Mom was standing over the wash pan cupping water in her hands and lifting them to her face. "If you want," he said, "you can take a hot bath, and later I'll fill the reservoir for you again. It's dark, but it's still early. I can clear out and go over to Clever's. I oughta spend more time with Clever since the cross burning anyway."

Mom smiled, water still glistening in little droplets from her chin and nostrils. "Well, that does sound good to have a private bath in my warm kitchen on such a dark eve-.

ning." Wiping her hands on the tail of her apron in a pleased manner, she added, "I do feel like relaxing, knowing the Lord must have spared Mr. McMulty, since there ain't been a searching soul seen hide nor hair of 'im. And now Whit's making people stop their search."

"Like you spared us from Uncle Tut's coming and goings?" Rass said with a sly smile.

"Don't you ever get tired of sassing?" Mom asked, pleased. She handed him the five-cell flashlight, one of the gifts from Aunt Kate, and shooed him out the door. Rass whistled for Ole Coalie, and away they went. He hoped to beat the rain.

First he got Bill, then Clever, who said as he joined them, "As long as I get home in time to go to church with my parents tonight, I'm okay. We always hear Preacher Bloodworth preach when he comes to our parts." He gave each a shovel and led them across fields to the graveyard back of his place.

It was set off from farms by a woods. In fact, many trees grew near burial plots, a real hindrance, Rass realized, when traveling in the dark. Old leaves, which had been crisp and crackling enough to wake the dead last fall, were matted to the ground now and felt spongy to the foot. Accumulated year on top of year, the leaves nearly filled sunken graves. Spiders, snakes, and other vermin living around such sinkholes weren't visible, but Rass heard scurrying and hooting and, as the wind picked up, his own heart. He whispered, "Uncle Tut tells us a story of a ghost that roams that slough, just over there, and how it cries out in the night." Rass shuddered, then added loudly, "At least it got stuck in the graveyard and not in someone's house."

"I feel them spirits of my dead ancestors," Clever whispered. "They're watching to see if we'll do what we come to do."

Bill made his noises, and Rass made up a song to distract the ghost with his cheerfulness: "Ole Dan Tucker was a good ole man, but he got liver disease and his teeth rotted away and he died. Boy, can his ghost still fiddle away on a dark, quiet night." His singing stopped. "Listen." He moved the flashlight about.

"I don't hear nothing," Clever said.

"Me neither," said Rass, hoping he was right. "It's just dark clouds; it ain't really night!" Then he flashed the light over the entire vicinity. They sized up where the next grave ought to be dug, propped the light against a willow, and started the hole.

Rass and Clever were digging, but Bill just stood there. So Rass waved his arms back in the direction of his home, hoping Bill would understand that Mr. McMulty was not dead. Next he threw himself across their first diggings and laughed, hoping Bill would see this was all to be a joke. But the light let Rass see that Bill understood no such thing.

Clever said, "Bill ain't going to understand. It cain't be helped. I don't hardly know what we're doing, and I ain't deaf and dumb."

"Bill ain't dumb!"

Bill made a cry, reached into his pocket, and pulled out a new plug of chewing tobacco and started to unwrap it. Rass threw down the shovel, grabbed the tobacco, and threw it into the hole, saying, "You swiped your pa's to-backy? You know it's bad! Start shoveling, Bill!" He forced Bill's shovel into the ground. Ole Coalie sniffed at the tobacco.

Bill began to shovel slowly, in the same way he went along with Rass on other things he didn't completely comprehend. Rass valued that kind of friendship, but his heart broke because Bill had to do that without understanding. Again Rass shoveled fast. So did Bill, who soon made it a game to see who could shovel the fastest and deepest. He was more an expert than Rass or Clever.

Rass, thinking of the power of the Klan, began talking of those live men who dressed like ghosts. Felt their power. Clever mentioned the evilness of it, too. After a bit, it seemed Bill felt some foreboding as well. None of them had ever dug a grave before. Toilet holes, for reseating, sure. But never a grave. Never dug anything in the dark.

To ease his growing fear, Rass tried a little light talk instead, in the manner of Preacher Bloodworth, about how a toilet hole would be a better thing to dig. That, along with hard work, almost convinced him he wasn't scared of a ghost, living or dead.

They weren't long into the competitive digging when he also realized he was tired out. Neither muscles nor mind were in for any more playacting. In spite of his light talk, truth was, the darkness coming so early had him really scared.

Among all their huffs and puffs they could hear a distant howling of dogs. Maybe Uncle Tut's hounds. Maybe Preston's. Maybe Nert's. Maybe bloodhounds. New fear filled Rass. Clever had slowed as well. Who knew when things would blow wide open? It was too much—this waiting, not knowing. How could Bill bear such all the time?

"Those dogs are getting louder. Maybe we ought to get out of here," Clever said, breathing hard, but didn't lay his shovel down.

"We ain't hardly three feet down," Rass answered. "Boy, those dogs *are* getting close!" He looked toward Bill, but kept shoveling, too. Then Rass had an idea. He started to shovel the dirt back in.

"What you doing?" Clever demanded. Bill stopped.

"Ain't nobody going to dig it out agin! Who knows if the grave's six foot down or not?"

Immediately Clever's shovel was lifting dirt back in, too. Bill made his noise and did likewise. But Rass and Clever stopped. The dogs were within yards. Clever shouldered his shovel, picked up the flashlight, and took off. Rass grabbed for Bill, whistled for Ole Coalie, and they were out of there, too, following the one with the light. Three pairs of feet went at top speed out of the colored people's graveyard, then across the white people's graveyard. The dogs were tailing them, gaining on them, till they had to drop shovels in the road ditch. Once on the gravel road, they fairly flew. But the dogs didn't give up. Ole Coalie's howls were blending with the others.

Then Rass, Clever, and Bill got caught in the headlights of a truck coming down the road. They dropped and rolled into the road ditch. Clever put the flashlight down, pulled something from his pocket, took a bite, and ordered, "Here, take a chaw, quick!"

Bill did. Rass took a big bite, half swallowed it, and gagged. "Chaw tobacky! You picked up Bill's pa's—?"

The truck had skidded to a stop. It was Maggie Porter, the woman Rass had feared all his life, who got out and walked into the beam of the truck's lights, pistol drawn. Maggie wore a tan sweater, tweed skirt, low-heeled brown shoes, and her hair was cut like a man's, but it was a woman's voice that spoke. "Get up holding your hands high, and walk into the light."

They did with no sass. Maggie was the law. Rass was gagging and spitting something awful. It wasn't playacting.

"Well, Whitley, Brown, and Dumas! What are you boys doing out here?"

Bill spit out his cud right in front of her.

Clever said, "I won't lie and burn in hell. Trying chaw tobacky."

Maggie laughed. "How old are you?"

"Bill turned eleven and I'm past twelve," said Clever.

"*Ah-h-h-urp!*" said Rass, and lost it right in front of the sheriff.

"Get in the back. It'll cool you off taking you home. Your pappys can settle this with you. That your dog?"

Rass nodded, and felt sicker having done so. The other dogs had melted back into the darkness when Maggie had gotten out.

"Well, I guess your dog's got the good sense to find his way home," Maggie said. She pocketed her gun in its holster, climbed in.

Clever jumped into the truck bed. So did Bill, and both helped Rass.

Clever laughed along with the truck roar as it zoomed down the dark road of night. "Mama says tobacky will kill you, but tonight it saved our skins. Supposing them dogs had got us! Nobody can outtalk a dog. You suppose Nert's dogs just got our scent somehow?"

Bill nudged Rass as if he should talk back, but Rass couldn't.

"How we gonna get our shovels back?" Clever asked.

Rass just let him talk. Let him settle all the problems. He wanted only to curl up in the corner of that truck bed and die.

As they rode along, the sky lightened some and some moonlight was seeping through. The rain was passing over. Night had evidently come. It was probably about seven or seven-thirty. Shortly the truck stopped.

Bill jumped out and Maggie didn't even bother talking to his parents, but when Clever's turn came Maggie had a few words to say to Mr. and Mrs. Dumas. Mr. Dumas, standing there beside his wife in the headlights' beam, wore a loose long-sleeved shirt; not a bandage was notice-able.

Only a couple of minutes later, Maggie was hauling Rass out of the truck and pushing him toward Dad who was in the backyard with Marylu astraddle his neck, run-ning around the wood block, playing horsey. She told Dad how she'd caught Rass hiding out with some boys chewing tobacco.

"Had to get my baby here wore out," Dad explained his actions.

Rass's head cleared enough to realize luck was with him. Dad was in a fine mood!

"Them black clouds being out made our baby fall asleep early. Now she thinks it's daytime. My wife's wore out and needs her rest. Like I told you in town, Maggie, my Helen's had a hard time sleeping at night. If'n it tweren't people here a-searching, 'twas Tut's boys breaking fruit jars. Then that cross burning set her to worrying about the Klan!"

"You told me all that before, Whit. Let me get a word in edgewise."

But Dad wouldn't. "Worry's why she's put all the blame on my kin. Blame oughta been on your deputies' senseless prowling. More blame will be on you if'n you don't put a stop to Miss Esther's gossip."

"Whit, like I said, you see to your job, and I'll see to mine. Now, settle things with this boy of yourn."

"I'll see he gets the licking he deserves. My pa give me a good thrashing the first time I tried chewing his Bull Durham. Learned my lesson."

Maggie seemed satisfied with that and headed back to her truck, but paused to have a last word. "Sorry to be ruffling your feathers twice in one evening, Whit, but I cain't say me nor my deputies won't be out bothering Helen again. Right after you left I called for bloodhounds to be sent in by train. Law says I have to make this search thorough, your place same as your neighbors'. Like Tut told you, the KKK will finish things if I don't. I'll do my duty." She stepped high into her truck.

Dad immediately grabbed a stick that Chrissy had been riding for a horse that very afternoon, and before Maggie had the truck engine turned on, he grabbed Rass and held him down. The wood yard exploded with sound. Rass howled and howled, never hearing the roar of Maggie's leave-taking.

"Dad, you're killing him! Stop!" L.G. screamed as he came running from the house.

Right then Rass saw Mr. McMulty about to walk out of the barn.

# 18

"STOP! STOP!" Rass cried out.

Mr. McMulty receded back into the barn, and the sounds of the beating stopped. Rass suddenly realized that none of Dad's licks had hit him—just the chopping block beside him. Was Dad playing a practical joke on Maggie? No. He would on Mom, or the girls, but...Oh, no, Dad had seen Mr. McMulty and got his aim thrown off? Rass broke loose.

Dad ordered L.G. back inside the house, then scooped up crying Marlyu and fought off her clawing at him, saying harshly, "Shush! Shush, child. I mean it!"

Marylu's fight stopped with a gasp of fear. For a moment Dad looked again as he had looked there on the ditch bank, right after Rass had saved his life, a man of total despair. Then, letting go of his toughness, he sat Marylu down and looked directly at Rass. "You wondering why I didn't thrash you good? Why I hit the block instead of you?"

"Yes sir, I'm a-wondering," Rass answered, trying to catch his breath. Some miracle had surely saved him.

" 'Cause earlier tonight Maggie Porter told me you told Nert that we saw the calf a-hanging over his front stoop."

"Yes, sir."

"Well, when I heard that I *was* ready to thrash you good. You put me on the spot, boy."

Rass nodded, but said nothing.

"But when I got back home from seeing Maggie, I saw your mother looking so ragged and wrung out, and her not having the chance to use the water you'd brought in for her bath. She was still hoping to take it, if I'd quiet the kids who was arguing and the baby who was a-screaming. I softened." Dad twisted in his discomfort at showing emotion.

"So's I sends the bigger ones to the library table to do their homework and put L.G. in charge whiles I takes Marylu off'n Helen's hands, and I come out to the wood yard to set awhile. And it was right here on this chopping block that I set until my mind clears and I start to thinking what a good boy you was, getting in that bathwater for your mother. And I thinks how words come easy to you and you're always spouting off, but you ain't mean a'tall. I always taught you to pay respect to your elders, so you telling the truth to a landlord was natural. I couldn't give no licking to you, boy, for telling the truth. Not even when you'd chawed tobacky."

Dad had never spoken in this manner before, nor taken blame unto himself. Rass wanted to touch Dad as he had on the ditch bank, though touching between father and son wasn't proper. But it wouldn't hurt to reemphasize his truth telling. "And I was honest when I told Nert *you* weren't hiding out no one, even when Miss Esther says you was."

"Well, it all explains why Maggie ain't been out here again looking personally and Nert ain't come back a second time." Dad let go a chuckle. "Boy, your honesty has set Nert off us! I oughta known—he'd a-been setting on our doorsteps all night long if'n he'd really thought McMulty was here."

Rass dared not say a word. He might wake up and find this just a dream.

Dad looked at him and added, "I been hoping all along that McMulty makes his escape and never has to involve us a'tall." He stood up, moved closer. "Tut told me yesterdy Nert ripped out a toolbox built under someone's wagon, again looking for McMulty, and never even offered to tack it back on." Dad picked up Marylu in spite of her protest and the lantern and went toward the house, saying, "Come on, son, you need to get your homework done. It's like I told L.G., tomarr's Saturday and we'll need a full sunrise-to-sunset day of work and we still got to get over to Five Ditch to fix our neighbor's planter, so's they can get in a full day, too."

Rass started to follow—but on second thought, seeing Marylu fighting to get down again, he said, "Let me keep Marylu outside until she runs out of steam, then I'll bring her in."

Dad handed the child over at once. So Rass took her chubby little hands and started walking her about—right into the barn so he could have it out with Mr. McMulty.

Mr. McMulty walked a few steps to meet him, doing

fine, albeit he limped. His clean bandage shone in the light.

"What did you mean by showing yourself?" Rass demanded, not even bothering with politeness.

"I couldn't stand by, let my friend be beat by his daddy!"

Rass caught the compliment about himself, and it was almost more than he could hold.

"And I couldn't let Whit set his father's heart on revenge that'd just fill his soul."

"It weren't as bad as it looked," Rass said, though it was still a bit frightening to think Dad had changed so much, even to believe in sparing the rod. Dad's licks had *always* hit. "Your stepping outside like that was bad! I don't want you hung, Mr. McMulty! Us boys dug the grave to get you free time to heal and then escape. You know what it'd be if you got caught." Rass fought with Marylu wanting to be lifted up into the corncrib. She won.

"Back a couple year"—Mr. McMulty spoke softly—"Whit save my life, when he ask Nert to make me his cropper. I wishes to return the favor by not letting him be harsh on his son. A man need the love of a son. I figgers it the trouble I cause what churns anger in you and set yo' mind on rebelling. With rebel fire a-raging, hands clasp on to sin like a lost chile. Yo' trying tobacky come out of that grave digging to spare me." He lowered his head and leathery old hands nimbly stuffed in his pant leg.

"I ain't ever gonna use tobacky agin," Rass said as he twisted about on some corn kernels dropped by Marylu. "Mr. McMulty, you wouldn't want Dad to turn you in.

You wouldn't want Maggie to get us for harboring. You got to think on that part."

Mr. McMulty said, "I jist tard letting you take the consequence when I be the one what done the wrong."

"But *you* took the consequence for *us*!" Rass was raising his voice in reasoning. "We got hit by the flood, not you. And you lost your home and job, and we let you do it!"

Mr. McMulty rocked a bit on his heels, then spoke softly. "That be true, but then I step out o' line. I wishes I could tell you and my neighbors, tweren't my *natural* self what done that. It be my angry self who visit Nert's place and done that deed. I always been a man o' reason—even use reason to blind myself and excuse Nert's acts. But weren't no reasoning left in me for what Nert done to me when I get ousted." He paused, but Rass didn't speak. "I starts moving my belongings, and my anger does my thinking. I thinks I be a blind man and never be no man o' reason 'fore that moment. To simmer, I go hep with yo' salvaging. But my simmering blooms full, and I rushes off and do that deed."

"Nert caused you to," Rass said. "He deserved what he got!"

"I thinks that be true, Rass, but Lord hep me! I goes outside the law and I involves my friends." His voice got so sad the mules shuddered and stamped in their stalls. Rass knew he must be thinking of Mr. Dumas, as well as the Whitleys. "I ready now to turn myself in, boy, and bear the consequences for doing it a wrong way. I through with hiding." His hands reached forth as if to be handcuffed.

"No! No!" Rass jumped back.

"I got to do it, son! You didn't make me hang no calf. It be a crime. Let me face up to it!"

Rass turned his back to fetch Marylu, who was crawling to the other side of the crib, but his words came forward. "Nert ridded you of your mule colt, and that's a crime, too! Nert didn't honor his contract with you, and that's another crime! It was me what involved us, not you! You don't need to face up to nothing!" Rass sat Marylu outside the crib, picked up a small piece of straw, and broke it into halves, then quarters, then eighths, squeezing and twisting it tight until no air remained in any portion of it.

"Son, that part o' me what wars agin my Maker didn't face up to no laws." McMulty's voice changed, became angry, harsh. "That part shouts justice! Time of my bad deed, I feels like a free man for the first time, a-standing up to *the* man, destroying his property, like he do mine. I thinks it be an eye for an eye, my mule and dreams for his calf and dreams. That all be true."

Mr. McMulty's face shone filled with emotion there in the lantern's light. "Don't tell me my right to revenge, boy. I knows it. But revenge don't heal me none. Nert's evil smiling face be with me all the hours in my hiding. Scarier than spiders or rats. I gonna see it till I be dead and buried. Cain't go on hurting others. Cain't go on letting my friends chance being cotched. Best I let yo' daddy see me." He stood solid.

Rass, wanting to ease his pain, embraced the feeling that flooded him. "Mr. McMulty, you're wrong to ever think of giving up! You got to resist! Maybe you protested wrong, but you did stand up, and that's all that matters.

Dad had us standing up to Nert today, working where Nert said not to. Pay the way of it no mind!" Rass grew silent.

"Rass, you a good boy, pointing out truth like you sees it, but Preacher Bloodworth preaches a new way," Mr. McMulty said. "I feels sorry I let my festering reach that point where it brake loose in such a violent way. Things 'sploded in this old head, my mind so set agin my enemy. Nert be wrong. I be wrong."

The need to stop such talk shot off like a cannon in Rass's head, making his ears ring, his heart beat faster. How was he to talk sense into Mr. McMulty?

"You killed a calf, not a human," Rass exploded. "Turn yourself in, the law won't give you no day in court. The Klan'll lynch you! You ain't no criminal! You ain't done nothing to hurt nobody, like Nert does. That makes a big difference. Us boys dug that grave tonight and we'll help you escape outa Missouri, too. And we got to do it fast, 'fore Maggie gets her bloodhounds and searches our place. If I could drive like L.G., I'd help you escape, right now, tonight!"

"Argument over." Mr. McMulty's voice came mild in contrast to Rass's. "I gwine let the Lord pave my way. If'n it be right I leave, I leave. But if'n I do, I be back later to fight Nert's evil with the law. Preacher Bloodworth have a say on how laws can be the first change. So set yo' mind to peace, Rass. The Lord be my sanctifier, who radiates an understanding heart and ransoms my soul. I trusts the Lord to open the door of my prison one way or t'uther. Preacher Bloodworth done say, 'Get right with the Lord,' and now I do be right with Him. Leave me be."

Those words didn't set Mr. McMulty free, nor get the foul taste of chewing tobacco out of Rass's mouth, but they did allow him to carry sleepy Marylu back to the house, give her to Mom, who sat in the kitchen talking quietly with Dad, and go himself to the library table for memorizing his state capitals. It was almost eight-thirty—bedtime. But his mind trailed from capitals to Preacher Bloodworth, till it suddenly became clear what the man meant by passive resistance. It was like Mr. McMulty out there in the dark quietly talking to him, until he had finally listened. It was like Sally gagging on the molasses and lard, or himself gagging on the tobacco: It focused attention elsewhere. If Maggie returned, they'd keep on gagging till she called off her dogs.

He bounced up from the table, slammed his geography book shut. That wouldn't work for the Klan. When the Klan got a belief, they'd never let go because of reason, nor be diverted by soft talk. *They had no need to answer to laws.*

Dad's voice from the kitchen grew loud. "...And if that weren't enough, Maggie says the town's on edge 'cause newspapers in New York, Chicago, and Los Angeles has copied a picture of McMulty lifting up a white girl, and that girl's our Sally!"

The girls stopped their chatter in the bedroom, as they did at times to hear Dad's storytelling. The nice voice Dad had used in the wood yard when talking to Rass was put aside now. "I cain't stop what the paper's already done, but Helen, mark my words, I ain't letting Maggie bring out no bloodhounds!"

"Why would she do that?"

"Why?"

"Why?" The little girls were in the doorway, wanting to know. Especially Sally.

Dad answered sharply, "Let your studies stop your whys!"

The girls took that as permission to come sit again at the library table. When Mom came in and suggested they say their prayers, Dad yelled, "Don't go mouthing off to God, Helen! He cain't change a town of set people, lessen you want Him to wire Miss Esther's mouth shut."

"What'd Miss Esther say?" Sally demanded.

For an answer Dad said, "Rass, take that flashlight and trot over to Preston's and tell him Sally ain't going to no fair. I need that chore off my mind."

Dad went on, directing Rass how to put it so the rich neighbor took no offense, but Rass heard none of it. For right in the middle of those instructions, and Sally's wild protestations, it came to Rass: *Such an assignment was a miracle!* There for the taking! A way had come to smuggle Mr. McMulty to New Madrid, a river town. He'd trot over to Mr. Preston's all right, but one more time he'd have to disobey Dad.

"Yes, sir," he said quickly. "I'll take the flashlight even though I ain't afraid of the dark, nor Mr. Preston's dogs."

Rass took off quickly, controlling his urge to shout, until he got out of hearing distance of the house. Then he let go: *"Yahoo!"* He spun around three or four times, then quickly explained to Ole Coalie, who'd caught up with him. "We're going to get Mr. McMulty outa here in the trunk of Mr. Preston's Lincoln! What do you think of that? It's a splendid miracle. There's not a law officer in Missouri what'd stop Mr. Preston's car for inspection, Nert's orders or no! Course, we got to get him to insist on taking Sally. Dad'll agree with anything that rich man says. Nothing can go wrong!"

The light of the flashlight flicked quickly to Rass's walking motion, which had caught the speed of his excitement. His thoughts set on how to get Mr. Preston's consent. He'd do it. He'd had plenty of practice getting himself out of a jam. "Coalie, I'll just go tell Mr. Preston that Sally cain't go," Rass said. "You know I'm obeying what Dad told me to say, but then I'll add, 'It's 'cause she's got no ride and cain't go without me going along, too.' "

Coalie and he trotted on for quite a while, silent.

As they came within the rays of the electric lights that surrounded Mr. Preston's cotton gins, those buildings where seed was separated from the cotton and then the cotton pressed into five-hundred-pound bales for shipping to mills, Rass began doubting. He was beginning to realize what a daring and irrational thing it was for a boy to try to sneak a black fugitive into the car of the most prestigious white plantation owner in the area. But an opening was an opening. He had to do it. By tomorrow Miss Esther would be pointing out the exact spot Mr. McMulty was hiding, and Mr. McMulty would not stay hidden, and he and the whole family would suffer.

The first part of Rass's plan went fine. Mr. Preston instantly insisted he'd take Sally. When Rass explained how, Sally being a girl and all, he'd need to go along, too, Mr.

Preston agreed to that condition as well, adding, "I have to leave early, five o'clock, to tend to the readying of my bull."

Rass was back home shortly after nine, whispering the news to Mr. McMulty, who was joyous and said, "The Lord done pro-vide the way!" He scrubbed his boot on a piece of broken glass, pulverizing it. "Well, we best talk this over to the last hair—how we gwine not get caught."

Rass set his mind to this next big matter. He made suggestions and heard Mr. McMulty's counter suggestions. By nine-thirty a plan was set, but it would work only if Dad and L.G. left before Mr. Preston arrived. They had no solution for that. Mr. McMulty ended with, "Lord gwine provide the way. If'n it don't come out right, it not meant to be." Such a statement no longer seemed irrational.

It had to work.

Of course it would work.

Rass said, "The earlier we get up in the morning, the better." Then he crossed his fingers for luck that Dad would let Sally go.

When he told Dad, Sally got so wound up Mom had to school her on proper behavior. Dad couldn't refuse her. Even when Sally insisted on sleeping on the floor in the living room, next to Mom's and Dad's bed, Dad said, "Sure, you can fall asleep here, big sister."

Kids were never allowed to sleep there! Then Dad touched Sally's beautiful red hair and said proudly, "Never thought none of my kids, lessen it'd be L.G. who knows motors in and out, would ever 'mount to something. Well, looks like you're gonna have your first big outing tomarr."

He pulled her to her feet, danced her merrily about, then let her down easily. It was okay for a happy father to do that with a daughter.

"Good-night, Daddy. Set the alarm for four-thirty," Sally said, and curled up on the floor and fell asleep.

Dad said, "Rass, you watch out for her. Mark my word!"

"Yes, sir. I'm sleeping in my favorite spot, too, behind the kitchen stove, soon's I come back from the toilet," Rass announced. It was his good-luck space at McMulty's. Hearing no objections, he picked up the lantern, though its wick had burned low, and raced the rising wind toward the barn, not the toilet.

"Mr. McMulty, we got to rehearse this all one more time. My thinking makes me nervous. I'm sleeping in my clothes, so no time's wasted dressing. A hundred things can go wrong, you know? It's too long a way from road to barn. How am I gonna get Mr. Preston's Lincoln backed in that far? You best stay safe in the barn all night, but be awake and be close by under the house just before time to leave. Okay?"

"I be awake, God willing. Sleep be better in the crib than under it! I be there and my cotton sack with me, as planned. Under the house is chancy, but less chancy than t'other way. No question 'bout it." He touched Rass's shoulder, forcefully digging his fingers into the flesh. "I feels like I sending my boy off to war. Get in the house before that lantern wick drop into the oil and start a fire! We both best sleep some, if'n we can."

Rass blew out the dying flame and it seemed night lowered close to hide him.

As he quickly picked his way back toward the house in the dark, he recalled things that had worked out fine—he'd found Dad's contract, he'd gotten no licking for using chaw tobacky, and even L.G. had gotten to claim his acres in spite of Nert. Still, he was dead tired. Couldn't think anymore. Life was serious business.

Getting near the pump he felt his thirst rise, so started to prime it. Then he remembered to make no noise. He couldn't let Dad, nor anyone, get suspicious. So he got his drink from the bucket on the back porch. Then, assuring himself that all preparations were done and sealed by the night, he settled in behind the cookstove.

THERE CAME the barking of dogs, and Ole Coalie set up a howl in response. "Maggie couldn't have her bloodhounds tonight!" thundered Dad as he stomped to the door. Rass was there, too. L.G. as well.

"Stay inside!" Dad scolded them. "I'll handle this."

Then came the clopping of horse's hooves. And out of the darkness came Nert's white horse. Above the barks of dogs, Nert shouted, "Whit, step out here!"

"I'm out here," Dad said. "It's near ten. What's wrong?"

"I was over at Preston's to get information since I'm leaving tonight for the fair. He says he's taking two of your kids to it. I cain't allow that. L.G.'s to be on that plow come sunrise. Let the little squirt go—he don't move too fast as it is."

Dad shouted back, "Preston weren't taking L.G. and Rass—it's Sally and Rass." The dogs went sniffing and whining around the house, and Nert's response was just to order them home and leave.

L.G. went back to his mattress in the loft, and Rass lay down again behind the kitchen stove, felt the darkness grow deeper and deeper until nothing was left but endless rehearsals of getting Mr. McMulty to New Madrid, getting the keys from Mr. Preston, and getting his friend out of the trunk.

It was being called "a little squirt" that gave Rass the fire to believe that he alone could do the job. While checking and rechecking for loopholes, he slept off and on. The dark holes between were filled with horrible dreams of failure and the consequences. Then Rass suddenly awakened, sniffing a burning pine smell drifting in, hearing the cry of animals. Surely he had blown out that lantern.

He screamed, "Our barn's on fire! Wake up, everyone! Fire!"

As he shot out the door he heard Dad shout words that struck his heart. "Save the mules!"

Rass's own cry was "Mr. McMulty! Mr. McMulty!"

# 19

M<small>R</small>. M<small>C</small>M<small>ULTY</small> didn't respond to Rass's calls. Covering eyes with arms, Rass dashed inside the barn, directly to the corncrib. The stalls were not locked, but the mules were crazed by the flames, rearing and pawing the hot air, their whinnies a cry of death. "Mr. McMulty! Mr. McMulty!" Rass continued to shout as he instinctively turned the mules toward the entrance. L.G. was suddenly there beside him, hitting their rumps, sending them charging off, braying, across field. Then, clamping his hand over Rass's mouth to silence his screams for Mr. McMulty, L.G. pushed him to Dad, who yanked him to safety, shouting, "You saved Nert's mules!"

Then Mom was there. "No injuries," Dad told her as he pushed Rass into her arms and ran back to the fire. Mom rubbed smoke smudges from Rass's face, then held him close as she yelled, "Where's Sally and the little girls? Don't let them outside!"

"Sally's right over there." L.G. pointed at Sally, who was emptying the slop bucket into the flames.

"Grab buckets! Start pumping water, L.G.! Dad! Rass!"
Sally shouted her commands, then suddenly stopped.

Rass saw white robes of the Klan just as Dad soberly
announced, "Oh God. The Klan must have McMulty on
the run."

The flames leaped brighter into the dark night. Mr.
McMulty was in the crib! Flames were too high. Mr.
McMulty would be roasted alive. Rass clung to Mom and
wept.

When Rass pulled loose to look about, he saw past the
pile of lumber by the outhouse and behind that scrawny
little poplar tree, five horses stamping impatiently and ner-
vously neighing in response to the brays of the crazed
mules. Wind whipped the white robes of the horses' riders.
No faces could be seen. White hoods covered their necks
and came to a point on top, with slits only for eyes. No
regular clothing was visible as identification. Their robes
dangled low, past the horses' bellies. Rass looked further
and saw other white forms positioned to surround the
barn.

Now ghostly shapes moved beyond the smoke and con-
fusion. Like specters in the smoky air, more white-robed
creatures stood vigil. One was right next to the pump,
gun drawn, allowing no water to be pumped. So all the
Whitleys, even the little girls near the back door, stood at
gunpoint while flames grew larger and wilder and ate
deeper, burning a man, destroying tools and harness along
with the scarce supply of hay and feed. Rass's scream on
the air produced no sound. His body had no ability to
move. In the midst of that burning barn was his friend,

whom he loved and the Lord hadn't spared. Rass moved toward the blaze.

Defying guns, Sally and Mom rushed the little girls into the house, where they'd be safe, unless sparks carried. The barn didn't seem so far from the house now.

"Mr. McMulty! Mr. McMulty's in there!" Rass finally had voice, and he didn't care who heard him.

"He's not!" L.G. shouted. "Rass has gone crazy!"

"Course the nigger's in there," sang back a Klansman. "But the cracks in that barn's big enough to throw a cat through. He'll come through one, wait and see. Whichever board's above his hidey-hole."

"Shush, Rass!" Dad hissed. "They'll shoot you! Get inside the house with Helen." But there were Sally and Mom back outside.

Already two cars had pulled up: Mr. Preston's Lincoln and Uncle Jake's Chevy. Both were stopped by the Klansmen's guns. Those hooded men by the trees still talked, but not loud—just sounds of coaxing and peevish jawing to one another. A colored man's life had no value.

Then came a shout: "Hot enough, nigger? Minute he comes out, grab 'im. Git the rope ready." The horses and mules of the Klansmen surrounding the barn danced in readiness.

From the robed figure remaining nearest the scrub poplar came John Henry Litikin's stringy voice, the same man who had once told Rass he was white and Clever was black. Baying loud above the increased crackle of the fire, like a hound dog awaiting a sign of the squirrel he'd treed, John Henry said, "Come out, nigger, er git your black hide roasted off! You got 'bout one second 'fore we grab your horns and shoot your pigtail off your be-hind!"

Hee-haws followed, and Dad, Uncle Jake, and Mr. Preston shouted threats back as timbers crashed, drowning their voices and changing the patterns of the flames. The falling hay momentarily smothered the center of the fire, blurring sight as it hid the flames, but then it ignited and smoke billowed, flames returned, and the fire grew greater and hotter. Guns were lowered.

Rass moaned. There was no way Mr. McMulty had the power to run to safety now. Besides, there was no safety.

Rass's sobs grew loud, and the little girls' sobbings could be heard, too, from the windows and doors of the Whitley house. Dad came up, touched Rass, and said softly, "The old man's done for. Rass, I'm a sorry soul!"

"Oh Lord, oh Lord, oh Lord," cried Mom. "Whit, don't tell me Mr. McMulty's in there!"

Dad nodded. "Klan had him on the run."

Mom held Rass close, her grieving voice rising higher and higher, making a sad song in the night.

Rass looked to her face. The firelight heightened and brightened some features and set others into shadow, giving her an eerie, foreboding appearance, with eyes set in deep sockets and gaze as afar off as her keening. He loved his Mom. He loved Mr. McMulty, and he'd not helped either of them.

Dennis and L.G. tried to pull Rass free, but Aunt Kate stopped them. "Let the boy be," she said, then began yelling in a most un-Christian way, "You men get the hell off this place and back to your families! I don't care who you are. Damn you, get!"

There came even a stronger voice of authority—Preston's. "What the hell do you idiots think you're doing? You've burned down Nert's barn, and him just left for the New Madrid Fair and not here to defend it! Go home!" His head high, his cape flowing, he was a giant to be reckoned with.

"It *is* Preston!" one Klansman shouted.

His presence shocked riders nearby. They jerked reins, and restless pawing and fidgeting switched to rearing as they moved backward. But then came, "Nur do we keer who you be, old man! We come to finish off'n a job sheriff couldn't. *You* better git!" Riders fought mules and horses, ordering them to stay put. More neighbors gathered.

"Don't threaten me!" Preston's voice carried above all sounds. "I know who you are. Every one!" No one moved back. A hot cinder hit Rass above the ankle; he slapped at it, but his sock top and pant leg were melted away.

A voice like Big Red's called from the other side of the barn, "You black-hearted shoat, stick that black neck out here and—"

"Hey, McMulty, come on out! You're not above the law!" That demand came from a more refined voice.

Then from the farthest point came a shout: "There ain't no sign of 'im. He ain't in thar, or else he's dade. Or else he's slipped us. We'd a smelled him cookin' if'n he war dade. No nigger gonna roast if'n he got legs, even little bitty short cutoff legs." Another Litikin. "Hit's hotter'n hell here."

Mr. McMulty wouldn't come out to be hanged when, by staying hid, it would spare the Whitleys. "Don't spare us, Mr. McMulty!" Rass cried.

While the blaze drove the mounts of the Klansmen back, John Henry whipped his mule in closer, singing out his mocking taunts above the rest. "Calf hanger, come outa yur dug hidey-hole. Jist creep out nice 'n' easy." Then, feeling the heat: "Snowballs in hell ain't getting him to come out. This ain't no regular animal we treed."

"And you're no regular human, trying to burn a man!" came the mighty voice of Maggie Porter. "John Henry, I'd know your voice anywhere. You better leave now and stay clear of Parma. I won't have you here organizing! By morning bloodhounds could have proved no one was hiding here. But you couldn't wait. Burning Nert's barn is as criminal an act as killing his calf. I'll run the lot of you in!"

Then Rass saw Shark, right beside her, his Box Brownie clicking away in the great light of the fire. Lots more people were gathering.

"Maggie Porter, John Henry's coming after you!" Sally wailed.

Maggie took a step toward, not away. A garter snake slithered out from the stacked wood and was roasted alive by flames licking across Maggie's path. She never halted. She shot her pistol twice into the air.

Now the entire Klan, as many as twenty men, moved back near the barren dirt of new-plowed ground. Not from the sweeping flames, which had come to a dead stop before reaching the Klan, but because they saw Maggie's walk, the walk that had scared kids for years. Standing beside her was Preston, the other great representative of power, not only in Parma but in all Missouri.

"I got pictures!" yelled Shark.

Rass said nothing. This was not real. He was still behind the kitchen stove, having a bad dream. A flame seared his pants leg, demanding he not hide from knowing the worst.

John Henry whipped his mule; it whinnied and reared, giving him a better view of whom he was challenging. "Horse manure! Old man Preston's backing her up!" At that, he dug his work boots into the mule's sides and took off into the night. There followed much cussing and a great clamor as other mules and horses, already being turned about to escape the heat, were kicked into a gallop in pursuit of their leader.

Dad, jerking and gesturing, shouted, "I'll shoot you full of holes, John Henry, if I ever lay eyes on you again!"

As the white robes faded into the dark night, the last call heard was, "Nigger lovers, you ain't heard the end o' it!"

"We'll see that they have," Maggie declared to those who remained.

Preston gave her a wry look. "Maggie, no sheriff can match them single-handed. The savagery is awful. I'll call my son in Washington."

Suddenly there was Tut, swiping sweat from his forehead, eyes full of panic, demanding of Rass between hard breaths, "McMulty? They burn him out?"

"They thought they was, but thank God he wasn't

here," Aunt Kate answered, but Rass could see Uncle Tut didn't believe her.

"I'm telling you, Uncle Tut, he ain't here," L.G. said. Uncle Tut calmed down. Everybody believed L.G.

Mr. Preston put a hand on Sally's shoulder. "I'll see you and your brother in the morning, if you're still up to it. Best I get going while I still can get my car on the road." People kept streaming in, blocking his exit. To Maggie Porter he said, "We need to talk with our congressman about the Klan, as well as the government parity checks."

"Mr. Preston, can you give us a new barn and hay for the mules?" Sally said boldly.

"Sally, that ain't proper! People takes care of their own," Mom said. Then Mom and Dad immediately began begging pardon for Sally's inappropriate behavior.

Rass thought, If Mr. McMulty were alive he'd have said, "The chile don't know what she asking."

Mom said, "We can use our old barn, Sally. It's still a-standing. I never did like a barn too close to the house." She looked right at Rass and cautioned, "What a chile don't know cain't hurt."

There was an awkward silence, which Dad filled in quickly. "The mules is Nert's. He's got hay aplenty. Ever' landlord takes care of his own business, daughter."

"She's all right," Mr. Preston said. "Sally here is a fine little artist." Artist or not, Rass felt Sally was ignorant of life, and at this moment he didn't want to change that.

Mr. Preston had to walk past more neighbors gathered to watch the fire. Some turned to watch him.

Rass had the urge to offer to take Mr. Preston's keys and open the trunk, just so Mr. Preston would find him acting no different in the morning. Foolish thoughts. His old friend was dead; he couldn't change that. Just as he moved nearer Mom, a great roar sounded, and the sides of the barn caved in. The heavens lit up and one could see as clearly as noonday. Sparks rose like fireworks on the Fourth of July. There was Dennis, the rocket maker, looking on in awe. Shark was still snapping pictures.

Beside Rass now was Bill Brown, whose family had just arrived. Rass pulled him close, as Mr. McMulty would have done, held him and cried. Bill was crying, too.

In the burning light of the barn, Rass remembered all the wise words Mr. McMulty had poured into him. A belief formed in him that was clear and right. Mr. McMulty was a man of his word, never a fugitive from the law. He was just trying to escape from men who acted outside of the law, who tore down and destroyed others just to up themselves. Nert. The Klan. Rass promised Mr. McMulty, still very alive in his heart, that he would always do his utmost to be a man of his word, too. Not be mean-spirited nor cruel to anyone. Rass tapped the carved willow whistle Bill kept in the pencil pocket of his overalls. Bill nodded, and both wept anew.

"The fire won't spread no farther. The Klan's gone," L.G. said just as Maggie Porter yelled, "There's nothing here that anyone can do, and we can't change the world tonight. Go on home. Let this family rest. They been through a lot. Shark, I'd best get you home, too."

"I'd like to see John Henry hung," Shark said. "Maybe Big Red and Rooster, too. Them acting so normal, then switching like they done."

"I know that killing's wrong in all its forms," said Aunt

Kate. "But I tell you, I'd like to see the whole lot of 'em dead! But a few dead men wouldn't change a world's ignorance. Would it?"

Sally began quoting Mr. Aaral in such a way that all saying good-bye stopped to listen. " 'Let one man stay ignorant, and meaningful change cain't follow!' " Now she'd be quoted. It was a perfect time to do so, but Rass didn't declare her ignorant of life. He himself was not wise. He was empty. He had lost his best friend in all the world.

Uncle Jake said, "Whit, the barn is leveled. Tomarr me and Tut got to set to and come help you clean up."

Dad pulled Mom close, pressed her head to his shoulder, and thundered to Jake, "I can take care o' my own! We'll manage fine. Don't go feeling sorry for us. Nert'll want his crops in the ground. We're setting good till then. We got a place to lay our heads tonight, and I got other work to do tomarr. We'll clean up after crops are laid by."

Lightning flashed in the sky. Thunder bellowed in echo. More lightning. More thunder. Kin and neighbors barely made it to their cars before the rains that had threatened all day came down in a great wash, making blistering, sizzling sounds as flames were extinguished. Smoke arose and the blackness of night returned before lights of cars and wagons could be lit.

Bill protested leaving. His folks couldn't stand in the rain and argue, so let him stay.

Dad patted Rass's shoulder and said, "I know it'll be hard after your seeing our old neighbor run into that burning barn, but try to get some sleep." Mom offered her sympathies, too.

Bill was tugging hard at Rass and making his noises grow very loud. Rass turned and looked. *Under the edge of the house, right in the place he was to be the next morning, pretty well covered by a cotton sack, lay Mr. McMulty!*

# 20

By the whistle of the earliest morning train, Mom had breakfast made and all but the little girls up. Though the fire was squelched by the rain, its odor filled the air on this overcast and misty morning. Mom's prayer on the food was the longest and strongest, which didn't please Dad, who was in a hurry to leave, but it pleased Rass plenty. He had slept little. He kept being thankful that Mr. McMulty was alive. He must have decided to sleep under the house, instead of waiting for morning. Mr. McMulty had been lying at the very spot where Nert's dogs had sniffed and yelped till Nert made them go home. Of course they hadn't protested. Mr. McMulty was their old friend.

Rass had to tell his parents something to ease their worries, so had told them it wasn't Mr. McMulty he'd seen run but a Klansman. Dad was still mad that he'd caused them needless worry. And Bill might not be the best person to try to help. Bill's mom had used the finger-to-lips sign to shush Bill so often that Bill understood it meant "stay calm." Rass had used it every chance he got since Bill awakened beside him behind the kitchen stove. Rass's own nerves were strung tight.

After they ate, Mom swung into action, commanding them all: made Rass comb his hair—Bill, too—then criticized Sally's painting, saying, "You need to darken the fencerows. They don't hardly show." Sally, hurt, got out her paints again.

Dad and L.G. hurried to escape being next, and Rass was beholden to Mom.

No sooner than Dad had pulled it shut, the door opened again. It was Clever. His folks had left early to take Preacher Bloodworth the long trip back to Sikeston, so Clever had come to see Rass and check on Mr. McMulty. On seeing the burned barn he'd burst into Rass's house without knocking.

Rass pushed him back outside and told him all. They stood within hearing distance of Mr. McMulty, but Rass didn't dare speak to the man outright.

Tears shadowed Clever's eyes as they waited for sounds of Preston's car. He said, "Last night shows what woulda happened if Maggie let the Klan get control."

"But Maggie didn't arrest anybody. And if Mr. Preston does call Washington, how's that going to put an end to the Klan?"

Bill joined them, then began easing closer and closer to Mr. McMulty, but stopped at Rass's signal.

"You're doing right. We got to keep on keeping on," Clever said, his voice low, "and I can help. We ain't so much boys no more. We been through a night worse than this fire, and I'll help get you through this thing, too! Have to. A man's life's at stake, and life ain't cheap. I'm good at distracting. I'll distract Mr. Preston, easy. I know big talk. You just go on and do what you planned!"

Rass was welcoming that idea just as Mr. Preston's Lincoln stopped out front. Quickly he dashed in, grabbed up Sally's picture, and was out the front door *as planned*. Clever and Bill were right beside him. Ole Coalie was tagging along, too. "Remember to make your big talk, Clever," Rass cautioned. "Big talk might work." Then to Bill he said, "You talk big, too! You don't need to stay quiet no more, Bill."

Clever was already making his voice loud even before they got to the car. Suddenly Ole Coalie growled. Yips of dogs were heard. Maggie's bloodhounds? Clever and Rass froze. If anyone turned his back on barking dogs, they'd be on him in a minute. And if those dogs noticed Mr. McMulty, the whole plan was gone! Rass steeled himself. He had to play things out as they had rehearsed. He couldn't let fear of anything get in the way.

Growls and yips reached a higher pitch, blended with Rass's racing heart. Why—those weren't Maggie's dogs! They were Mr. Preston's big long-haired German shepherds, specially trained to chew up any prowler who came near the cotton gin at night!

Instantly there was Bill, befriending them!

Rass pranced back and forth, wanting to yell thanks, but controlled himself and moved quietly toward the dogs as his friend Bill did. "Hey, King. Hey, George. Good dogs." The dogs calmed down, so Rass calmed himself and called to Mr. Preston, *as planned,* "Mr. Preston, if I'm to get the picture in the trunk, you'll need to back in the driveway. Sally'll be out directly. Ain't much space to turn around. What with cinders and hot ashes about," he added.

Clever joined in, "Delicate thing, backing this big car in. Come along—I'll keep an eye on your wheels." It was something to see, Clever nervous as the weather, motioning like mad, trying all he knew to help.

Bill watched a moment, then joined in with the motioning, backing along with the car same as Clever. Rass was amazed. The only thing was, the dogs marched along with him.

Rass had to ignore them, but to do so was as hard as ignoring the big fire smell in order to catch the odor of ash wood from the breakfast fire, a good smell. Mr. McMulty would have pointed out that good natural smell, as a proven way to ease fear. Rass paused near the house, feeling Mr. McMulty's presence. The dogs left Bill in order to growl and nip at the wheels as Mr. Preston brought the car to a stop. But he was only halfway to the desired spot. Rass couldn't ignore these dogs. They'd sure ruin his plan. They must leave.

Mr. Preston, looking as formidable as ever, was rolling down his car window. King leaped up; George did likewise on the passenger side. The fawn fringe on their lower legs showed in the light. The old man shouted, "Stay, dogs! Down, fellers!" The dogs obeyed at once.

"I'll send them home for you," Rass offered.

"There now. Don't bite Sally's brother! Soon as Sally's ready," Mr. Preston said to Rass, "we must get going, if we're to take tops at the fair." Preston had his cape pulled tight over his shoulders, but Rass knew he was also wearing his pinstriped pants and sporty black leather shoes, shined to a fare-thee-well. The trademark of a rich man.

"I ain't afraid of your dogs," Rass said, very much afraid. "It's just—"

Sally dashed out in her starched yellow dress, showing no evidence at all of the mud she had washed from it after it was salvaged. She got into the backseat and began talking about the fair, about Mr. Preston's nice bull, about her fine painting, about how L.G. was having to stay home and work, but how Rass, who wasn't so much good in the fields, got to come. *Not part of the plan. Mom had let Sally outside too soon.*

"Could you move your car on back a bit?" Rass asked, then added cheerful big talk in the manner Clever used: "If Sally takes tops, I'll grow hair on a doorknob, but I'm sure your bull will win hands down." The dogs were on him. How would Mr. McMulty make it to the trunk? "I love dairy cows. Someday, I'd like to have my own dairy herd. But I guess I'll have to wait to have a house full of boys to help with the milking." Big talk was spilling out fast, easing the way to him sending those dogs home.

Mr. Preston's interest perked up at the mention of milking. He moved his car a little and said, "Not necessarily so. I'm thinking of buying some of those new milking machines. Only one man needed."

"Mr. Preston, you want me to make your dogs go home?" Rass blurted it out, and made a motion with his hands.

"I'll do it," said Sally, and was out of the car at once. *Not part of the plan.* One slip and those dogs would be at Mr. McMulty's throat.

"Get back in, Sally. I can do it," Rass whispered desperately, forgetting the cheerful talk. He still tried waving the dogs away.

Clever took over the talk, chattered away giving directions. "Just keep moving back. Keep it coming." His talk rose high. He'd always been scared of Preston's dogs, too.

"Neither of you can send my dogs home! They won't obey anyone but family," Mr. Preston said. He stopped his car and began ordering the dogs home himself. No effect. They were too excited. Already the car and dogs had gotten very near to where Mr. McMulty lay.

Then Bill touched King, gave him a gentle shove back, and made a sound. The dogs took off toward Preston's mansion. There was silence from all. Rass wished Bill could tell him his secret.

Mr. Preston said, "Well done. Wish I could relay my admiration to the deaf boy. Now, Rass, what are you waiting for? Load in your sister's art," Mr. Preston ordered.

"Back a little more—then Rass can open the trunk," Clever answered. Clever had gotten it wrong. Too far back! Now if Mr. McMulty tried to get in from this spot, he'd be seen.

"Ah, er, ah . . . we need the keys to open the trunk." Rass put out his hand, then turned and yelled, "Clever, get a cotton sack for the floor of the trunk. Sally had to go put more paint on, and it ain't quite dry yet. Mr. Preston, could you move up just a little bit to where it's dry ground?"

"No, I'm all right. Just get that trunk open before your friend drops Sally's painting. Sally, you better get back in."

Sally started protesting that she'd not put on so much new paint but what it could be slid in the backseat in front of her legs. But Rass outyelled her. "Move on up just a little bit more till you hit dry ground, please, Mr. Preston, so Sally can get in." Somehow he had to get Sally back into the car so she couldn't see what was about to happen.

"Well, let me get these wheels straightened into the lane better. Does seem to be stuck in a mud hole. Doesn't Nert keep up this place?"

"Mud's from the rain, but we ain't complaining," said Rass.

Mr. Preston agreed and jockeyed the car, getting it closer to the place under the house where Mr. McMulty lay. Rass yelled, "There!"

Clever quickly added, "A little to the left. Too far. Back 'er up two feet."

Bill waved his arms wildly as well.

Mr. Preston revved the engine and went spurting back till he almost hit the house.

"Fine!" yelled Rass and Clever together. Even Bill's hands were held up in a stop signal. "Sally, get in the car!" Rass ordered.

But Sally had got splattered with mud and had to go wash it off. *Not part of the plan.* Still, it couldn't have been better. "Okay! Stop! You're okay. Ground's dry. You'll be able to pull out," Rass shouted. This was the exact spot. Clever grabbed the key, opened the trunk. *Not planned.* But Bill had distracted, what with all his arm waving.

"The car my landlord Jake Whitley drives ain't quite

so wonderful as this one," Clever said as he ran to return the key and stayed right by Mr. Preston's window. He kept talk of Jake's Chevy flowing as Rass went into action *as planned.* He slung the cotton sack full out behind him, as if he were about to pick a field clean, and Mr. McMulty got under it. They moved to the trunk.

"Lord, stay close," Mr. McMulty whispered, though plans were, he wasn't to say a word. But Mr. Preston couldn't hear, for Clever handed Sally's picture over, saying, "Now you be careful with it, Rass! Don't smudge it! Sally'd be heartsick."

Rass joined the big talk. "I'll just put it right in here and try not to get paint smeared in the trunk of Mr. Preston's nice car. But first, let me get the sack in there good. We cain't have paint all over."

"No, I don't want paint all over," Mr. Preston called out.

Clever stood tight by that window. "Yes sir, Mr. Preston, we sure do appreciate you giving Sally a ride to the fair, and Rass, too. Rass needs to keep an eye on Sally, or his Dad'll do him in. The two of them ain't allowed to part. If they do, they'll be sorry when they get back home."

Rass put the sack in and around Mr. McMulty. It was as if that bed had been prepared for someone just his size. Then in went Sally's picture. A second later Sally came running out and jumped into the backseat of the Lincoln, where she always rode.

Clever yelled, "Rass! Get a move on!"

And Rass answered, "I got to be careful how I wrap this picture!"

Clever played it all the way. "See how you take it out

when you get there, too. Sally'd want it in top condition."

Mr. Preston said something that Rass didn't hear, for Clever's talk kept flowing. "Never thought I'd live to see the day that Sally'd get noticed for her drawing. No one in our town ever has. Sally has the gift." On he went, fast-talking, slapping the side of the car, saying again and again how it was such an honor for him to even talk to a plantation owner.

Bill managed to do some car slapping as well, and Mr. Preston managed to nod a time or two.

Rass fixed the trunk for air for Mr. McMulty to survive the long trip. He'd already shortened the strap on his cotton sack by knotting it to the right measure to fit his shoulder. Now he placed that knot in a manner to leave air space, but also in such a way that he'd need no key—the remaining piece of strap hooked to the license bolt.

Clever rocked the car with a resounding "Thanks agin!" as the trunk lid shut.

Each step had eased into the next like well-oiled farm machinery doing its job, natural as could be. No words from Rass as he started to get in, but relief drove Clever's voice high. "Yep, Sally'd sure not been able to pull this trip off without your generosity. We're beholden." Then, as if an afterthought, Clever added, "Hurry! Time's a-wasting. Take it easy now." Clever was overdoing it. In fact Clever continued bumping against the car as it moved.

"Boy, don't be so nervous." Mr. Preston had his head out the window trying to assure Clever. "Cain't say I blame you, though. We're all proud of Sally. I reckon she's not all that calm about it herself."

"Me neither," said Rass. "Ain't no other artist in our

family. Who'd ever a thought my sister'd be going to show a picture at a fair?"

Sally kept saying, "Rass! Why, Rass, I didn't even know you cared."

For several long seconds Rass just sat there in wonderment. It had worked. Then he stuck his head out the window and yelled good-bye to Bill and Clever, whose faces held big smiles and they were jumping around and back-slapping. What great friends! It allowed Rass to smile same as Sally as he waved to his family. Even the little girls had their faces squashed up against their bedroom window. Then they were off, and Mr. Preston was assuring Sally that her flat painting might win.

Sally said, "Yes, I guess I'm going to get a blue ribbon. Rass nor his friend never have took on like that before."

"If I'd known it would have meant this much," Mr. Preston said, quite touched, "I'd have done it last year. But then, you didn't have a picture last year. Yes, I think you might get a blue ribbon."

Sally leaned against the front seat and continued talking to Mr. Preston. Within seconds Rass thought of a thousand things that could go wrong on this long journey to New Madrid. For one thing, Sally was unpredictable. Rass crouched low in the seat and shivered. A crick caught in his neck. Mr. McMulty could get caught getting out of the trunk. How was Rass going to be free of Sally long enough to make sure that part went right? Especially since Clever announced Rass had to stay near her. He was going to get caught. No more plans to use.

Well, if he got caught he'd take all the blame, swear his family knew nothing. He'd swear Mr. McMulty just happened to be standing by the house and he had a sudden wild urge and pushed him into the trunk. He was known for being wild. He wouldn't do what Dad would have— pretend ignorance and let the law argue with powerful Mr. Preston as to why he'd carted off a colored fugitive. This nice old rich man who hadn't said one word about the Klan nor the fire, nonetheless, he was mighty good to Sally. He just didn't know a thing about nothing.

Being skilled at figures, Rass talked of milking machine prices to mask any noise made by Mr. McMulty.

Sally listened to the talk for a while but finally drifted off to sleep. After another thirty minutes, so did Rass. Immediately he got awakened by sirens. Mr. Preston eased over to the edge of the road. And Rass had thought nobody in the state would dare stop Mr. Preston!

A policeman leaned into the window and said, "You know your trunk's not closed, sir?"

"Why, no! I thought I was hearing too much of an air drag, but I attributed it to old age. Want to close it, Rass?"

Rass was out of the car in a flash. At least there had been no rain in this part of the state. The shoulder of the road was quite narrow and there was no guardrail to protect him from a sharp fall into the water. Good gosh, they must already be at the levee on the Mississippi! Rass clutched the car, made it to the trunk, unhooked the strap, stuffed the knot inside, and slammed it shut. Enough air for the remaining short trip. However, a shut trunk meant getting the keys again from Mr. Preston. *Not part of the plan.*

The police waved them on and Rass said, "I'm sorry it wasn't tight."

All Preston said was, "Fog's picking back up here a

little, being so near the river." Rass looked at the sky, still a glazed gray-green. Shortly Mr. Preston turned into a gas station. Again Rass was out in a flash, cleaning bugs from the windshield and lights, dancing and talking as lively as Clever or Uncle Tut, as he stood guard on the attendant filling the gas tank. The attendant spoke of the bugs, noticed nothing.

At their next stop Mr. Preston said, "Well, here we are, kids. Fairgrounds won't be officially open for another hour. If you want to wait for me near here, I'll be back to get your picture entered, Sally."

"We'll just wait in the car, if you'll leave the keys," Rass said.

"Leave the keys? No. Can't chance children in a vehicle alone. Certainly not with keys to the ignition." He pointed to the sun rising. "The day's opening up nice here in New Madrid. You kids play outside near here. Watch the trucks coming in to unload. My own driver should already be here with my bull. There he is."

Sally and Rass both got out, and Mr. Preston locked his car.

Drat! And they were parked near a clump of bushes, a perfect place for opening the trunk.

"White horse, Rass! A white horse. Come make a wish on it, Rass!" Sally went flying away to be closer to the horse. If that turned out to be Nert's horse, they were in sore trouble. Whoever came up with the idea that white horses meant good luck had holes in their head.

"You get back here! Dad says we're not to separate. Obey me!"

"You obey *me*, Rass, and come wish on the white horse.

Wish me to win!" All their praise of her painting had gone straight to her head.

"We can wish on it from here. No one says you got to be right on top of the horse to make a wish come true." Rass humored her since it wasn't Nert's horse and made a silent wish on the horse for Mr. McMulty, and for his sister's painting. Then he made another wish that he would be the one to get Sally's picture out of the trunk. What if, when Mr. Preston returned, he wanted to do it himself?

Rass looked around for something interesting he could send Mr. Preston to look at so he could say, "You just go on, look that thing over good. Sally, go show Mr. Preston that very interesting thing. Hand me the keys, Mr. Preston. I'll get Sally's painting out of the trunk."

"Answer me, Rass. You ain't listening to a word I say. Don't you wish we had money to spend? Wouldn't it be nice? I smell popcorn."

"We don't need no popcorn. L.G.'s planting popcorn on his whole five acres. He told me Mr. Aaral had told him to do that. Come fall, we'll have more popcorn than this whole fair could eat."

"I want some now," said Sally as they moved back toward the car. Right then Rass noticed the trunk was ajar. "Sally, get over yonder and find something interesting to look at. Stop your whining."

"I ain't whining! Dad said we wasn't to separate! I won't go."

"You got to go, Sally. Cain't you take a hint? I got to use the bushes. Now go over yonder and don't look back till I call all clear."

"Well, I got to use the bushes, too."

"Sally!"

She went. Acted proper.

Mr. McMulty pushed the trunk lid up a little and asked, "Ever'thing be clear out there now, boy?"

"It is," Rass whispered. "How'd you do it—get the trunk open?"

"Hold this sack up for a cover, chile, and I tells you. I hears them sirens. I hears you leap out when Preston say close the trunk. I makes right sure the sack gets caught in the latch, make it easy to spring." Mr. McMulty was out, the sack draped over him.

Rass directed him toward the bushes and once there said, "I'm sure glad you got under the house before the barn was on fire, with nobody seeing!"

Mr. McMulty removed the sack. He had L.G.'s red bandanna tied around his head. Quickly he rolled the cotton sack and put it under his arm. "Yeah. Me being afraid you be late to wake me for this trip turn to a blessing."

He did the strangest thing then: took the small carved calf from his pocket and pressed it into Rass's hand.

Rass was shocked.

"No, Mr. McMulty, you cain't! This is for Miss Greene. It's the finest carving in the whole world. I cain't take it."

Then sorrow filled him. "Mr. McMulty, you're leaving! I'll never see you again!" He'd been too fully occupied with the escape to allow this loss to be felt. But feelings engulfed him now, like the raging waters of a broken ditch. He couldn't bear it. A slow moan arose from his chest. He hated Nert for causing this. Nert, nor anyone, knew what Mr. McMulty meant to him. He...

He should not halt his friend's escape. He should straighten up and act civil... but he held on to the wooden calf and cried.

"It be yours." Mr. McMulty looked him straight in the eye and said, "No more sorrows over me moving far away. There be a time for joy and a time for pain. Fear cain't rob us this time for joy. Think on the good things. Miss Greene. Honeysuckle near the river down there, look! You a brave boy, risk yo' life for a friend. There be no better person. I beholden."

"Oh, no sir. It's me what's beholden," Rass whispered.

A gentle touch to his cheek, then Mr. McMulty took in a deep breath of air, stretched, brushed through and to the other side of the remaining bushes, and, limping slightly, he sauntered away, heading for work on the river barges.

He didn't look back.

# 21

IN SPITE OF winning only a white ribbon, Sally did have a nice day at the fair. As they drove home along the river road, they saw two showboats and five barges— two being loaded by black men. Mr. Preston stopped so they could look, saying, "I stood fascinated, watching those barges when I was a boy, myself." Other people, mostly colored, stood on shore watching, too. Several of the workers wore bandanna handkerchiefs on their heads. A couple of them were very short men. One of those had a slight limp. *Mr. McMulty?*

Mr. Preston insisted on treating them to a celebration-of-the-fair dinner. "Why, yes, thank you, Mr. Preston!" Sally said before Rass could think of a way to say they ought to hurry home. He wanted Clever and Bill to know Mr. McMulty was free and set their minds at rest. However, the release of tension within himself demanded expression, and Mr. McMulty would have said, "Go on, son. Celebrate in this catfish restaurant on the riverfront," so Rass didn't fight it.

"Now, this is the sort of meat I was raised on. My wife never cooks it anymore," said Mr. Preston, greatly enjoying the food.

By the time they finished eating it was getting dark— Mom and Dad would be worried sick. It turned night during the drive home, too dark to know when they were passing things familiar. Perhaps he slept a little, for suddenly Mr. Preston's car stopped on the road, right in front of the Whitleys'. He didn't turn into the driveway because Uncle Jake's car was parked in the entrance. Other cars and wagons were there, too. How could his family be entertaining company with the smell of burned barn still in the air?

Again Rass could hear Mr. McMulty saying, "The mules saved. The house not cotch on fire. It be time to rejoice. Cain't let life stop, son, or our enemy claims us."

Mr. Preston handed Rass the keys to the trunk. But once Rass had it open, Mr. Preston was there, reaching for the painting. He held it for a moment before saying, "Sally, I can't part with this. It's truly a fine piece of art. The judges are ignorant of this style. May I buy it from you for my office?"

Rass didn't know if Mr. Preston was buttering Sally up or if he actually believed the picture laying a plantation out flat like that looked pretty. But he was a rich man, so Rass whispered, "Say yes."

So Sally said yes, but she also added, "I give it to you, Mr. Preston." Rass almost died.

"No. I want to buy it. Now, how much do you think it's worth?"

Sally said, "You can just have—"

"—it for the trade of a milk cow!" Rass finished for her, having learned from Mr. McMulty that pleasing too much gets you nothing.

Mr. Preston chuckled. "I believe I do have a young Jersey heifer—if that's a fair trade, Sally?"

"Why, Mr. Preston, that's just fi—"

"—fine if you could also give one breeding," said Rass. It didn't cost no more to Mr. Preston, if you thought about it.

Mr. Preston made no comment on the breeding, but he did hesitate before he told Sally, "If you'll come over tomorrow, you can take your heifer home. Do you want to keep this picture tonight until the trade is official?"

"Naw, she don't need—," Rass began, but Sally cut him off.

"I'd like my whole family to see it once more, since Rass loves it so," Sally said. Rass couldn't bear to hear any more, so quickly thanked Mr. Preston for all his help and kindness and left Sally to tell him good-night herself.

The moon and stars seemed brighter, though. Dad was showing the charred remains of the barn to some people, using a lantern for light. "Let them Klansmen think they burned McMulty," Dad said, "but he weren't in this barn a'tall. He's outfoxed 'em!"

Happy sounds arose, so Rass chose this moment to greet everyone, especially giving Bill and Clever a quick hi, plus a motion for them not to rush to him yet.

Without skipping a beat, Dad said, "Time to celebrate McMulty not being cotched and also Sally's blue ribbon. Ask Preston to join us, son."

Right away Rass was back to the Lincoln asking,

knowing a rich man couldn't accept. But asking was always proper.

"Thank you kindly, but I have to get home," Mr. Preston said politely as he left. Sally waved as best she could holding her picture. Mom gave her a hand. She'd come to thank Mr. Preston as well.

Going back to join the others, Rass told Mom, "It was a perfect fair... except Sally didn't win no big prize." Mom understood, but Sally called him a liar and told Mom all the details of how Mr. Preston had traded for her prized picture and where he was going to hang it.

"I knew you'd make it!" Mom said, then hurried on carrying Sally's picture high as they joined others near the burned barn. "Whit, L.G., look! All went well. The Lord's give us a sign! Sally's picture's to go in the plantation office. Not Nert's office, but the gentry Nert hopes to be like. If Nert should ever truly be like him, maybe the lion and the lamb could lie down together," she added. "And there wouldn't be no KKK and barn burnings."

The people gathered close, and Mom demanded, "Daughter, share with ever'body what you told me. Our Sally was a-sharing her beautiful painting with Mr. Preston and..."

"I traded it to him for a Jersey heifer!"

It was a soft, wonderful moment there in the night. The warm gold lantern light only mellowed the darkness, making Sally look beautiful.

"Hold on just a minute! New Jersey's mine. You was gonna *give* the painting to Mr. Preston. I bargained for New Jersey," Rass said, and grabbed for the picture. But

Sally quickly put her treasure into Dad's hands, and ordered L.G. to hold the lantern near it.

Then, while the grown-ups gawked, Rass and Sally had it out in a wondrous carefree way. "New Jersey is the name of a state, Rass. The cow is mine because I made the picture."

"But you cain't milk. You pinch teats with your fingernails."

Sally stood tall and meditative. "The cow's still mine. You can be responsible for feeding and milking her, Rass, as your reward."

Rass was about to continue teasing Sally by declaring, "And I get all that comes out of her," hoping Mr. Preston would allow one breeding. Instead, he thought of Mr. McMulty's counsel that owning things didn't make him good, but fairness and kindness did. It was Sally's heifer.

Using a long stick to pull out the metal parts of a burned harness from the ashes, Rass felt again his loss when he'd thought Mr. McMulty was in that fire. He laid the metal over near the hoes and shovels, now missing handles. Lots had been won and lost this past week. He hadn't lost Mr. McMulty. He'd be with Rass always.

"Now listen." Dad pranced around with the picture held high in one hand. "I was just telling Helen here that the barn being burnt might give her a little space to put in a garden." Dad in prime storytelling manner. Center stage. A man alive. "As we've all heard McMulty say time and agin, we cain't never make it seeing only the dark side o' things, now can we? I know some of youns' beds is awaiting, but I'd like who can to stay and hep us celebrate McMulty's not being in that barn and also celebrate my little artist's prize painting."

Some folks sighed, made more well wishes, praised the painting, then went home. The closest friends stayed: Uncle Tut and tribe, Uncle Jake's family, the Browns, who had arrived late, and Clever's parents, who'd just arrived at about nine o'clock.

Mr. Dumas said to the crowd, "We just heard of the barn burning. We took Preacher Bloodworth home to Sikeston and went to a farm meeting today. Looks like we're always gone to a meeting when things happen." Rass felt Mr. Dumas's quick gaze of approval.

"Night riders doing this! My lans," said Mrs. Dumas. Her wide-set eyes grew large, and she hid her mouth.

Rass wished he could tell everyone outright that Mr. McMulty was free. But he and Clever had agreed that they would never spread things by talk. He must live with secrets, though this was a mighty painful one. Rass felt more natural with open words. Still, his friend Bill lived with his secrets all the time. Rass would be strong, like him. He stood next to Bill, who understood, and together they tossed a few rocks into the ashes. Bill picked up some ashes and rubbed them on his lower leg. Rass nodded, smiled, and acted out freedom the best he could. Happy sounds came from Bill. And Clever made no effort to hold back his smile, either.

"Forget them night riders. Like your dad says, it's time for a party."

Aunt Kate was hauling out jars of rhubarb and cherries

from her car. "I made the trip over here to deliver these in the first place."

Mom saw and said, "Rass, go stir up coals in the cook-stove so's I can bake a cobbler from the things Kate's brought."

Dennis was showing L.G. and Louie a new game he took out of the car. Bill stayed near Rass. Rass quickly pulled Clever in to be with him, too. The three of them built a fine roaring fire in Mom's cookstove.

Mrs. Dumas came to Rass. She touched his face, giving him a proud little smile. "You've acted like a good man, Rass, just like your daddy. You both fine men."

Dad heard and was pleased.

Rass knew she'd mentioned Dad to keep the secret safe. Word must have traveled fast among the black people to their leader, Preacher Bloodworth. Dad showed his plea-sure at Mrs. Dumas's compliment by grabbing Mom's hand and singing, "A Hole in the Bottom of the Sea," her favorite song. She proudly caught up the tune, and every-one chimed in. Bill made happy noises in his own way. A party was really on after that.

First Dad placed Sally's picture in the center of the library table and said, "This is what a Whitley done!" The little kids clamped on to Sally and worshiped her, dancing around, hollering and screaming. Marylu was crawling be-tween their legs. Then Dad placed the picture on top of the food safe, using as props Mom's prized blue pitcher and covered oriental blue bowl. Amazingly, the painting truly looked like a prizewinner, too.

Sally caught Rass's admiration and smiled.

"I do fear my daughter is reaching above her raising," Mom said. Then she grabbed Sally and hugged her. Mom looked so pretty, so Rass told her that. She grabbed him and hugged him, too, though such wasn't proper, but it made him know this party wasn't just for Sally. He remembered Mom's relief when he'd assured her and Dad that Mr. McMulty hadn't been in the fire.

"Well now," said Mrs. Dumas, "let's remove this cobbler from this ole bread pan and put it in this oriental dish, proper like, for a talented young lady." Mom, loving the idea, responded to Bill's joy noises and allowed him to fill her treasured blue pitcher with water also. Amazing.

Aunt Kate and Uncle Jake, Uncle Tut and Crystal, and all the kids joined in the talking. Everyone thought Sally had traded for exactly the right thing. No one mentioned Mr. McMulty. As far as that went, no one even mentioned the Klan or the barn burning after that.

Certain bad happenings, like calf hangings and barn burnings, got quickly pushed into the land of no remembering. They all went right on, clamping on to any happiness as farmers would forever do, Rass thought. But he would never forget. Forgetting created a world where change never happened.

L.G. announced, "I just found out where I can get a used transmission for your Chevy, Dad. All I got to do is work on a truck for this guy what come here tonight."

Dad rah-rahed about that and challenged Uncle Jake, Uncle Tut, and Mr. Dumas to a contest spitting cherry seeds into the slop can, ten feet away. The kids joined in.

Aunt Kate said, "Ain't that contest the limit? And

people think I'm awful, never pitting my cherries a'fore I can them."

"All in all, it's been a good day," Dad said when the game was over. "A week ago today, I never thought to hear myself saying that agin."

"Me neither," said Rass. "I surely didn't."

Sally spoke loudly, drawing herself back to the middle of *her* party. "I'd think this is the perfectest night in the world"—she moved close to Rass—"if I knowed Mr. Mc-Multy was eating cobbler somewhere."

Uncle Tut spoke solemnly. "Sally, you can believe that if you want to, but I believe the man's gone to his rest. Word has it a shallow grave got dug by colored folk who buried him in secret. Then, a-fearing the Klan might want to claim his body, they buried him again in the woods. That grave may never be found. That right, Dumas?"

"Tut, we hear talk on the vine, that's all we know. He may be alive. I get hearsay, same as you," Mr. Dumas said evenly.

"And I say," said Uncle Tut, "that Nert's lost hisself a barn! You kids eat more cobbler. The Lord's taking care of McMulty. We need celebrate we ain't dead ourselves." Uncle Tut said more, storyteller that he was, and Rass didn't stop him, nor would anyone for years to come as he made a whole new history of things.

Dad ushered Rass away and to one side, awkwardly slapped Rass's back, and said, "Son, I'm thinking if'n I can get Sally's Jersey bred, you can claim the calf."

Warmth filled Rass to overflowing. He spared Dad by not telling him such was already arranged with Mr.

Preston. "I'll take care of New Jersey; she's my responsibility," he said. "But the cow is Sally's. You cain't give the calf to me—only Sally can." It took courage for him to say that. Mr. McMulty would have been proud.

His fingers traced the carved calf in his pocket.